To The Lesbian Bar Project and few remaining lesbian bars in the United States—don't give up. The safe spaces you provide are unparalleled and so desperately needed.

Special dedication to Jo & Coach for creating my favorite safe space at As You Are DC.

Author's Note

Dear Reader,

This book is inspired by the opening of my favorite bar and safe space, As You Are in Washington, DC—one of fewer than twenty-five lesbian bars in America. They had to fight their way to opening and now continue to provide an inclusive, safe space that listens to the needs of each and every person who walks in the door. It's the first bar I've ever been to that felt like a friend's living room—fiercely protected, deeply safe, and wholly genuine.

This brought me to discovering the docuseries and awareness campaign called The Lesbian Bar Project in 2020:

"In the 1980s, there were roughly 200 Lesbian Bars in the United States. Today, there are fewer than 25. As these bars disappear, filmmakers Erica Rose and Elina Street established The Lesbian Bar Project to celebrate, support, and amplify the remaining Lesbian bars. The Lesbian Bar Project believes what

makes a bar uniquely Lesbian is its prioritization of creating space for people of marginalized genders including women (regardless if they are cis or trans), nonbinary folks, and trans men. As these spaces aim to be inclusive of all individuals across the diverse LGBTQIA+ community, the label Lesbian belongs to all people who feel that it empowers them." - www.lesbian-barproject.com

We need more spaces like this in America, and we need people to advocate for their creation and continued support. If you love this book, consider helping to spread their message. Visit their website. Check out their merch. Follow them on social. And go find your closest lesbian bar and support them in person.

In solidarity,
Sarah Robinson

Chapter One

"I honestly don't understand how sour edible panties didn't take off," I said to my best friend and former roommate for the last decade, Rachel Blumenthal. "It was a one-in-a-million idea—if Shark Tank hadn't turned down my application..."

Rachel shot me a look as she placed the last box down on top of the stack of other moving boxes stacked against one wall of what would soon be my living room. "There was zero chance Mark Cuban was going to invest in that, Yasmeen. He's vegan."

I sighed and plopped down on the sectional couch, still in pieces and pushed against the opposite wall. Eventually I'd put the entire thing back together, but moving day had been exhausting enough just getting all my things from our former row home in Washington, DC to this new, larger apartment in Arlington, Virginia.

I'd crossed the bridge and become a Northern Virginia girl.

The irony wasn't lost on me given how often I make fun of people who can't stick it out in the big city—not that Washington, DC was that big of a city to begin with. But still, it wasn't

Virginia. *Shudder*. Despite the location, I had to admit...the price was right and the size was even righter. Real estate on this side of the bridge was significantly cheaper than in the city, and, frankly, that's what I needed right now.

That, plus a new idea for a business that would actually take off this time. The thought reminded me of the unreturned voicemail from my father on my cell phone about joining the family business, but I quickly squirreled that away to the area of my brain where childhood guilt permanently resides.

"I can't believe we're not going to be roommates anymore," I sighed, my voice stretching out like a whine. "And Mila's gone and started her own family. You and I are just...here."

"Speak for yourself, Yas," Rachel replied as she dropped onto another unconnected part of the sectional couch and tossed her feet up on a spare ottoman. "At least I'm still in DC."

I shot her a look, my eyes rolling back as far into my head as I could without getting them stuck. Was that even a thing? My grandmother had been insistent that it was, and I'd never been tempted to test her wisdom—may she rest in peace.

"Okay, but you got stuck with Macavity, so..." I gave her an evil grin, referring to Mila's cat who had refused to move with our former roommate Mila thanks to their frenemies bond with Rachel.

"The world's worst consolation prize," Rachel joked, though there was absolutely truth to it.

I still couldn't believe that the three of us had gone separate ways after over half a decade sharing the same roof.

Rachel had that environmental lawyer money and so she'd gotten her own place near Barrack's Row in Washington, DC. when we'd all split. She'd offered for me to move in with her, but it felt like time to start fresh. We were in our mid-thirties now, and I couldn't still have a roommate when I hit forty. Not that that was anytime soon since I'd just turned thirty-three last spring.

Please God, let time slow the fuck down.

Our other roommate, Mila, now lived on the East Coast half the year, splitting her time between Washington, DC and New York City, and then spent the other half of the year filming her television pilot in Los Angeles, California. Fancy as fuck, but I'm not jealous at all. Nope, not even a little...but maybe the smallest smidge. Plus, Mila had a wife and a toddler who kept her pretty busy, so I was trying to be understanding of the lessened communication from her and that it wasn't just about her going all Hollywood on us.

Still, I missed her and the life we'd had together.

"Have you heard from Mila lately?" I asked Rachel.

Rachel shrugged loosely. "Last time I FaceTimed her, she was breastfeeding Gracie while taking a shit on the toilet. I love boobs, but even that was a lot for me."

I grinned and shook my head. "Have you ever been with a mom before?"

Rachel shook her head. "Naked Becky was my last try for a MILF, but you know how that went."

Our former next door neighbor and her messy divorce was a story for another day.

"I think I'd make a great mom one day, but I don't want to be the one who carries it. I'll let my wife do that," I commented, musing at the idea of my potential future partner. "It's super hard to find Black sperm donors though, and I'd want a kid who looks like me a little bit at least."

Not that I blamed Black men even in the slightest for not trusting volunteering their DNA over to organizations. Still, it was a frustrating dichotomy for us Black lesbians.

"Hey—" I began.

The quiet room suddenly felt like it was split in two by the loud and low bass roaring of what could only be described as the Lord Jesus Christ returning and smiting half of Washington, DC.

"They have sonic jets out here in Virginia, too?" I placed both hands over my ears and groaned.

"What?" Rachel raised her voice to a near yell.

"SONIC JETS IN VIRGINIA?" I screamed back, but the sound had passed by the time I got to 'Virginia' so now I was just screaming into the void. "Oh. I mean, I didn't know they could hear them in Virginia, too."

"You're like less than a quarter mile from the Pentagon, and maybe three miles from the White House. You're going to hear sonic jets, babe." Rachel laughed and shook her head, but I just frowned. "Speaking of our beloved city, I should get home. I need to shower before my date tonight."

"Is this person from the kickball team, too?" I lifted one brow, because Rachel's hobby of intramural kickball had become more of a dating game show than an actual sport. "You know you're going to have to find a new team soon enough."

Rachel waved her hand as she stood and wove her way around the maze of boxes and scattered furniture. "No, this is one of my teammate's exes. She's not *on* the actual team, so it's fine."

I sucked my lips in between my teeth and shook my head. "Yeah, somehow I don't see that going the way you hope it does."

Rachel just shrugged, and I loved that she was naturally fearless in everything she did. "Maybe, but she's taking me indoor skydiving, so you know I'll try anything once."

She stood up and grabbed her tote bag that was sitting by the front door with READ QUEER BOOKS in rainbow letters across the side that she'd purchased last time we'd visited Little District Books—a local queer-owned bookstore that only sold books by queer authors or about queer characters. She slung the bag's handle over her shoulder and glanced at her phone in her other hand.

"Thanks for helping me move," I commented again as I walked her over to the front door. "Text me when you get home."

"Will do!" Rachel waved over her shoulder to me, but didn't turn to look back at me.

There was a row of haphazard electric scooters parked at the end of my street and Rachel hopped on one, linked it to her phone, and headed for the metro. I didn't trust those damn scooters as far as I could throw one—which was maybe an inch.

After she was out of sight, I returned inside and stared at all the boxes—seemed like a good day for ordering dinner in. I pulled out my phone and scanned the options on DoorDash in my new neighborhood. Definitely not as bountiful as DC, but it wasn't terrible either.

I was about to click on the dessert section when my sister's picture appeared on the screen—her incoming call refusing to be ignored.

"Hey, Nia. What's going on?" I turned the call on speaker and started opening one of the boxes in front of me to keep my hands busy.

"Dad says you haven't returned his call," my older sister spoke into the phone like she was exhaling all the stress she had been holding inside into that one sentence. "Why do I have to be the middleman? Can't you just call him back?"

"Absence makes the heart grow fonder." I sidestepped an answer like the skilled baby of the family that I am. "He's a lot happier with me when he doesn't actually know what I'm doing."

"Oh, god..." Nia groaned loudly and I heard her typing on a keyboard in the background. I glanced at the time on my cell phone, noting that she was nearing the end of her workday and there was nothing that was going to distract her from being Type-A productive. In fact, I'm pretty sure there has not been a single day at her job that she's even considered clocking out before five o'clock. Typical elder sister syndrome. "Does that mean there's something going on with you that would make him unhappy? You realize I'm the target left behind when you're missing in action?"

Maybe it was the birth order part of things, but there was nothing Nia wouldn't do for our family, and she cared for our father, my brother, and me more than she ever did for herself. Hell, it was basically the story of her entire life, including her career as an executive in the nonprofit world making a lot less money than she deserves. Outside of that, she lived alone and her life mostly revolved around taking care of us—a job that always varied depending on the day and the person in trouble at that moment.

"Why can't Demetrius pick up the slack?" I asked, referring to my older brother, the middle child and golden boy in the Kiani clan. "He's the one working for Dad anyway. He gets a paycheck to deal with his bullshit."

"Paycheck—something you really need to know more about," Nia added. "You know Dad wants you to come on board at the firm. He said you could start off as an executive assistant, just get your feet wet in the field, you know? You could shadow an investigator and get involved in the security side once you feel ready—no rush."

I rolled my eyes at the very thought of one day working in corporate security for government contractors and rich people Capitol Hill-adjacent. "Nia, the day I walk into a giant conference room full of White men in suits whose girlfriend meal-prepped them bland boiled chicken and unseasoned broccoli for lunch is the day I've given up all hope for happiness."

She let out a low chuckle, and I could imagine her shaking her head. "I mean, they're not *all* White."

"Everyone we contract with is basically a Ted Cruz looka-like," I countered, because while Kiani Security was a Black-owned business and made sure to staff BIPOC employees, there was still an abundance of government contracts we bid on that were basically white-washed. I mean, let's be honest, the entire Hill was.

It's not like I wasn't proud of everything my father had built as a single father—another thing I tried not to think about because the guilt itched at me there, too. Not that I could blame myself for our mother passing away shortly after giving birth to me—an unnecessary c-section that led to an infection she just couldn't fight and by the time I was six hours old, she was gone. I should blame the medical system and the disparity in care when it comes to Black mothers.

And yet, still, I can't help but feel like I'm here...and she's not.

It's not *not* unrelated.

My father had been working as a Capitol Police Officer at one of the Senate buildings at the time, but in the aftermath of my mother's death, he'd decided to leave the force and begin his own security consulting company. They'd started with physical security first, but eventually expanded into everything from private investigations, background checks, and, most recently, cyber and IT security.

I felt the familiar weight on my chest and my internal defenses kicked into gear—keep it light, keep it humorous, keep it at a distance where it can't hurt me.

"Plus, Nia, it's not like *you* work for Dad," I reminded her with a barely joking lilt in my tone. "You ran the moment you graduated college. Why do I have to be the scapegoat?"

"Because, first of all, I actually graduated college, and

second of all, I *have* a job, Yas," Nia reminded me. "You're living off the family trust and random dead-end jobs."

I bristled at the completely true accusation. "Okay, but I live pretty frugally for someone with a trust fund. It's not like I'm out here riding private jets all day. I pull my own weight."

"I know that." Nia sighed.

We both were more than aware that that trust fund was an incredibly thoughtful gift our mother put into place before Demetrius was born that she insisted her life insurance pay directly into if anything ever happened. She hadn't known things would turn out the way they did, but that small step had set up all of her children to continue to thrive after she was gone. My father said it was even one of the things she spoke about on the way to labor and delivery—making sure we were all taken care of in the unlikely event when she wouldn't make it through. She'd always been Type-A in that way—the exact opposite of me.

Nia's voice sounded heavier when she continued. "Can you at least give him a call back so *I* don't get the calls instead? Do it for me, Yas."

"Fiiiine," I replied, even though I was absolutely not going to do that. "We still down for bottomless brunch this weekend?"

"Absolutely not." She said her goodbyes and hung up the phone. We were still going to do brunch, but Nia was a one-drink gal before she was at her limit—the woman hated not being in full control of herself.

I could respect it, just didn't relate.

I shoved my phone in the pocket of my lightweight palazzo pants—which, remarkably, actually had pockets. Don't get me started on how women are expected to carry everyone's shit and yet are rarely given pockets in our clothes for just that.

The box I began opening was full of kitchen dishes and

bowls, and I immediately lost all motivation to continue unpacking today. Instead, I checked DoorDash again and saw that the Peruvian chicken place I've been eyeing was a quarter mile from me.

Perfect excuse to go for a walk and explore the neighborhood.

A convenience store, a hipster-type coffee bar, and a bank later, I came to the end of the block and crossed over to the other side of the street. On that corner was a sports bar, and there were at least ten mid-twenties former frat boys on the patio section.

Ugh, I immediately missed my old haunts. The main queer-friendly bar in Arlington was a gay bar in Crystal City—admittedly, they have great karaoke—but damn, I missed the lesbians and trans folks from queer bars. There's nothing better than a lesbian bar, which is one of the reasons why it's super irritating that there are only a handful in the entire country. Like, literally less than twenty-five. If you think I'm joking, they made a whole docuseries about it.

The damn patriarchy doesn't stop at pockets or sexuality.

Two more blocks down and I was almost at the Peruvian chicken place when I came across a storefront with a "for lease" sign in the front window. My steps slowed for a moment and I peered through the darkened window—the inside looked like a former hair salon with mirrors and spinning chairs and a shampoo station in the back.

I stepped back from the window for a moment, but my brain was already beginning to spin its gears. The front door to the empty shop opened and I jumped back even farther, not expecting someone to have been inside. A woman with dark brown hair that reached past her shoulder blades and hung in a heavy curtain across her back stepped onto the sidewalk and then turned to lock the door behind her.

"Excuse me, miss?" I called out.

When she turned to face me, I tried not to notice how deeply blue her eyes were but failed almost immediately. I wondered if they were colored contacts, because I had never seen eyes that shade of blue before that somehow perfectly meshed with the spray of brown freckles across the tops of her pale pink cheeks and nose.

"Yes?" She straightened as she looked at me, and I didn't miss the way she swallowed hard when her eyes found mine. *Interesting.* "Can I help you?"

"Are you the property owner for this place?" I asked, pointing to the "for lease" sign in the window.

She glanced in the direction I was pointing. "Uh, I'm the property manager."

"It's still available?" I asked—and why the hell was I even asking that? The idea was forming in my head quicker than my inhibition could shove it down.

She nodded. "Technically, yes. We've had quite a few inquiries lately, so I think it won't be long. Were you looking for retail space?"

"I'm Yasmeen," I replied, sticking a hand out toward her. "And I think I have the perfect idea for this space."

The woman looked hesitant, but shook my hand in return. "I'm Tyler, and I'm all ears."

I was still stuck on her eyes, but if she wanted me to look at her ears, too, I don't think I'd say no.

Chapter Two

"**N**o offense or anything, but I've never seen a property manager have a penthouse office before," I commented as I stepped out of the elevator with Tyler onto the top floor.

We exited into a small corridor with a large set of double doors in front of us and then a single door to our right.

"That's my apartment," Tyler corrected me, pointing to the double doors then redirecting her finger to the smaller door. "The property management office is here."

I lifted one brow toward the double doors. "You live in the penthouse?"

Tyler was already unlocking the smaller side door, her back to me. I noticed what appeared to be a light orange leaf from a tree outside stuck in between a few strands of her dark brown hair but I said nothing.

Had she just been at the park? Why? What did that mean? Why did I even care? I pushed the thought away.

"It's..." She shrugged as she stepped into the office and ushered me inside. "It's a family business."

That made a bit more sense, but I still had questions. "Oh, so your whole family lives here?"

She shook her head as she pulled out a leather chair in front of the large desk for me then circled around to the back of the desk and sat in a tall office chair facing me. "No. I live alone. I mean, Larry obviously lives there, too."

Shit. She was married. And to a man. Fuck me. "Oh," I replied as I sat down across from her. "Well, congratulations. I'm sure you're a very happy couple."

She glanced over at me from the desktop computer screen she was waking up by shaking her mouse. Her brow was furrowed and her expression looked like I'd said something wrong. "Larry is my chihuahua."

Of course he was. I will never understand people who name their dogs plain human names as if they are a roommate. And a chihuahua? Absolutely useless species of animal.

I couldn't think of a response that wasn't going to be snippy. "Oh."

We stared at each other for a second longer before Tyler looked back at the desktop. "Anyway," she began. "You said you had thoughts for the space?"

"I do." I crossed my ankle over my opposite knee and wrapped my fingers around it. "Was it a hair salon before?"

She nodded, then grabbed some pieces of paper off what sounded like a printer that must have been under her desk. "It was. Here's the paper application, but I'd need a copy of your driver's license as well and consent to run a credit check."

I pulled my wallet out of the side pocket of my pants—I was never one to use a purse, and people with penises who put wallets in their back pocket have clearly never heard of prioritizing a balanced pelvic floor. "I think the space would be perfect for a lesbian bar."

Tyler paused her movements as she was straightening the

paperwork out into one pile. Those blue eyes found mine again, and I was pretty sure now that they actually were colored contacts as I was looking closer. "A lesbian bar?"

I nodded. "And get this twist—we also offer hair services, but pro bono."

"I'm pretty sure the application won't be approved unless it's going to be a profitable business," Tyler immediately replied, now looking hesitant to hand the papers to me.

I pulled my license out of my wallet and placed it down on the desk in front of her. "Oh, we're going to be profitable. I can guarantee that. The drinks itself will cover the rest."

I wasn't about to tell her that the last three businesses I'd tried to start had gone under before ever making a dime, but there were ways to word it on the application that wouldn't make it sound so dire. Plus, it seemed like she wasn't the deciding factor of it all anyway. Someone else was pulling the strings of this building operation, so I wasn't about to put in a ton of effort convincing this one woman—despite the fact that I definitely didn't want to stop talking to her.

Man, I really needed to keep my hormones in check.

She finally handed over the application and I took it from her on a clipboard with a pen at the top. "Okay, well...I can't guarantee anything, but you can always apply. It is a fifty-dollar application fee."

I slipped my credit card out of my wallet and placed it next to my driver's license on top of her desk. "Charge it."

Her gaze was wary but she picked up my driver's license first, and I noticed her fingernails were painted green and dotted with pink polka dots. Seemed as pretentious as a chihuahua named Larry, but who was I to judge?

"Yasmeen Kiani?"

My name rolling off her lips sounded softer than I'd heard before as if she was cradling it with her voice. Or had I just made that up in my romance-starved head? It had been a while... I lifted my eyes from the application to her, and it didn't escape me that she was staring a moment longer at my photo than she needed to—or that her cheeks were tinging just a bit pinker.

No, definitely not all in my head.

"Problem with the license?"

She shook her head vigorously—too vigorously for the situation—and grabbed the credit card next. "Nope. No problem."

I focused back on the application, quickly filling in my personal information and general thoughts for the business I was proposing. Thankfully, the application cared a lot more about my financial holdings than it did about future plans, so I didn't have to have it all figured out just yet.

"I'll need a list of character references as well if the credit check goes through," Tyler added, and I could feel her staring at the top of my head as I was focused down on the paperwork.

I shrugged. "Not a problem."

"And we'd require a security deposit, plus first and last month upfront," she added. "The rent increases by three percent annually, too."

"Would you like a kidney as well?" I asked, lifting my gaze to her this time. "I have two."

Her cheeks turned an even darker shade of pink that I hadn't even known someone as pale as this woman could conjure. "Hilarious," she joked with complete sarcasm. "It's just...it's a long process and I don't get to make the final call."

"Who does?" I continued filling out the application as I probed.

"My father owns this property and a few others, so he's usually the final say so. There are some VPs below him though that might weigh in one way or the other first." The way Tyler had cradled my name with her voice earlier was noticeably replaced by the sound of distaste as she spoke about her father's business—maybe her father as well? I couldn't really tell just yet. "This isn't my full-time gig, you know. I just do it to help him out."

"And to live in that penthouse?" I let a smirk slip out as I glanced back up at her.

Despite her best efforts to stop it, I saw her smirk back. "It's an added perk of the job."

I nodded like that made complete sense. I mean, hey, I was a trust fund kid, too, so it's not like I was going to judge. "Sure. Sure. So, what's your full-time gig?"

"I have a podcast," she replied. "The bonus of the penthouse is the recording studio inside, so I can work from one easy place."

A podcast. Of course she'd have a podcast. Gen Z was nothing if not predictable in their trends.

"Oh, fun," I said, but the words didn't translate to my voice.

Tyler sat up slightly taller, almost defensively. "It's not *just* a podcast. It's very well-known. I'm Tyler Adams."

I blinked at her a few times before realizing she expected me to know who that was. Good lord, rich White girls were another breed. "I'm not really the podcast type...sorry. I'm sure it's very popular."

"It's the nation's most listened-to true crime podcast in the past year." She looked indignant now. "I'm practically a household name."

Oh, God. I was going to have to stroke her ego if I wanted this lease, wasn't I?

"That's awesome!" I put on my chipper voice that contained zero percent sincerity. "What's it called?"

"The Deviant Devotee," she replied. "I cover some of the biggest, most complicated and sometimes unsolved crimes out there. This week we're doing an entire episode on The Killing Fields in Texas."

Another reason not to visit Texas.

"Wasn't there already a documentary on that?" I pursed my lips and replied a half second before my brain reminded me that I should be in flattery mode right now. "I mean, I'd love to hear more about that. Definitely send me the link to the podcast!"

Tyler's expression went from frustrated to excited faster than a lesbian asking her girlfriend to move in with her. "Okay! Can I text it to this phone number?"

She pointed at the phone number I'd listed on the first application page I'd already handed back—my cell phone number. "Uh, yeah. Yeah, that's fine. I can't wait to give it a listen."

I handed her the rest of the paperwork as she finished running my card, and I consciously looked everywhere else but at her as she inputted my information into the computer. This woman was clearly not my type—probably sheltered, definitely a little naive, and she clearly had never had anyone let the air out of her ego before. Not to mention she lived a few blocks from my new place, and she might even one day be my landlord of sorts—absolutely not a situation to fuck around with.

And yet, fuck around and find out didn't sound like the worst plan ever right now.

"You know any good lunch spots nearby?" I finally asked, breaking through the sound of her nails clicking against the keyboard. "I just moved to the neighborhood from DC, so I'm still trying to find all the best spots."

"There's a great Panera not too far away," she said, still staring at the computer screen and typing away. "Literally nothing better than their macaroni and cheese."

Not exactly what I'd been thinking of, but doable.

"Oh, cool. Maybe I'll grab a bite there after this." I paused for a moment, the tips of my shoes fidgeting with the carpet beneath me. "If you're hungry, you're welcome to join me."

The clicking on the keyboard stopped and Tyler looked up at me. I wanted to tell myself that squint in her eyes was curiosity and intrigue, but it also could have just been confusion. "Join you?"

I shrugged, now looking away and feeling my own cheeks heat. "For lunch. You know. Meet new people in the neighborhood, no pressure."

Was I asking her out? Good God, I think I was asking her out.

She slowly resumed typing. "I'm, uh, I'm almost done here, and I could certainly use a bite. Why not?"

"Cool." My tone was playing it chill, but my body's inner workings felt like the inside of a puzzle box after a toddler had been shaking it. "Sounds good. Definitely good."

Stop talking, Yas.

"I'd actually love to hear more about the business plans. A lesbian bar in Arlington sounds like a dream," Tyler added, now finishing up and putting the papers together. "I've been out to the new one in DC several times, but it can be a hike."

"As You Are is one of my favorite places," I mused, kind of impressed she not only knew about it but had been there before. "I wouldn't have pegged you as the type of patron to go there."

"If I was straight, I'd never get asked to prove my heteroness," Tyler commented, a lighter lilt to her voice. "But us queers need visible proof, a signed affidavit, and a blood sample before we consider someone part of our tribe."

I grinned wide, because this was the first spark of attitude I'd seen from her that I could actually connect with. "Damn, well okay. You're absolutely right there. We're not a super trusting bunch."

"No, we're not," Tyler agreed, a smile also on her lips as she locked eyes with me. "And for good reason."

"You're preaching to the choir now," I joked as she handed me back a few papers and I stood up from the chair I was seated in. "Lunch is sounding more and more fun by the minute."

Tyler stood as well and grabbed a small clutch from the top drawer of the desk, slipping it around her wrist. She put the rest of the paperwork away in a filing cabinet before turning to me with a warmer smile than I'd yet seen from her. "I'm ready if you are."

I wasn't entirely sure how ready I actually was or what I should be getting ready for, but I wasn't saying no now. "Lead the way."

Chapter Three

"The green goddess salad, please," Tyler told the young man standing behind the register. "And can you put the dressing on the side?"

Panera is one of those places that no one dislikes. Doesn't matter who, what, or where someone is from—Panera has something sweet or savory that isn't going to break the bank.

"I'll do the half, half order—macaroni and cheese and the roasted turkey and avocado BLT," I added to Tyler's order. "Plus, a large sweet tea and a sugar cookie."

Tyler's brows lifted as she looked at me. "Actually, that sounds good. I'll do a medium iced tea—unsweetened—and maybe one cookie, too."

He finished putting everything into the registry and then glanced up at the two of us. "Anything else?"

"That's it," I replied. "She's paying."

"I'm paying?" Tyler scoffed, and her blue eyes looked bewildered. "Since when?"

I grinned and pushed my hands into my pockets as if to

reiterate I wasn't pulling out a wallet. "You can write it off as a business expense. Lunch with a potential retail client."

"Oh, so this is a business lunch?" That small smirk had returned to the corners of her lips, but she was already handing her credit card over to the cashier. "Good to know. Glad we set those expectations ahead of time."

Now I wanted to walk back everything I'd just said, because business lunch sounded like second place coming out of her mouth.

She handed me the black buzzer machine that would alert us when our food is ready and then an empty cup for my tea. We both headed over to the drinks station and filled our cups with teas at opposite ends of the sugar spectrum. She chose unsweetened hibiscus iced tea, which is basically flower water and I do not understand White people sometimes.

We found a booth off to the side big enough only for two people and slid onto opposite benches.

"So, tell me about this lesbian bar plan that also does hair," Tyler prompted, taking a slow sip of her liquid flower. "How exactly does that work? And how is it not a health code violation?"

I clapped my hands together, because despite the fact that this idea was less than an hour old, I'd already started to put together eighteen different pieces of it in my head, and the adrenaline of a new project was coursing through me more than the sugar from this sweet tea. "Okay, so picture this—bar and lounge in the front, private hair studio in the back, and a catwalk to go from one side to the other."

Tyler gave me a deadpan expression. "I don't get it."

I tried not to sigh, because this was good practice. If I was going to launch this business, I needed to be able to explain it in a way that anyone could get it. "Okay, so back story—lesbian bars are safe queer spaces in a way that other bars—even gay male bars—are not. Lesbian bars are sanctuaries for trans people, nonbinary people, queer folks with disabilities, kinky folks, and literally everything else on the spectrum. Gay bars just don't offer those same vibes."

That made Tyler's brows lift, and the sparkle in the irises of her eyes gave me hope. "That's interesting."

"Yup," I continued. "There's over a thousand gay bars in America marketed toward gay men and their straight female friends, and less than twenty-five lesbian and queer bars. It's bullshit."

She rolled her eyes. "Patriarchy."

"Right?" I pointed at her in excitement. She was following my wavelength and it was feeding into my energy. Somehow people thought being a lesbian meant I was exempt from patriarchal bullshit, but it literally meant I was entirely under a hairy male thumb no matter what I did or who I fucked. "But that's not all—"

She snorted a laugh, and, god, it was fucking cute. "You sound like an infomercial now."

I waved her off and kept going. "Another issue in the queer community is safe places to get your hair done—particularly for people who are trans, nonbinary, or just struggling with the motivation to get into a salon and not feel like they are being judged by everyone there. Same with people with mental health issues—depression can be a real fucker when it comes to brushing or washing your hair and the queer community has sky-high levels of mental health issues thanks to how the rest of the world treats us. This bar is going to provide all of that in one safe place."

The buzzer for our food went off right then, and Tyler stood up from the bench seat she was on.

"Hold that thought. I'll be right back with our plates," she said.

I watched her walk toward the counter and didn't judge myself at all for letting my eyes wander the length of her body. I don't think I'd ever seen someone with a flatter ass before, but it was working for her—and for me. Something about the way she walked with purpose felt like I wanted to be beside her, hold her hand, and go wherever she wanted to take me.

Jesus, I sounded like a corny romance novel.

She turned around and held up the platter of food, smiling at me, and I quickly tried to push away my thoughts. If this woman was about to become my new landlord, I really couldn't be lusting over her every time I was around her.

I mean, I could…I probably would, but I really shouldn't.

Get it together, Yas.

"So, how does the catwalk fit into all of this?" Tyler asked as she placed our plates down in front of us and slid back into the bench seat across from me.

I took a quick bite of my sandwich and swallowed. "It'll be a fun option for those who want to show off after a cut or style. They'll have the option of literally walking the catwalk into the bar, and everyone will be encouraged to clap and support them. But, of course, we'll have a small side door and a back door for those who just want to come and go with no fuss or attention. That's important, too."

Tyler chewed on the bite of salad in her mouth before swallowing. "So, the haircuts are free then?"

I shake my head. "They are by voluntary donation. If you need free, that's totally fine. If you can pay, great. If you want to pay ahead for the next person, even better."

"So, kind of like a community system to help one another," Tyler mused. "That would really add to the cohesiveness and sense of belonging for all the patrons."

"Absolutely," I agreed, because that was the part I was most excited about. "And outside of the catwalk, the salon part is private so people can get what they need without feeling judged or gawked at, you know? The bar side will have coffee and daytime spritzers in the afternoons, then switch to more liquor and all that in the evenings. All couches, lounge areas, community-style seating to really promote people coming together."

"What about people who want to be alone?" Tyler asked. "Some people are introverts, you know. They might want to be around people but not actually interacting with them."

She had a point. "Okay, so not *all* community-style seating. Maybe we'll have like a workstation area to one side or little cubbies for those who want to be more in the background—kind of like how the old libraries used to do it?"

"I loved libraries as a kid," Tyler added, her voice stretching out the word *loved*. "People were all around, but everyone kept to themselves and watched out for each other. Books, of course, being the glue to it all. But there was really something about just being around people who felt the same way you did and also required nothing of you."

"Well, now I'm thinking one wall of the bar area should be a bookshelf," I said. "Maybe like a take one, leave one kind of situation? We could even heavily feature queer reads, because God knows there aren't enough of those stories out there."

"But not just coming of age and coming out stories," Tyler replied. She was rolling her eyes again, and I don't know why it was so hard to look away from that deep blue. "Not that there is anything wrong with those, but it's like that's all the literary industry knows how to publish—stories of people realizing they are queer and going through some terrible tragedy to find their truth or live their truth. No happy queer stories are allowed, because that couldn't possibly exist."

"You're preaching to the choir," I agreed. "It's so annoying that the literary—and every other—industry seems to think our trauma is the only interesting thing about us."

Tyler's smirk was back. "I mean, I find some other things interesting, too..."

The lilt in her voice as she said that had *just* a hint of flirty to it, and my senses immediately went on overdrive. "Tell me more..."

She grinned at me and I felt like I'd stumbled down a trap door. Good Lord, since when did I become so easy to pull in like that? She knew exactly what she was doing.

"I mean, let *me* tell you more about the bar concept," I rushed to continue, as if I hadn't just leaned in and flirted right back. "We obviously need a regular karaoke night."

Tyler laughed and there was a piece of lettuce on her front tooth that for some reason did nothing to turn me off. She wiped at it quickly with a napkin, and then shook her head. "Your application is going to be a hard sell to my father. Late night noise, crowds, alcohol, sharp scissors and hair dye? It sounds like the beginning of a liability lawsuit. Don't even get me started on the gay thing."

I wasn't sure what the hell that meant, but I ignored it.

"What *do* you think it would take to push our application to the top?" I asked, finishing the last few bites of my macaroni and cheese as I eyed her. "You're the property manager so I'd imagine you have more than a little sway into the decision."

"You'd think, but no," Tyler confirmed. "Plus, I really only do it to have someone on site for the property, you know? My podcast is really where my passion is."

"Right. The podcast." I polished off the last of my sweet tea and cleared my throat. "Deviant and Delicious?"

She laughed again—this time no lettuce in her teeth—and shook her head. "The Deviant Devotee."

Whoops. "Oh, sorry. What got you into true crime?"

"Besides being a millennial?" Tyler said with a grin. "Actually, I think my therapist could answer that question more than I could. Or, at least, she's been *trying* to get me to answer that for the last few years."

"They *do* do that, don't they?" I said. "So, if I asked your therapist, what would she say is why you love true crime?"

"Not love necessarily...but fascinated." Tyler held up one finger, and her tone turned more serious than the joking manner she'd just been speaking in. "And she'd probably say my childhood has a thing or two to do with it."

Juicy. I'm in. "Your childhood?"

Tyler nodded, but her eyes stopped meeting mine as she pushed the salad around her bowl. "My ACE score is six."

Adverse Childhood Experiences was a questionnaire from the CDC that my therapist had also given me but I'd only ever scored a two.

"Oh." Well, damn. The pretty rich girl just got a few layers deeper, and I had a shovel ready to keep tunneling for more. "I'm sorry. Childhood can be...rough. Trauma is a bitch."

Tyler waved a hand, but she still wasn't meeting my gaze. If she had, she would have seen my apology was genuine and that she'd just hit close to my home as well. "It's in the past—mostly —but there's probably something to my desire to help rid the world of secrets and continued hurt. I kind of consider it my life's mission to give a voice to the voiceless and a platform to people who've been overlooked or felt unloved."

I shouldn't ask more questions, but I'm going to. "Have you ever done a personal case on the podcast—like someone you know or something close to you?"

"Definitely not," Tyler shuts me down almost immediately. "I'm a journalist, and an artist. My own life has nothing to do with any of that. I'm completely separate. My identity is completely separate."

I swallowed hard—the wall she was putting up felt impenetrable. "Oh."

The woman had a shield more impenetrable than I'd ever met before. It was like the moment I tapped at the door, she put up the gate.

"Sorry." Tyler looked up at me now and there was a firmness in her expression. "We should probably wrap things up here, because I have to get back and do some edits for next week's release."

"Okay." It had been a while since I'd heard my own voice sound so timid—almost submissive. Something about the way she'd shut down conversation felt like I couldn't push back—or maybe that I wouldn't? I wasn't sure what I was feeling right now, except that her word was law in my mind. And yet, the weight on my chest was unmistakable.

Tyler was nothing like who my first impression had said she was, and I wasn't even sure what that meant or who she actually was.

All I did know is that I wanted to know more.

"When do you think you'll have a decision made on the space?" I asked, changing the topic as we both stood and began cleaning up our place settings. "You know, just so I can plan and run things by our accountant."

Note to self—check in with the accountant.

Also, hire an accountant.

Tyler stacked her dishes at the receptacle. "He wants someone in by the first of July, even mid-June, so I can't imagine long. I've got your information, so I'll be in touch."

"You'll be in touch?" We were standing at the front door now, and I was holding it open for her as she walked through. "That's...okay, well, yeah. You'll be in touch."

I felt like a helium balloon slowly deflating from the smallest of holes at the professionalism of it all.

"Thanks for lunch," I added when we both got out on the sidewalk. "That was a nice change of pace from unpacking."

"Welcome to the neighborhood." Tyler offered me one last smile, but I'd seen her real smile already and this one was not that. This was forced and formal, and it bothered me substantially more than the lettuce-in-the-teeth smile I'd seen before.

"Thanks," I replied, but Tyler had already turned around and was walking away, back in the direction of her penthouse.

I watched her go for a moment longer than I wanted to admit, and then pulled my cell phone out of my pocket. "I guess I really should call an accountant."

I could already hear my father's voice chiding this as my next failed business, but my gut was telling me something different I hadn't felt before.

This idea had legs, and I was in this for the hike.

Chapter Four

"**H**is name is Blaine?" I scrunched my brows as I glanced across the kitchen island at Isa Reyes sitting on a stool on the other side. "That's basically just the rich, preppy version of a Chad. Red flag right out of the gate."

I'd met Isa originally a few years back through my former roommate, Mila. They were—still are—very close, so Isa was just around all the time and she's just weird enough to be interesting. Rachel, however, can't stand her, so that was always a weird sticking point in our group that, thankfully, isn't as big a deal now that I'm living alone.

"It is *not* a red flag. You know family is important to us Filipinas." Isa waved me off and turned her phone screen toward me to show me Blaine's Hinge profile. "He was named after his grandfather and father. He's like the fourth Blaine in the family lineage—that's kind of sweet if you think about it! Shows he's a family man."

"Does it though?" I countered in a high-pitched teasing tone, taking her phone and scrolling through the whitest man's dating profile. There were at least two taco references, his favorite song was by Drake, and one photograph was just him holding a fish that didn't look big enough to be proud of. *Straight people dating profiles are just sad.* "Oh, god. He's a consultant, too? Next, you'll tell me he went to an Ivy League college and it'll be the DC douche canoe trifecta."

Isa grinned, crossing her arms on the countertop in front of me. "He went to Columbia."

"That tracks." I handed the phone back to her. "I mean, he's cute, but I'd have my spidey senses on around him. He has all the makings of a two a.m. *'you up?'* text message a month after ghosting you post-coitus."

Something about Isa brought out a protective side in me. It's not that she makes bad choices—I mean, she definitely does when it came to her dating life—but it was her undeterred optimism that made me want to shield her. She was a rare gem in a place like Washington, DC—still completely untarnished by cynicism despite being a boss bitch in public relations and being an immigrant. It honestly defied logic, and therefore, she had to be protected at all costs.

"We've only been on a few dates so far, and I've been holding out." Isa looked proud of herself, placing the phone down on the countertop and looking up at me. "I know the signs could be there, but I see a really sweet side to him that I don't think he shows other people. There's more than meets the surface, you know?"

Of course. The damaged alpha who only she can coax out of his guarded shell. That wasn't an overplayed stereotype at all.

"Plus, we have a lot in common—we're even in the same podcast Facebook group," Isa added.

"Oh, I just met someone who has a podcast," I mused, the image of Tyler's blue eyes coming to my mind. I still hadn't listened to an episode, but I'd never really gotten into podcasts before so it wasn't top of my mind. "I promised her I'd listen to an episode soon."

"Ooh, is this a love interest?" Isa wiggled her brows and cooed at me. "I mean, everyone has a podcast these days though, so good for her. What's hers called?"

"Uh..." I racked my brain for the memory but it had been almost a week since we'd had lunch together and I still hadn't heard back about my application on the retail space. *Note to self, I should go check in with her in person if I don't hear back by the end of today.* "Direly Devoted? Or something Devoted. I can't remember, but it's true crime related."

Isa's eyes widened and she slammed her palms flat down against the kitchen island. "Please tell me you are *not* referring to *The Deviant Devotee* by Tyler Adams? You're not, right?"

"Yes, that's it! She lives really close to here." I gestured out the kitchen window in the vague direction of her penthouse a few blocks east of me. "I'm trying to get into business with her on a new venture I'm working on."

Isa put her hand up, palm facing me. "Okay, as your public relations representative, I forbid all of this. Start to finish—just no. Absolutely no."

I lifted one eyebrow higher than the other and offered her a small smirk. "Um, since when am *I* your client?"

"Since you decided to get into bed with Tyler Adams," Isa replied. "Wait...did you *actually* get into bed with her? Or is this just business?"

My gaze scattered off to the corner of the room as a guilty wave passed over me because bed-related activities were exactly what I wanted to do with Tyler, whether I was going to admit that to Isa or not.

"I definitely have not slept with her," I assured Isa. "We've only talked business."

And personal life details that left a palpable physical tension between us we refused to admit to. I left that part out.

Isa rolled her eyes so hard that my grandmother would have had something to say, but she seemed more at ease with my answer. "So, you're going into podcasting now? Didn't the edible panties thing just flail into oblivion?"

"*Chewing with Love* was a beta test that didn't pan out," I said defensively, walking over to the fridge and pulling out two hard seltzers. I handed one to Isa and then opened the other for myself. "It didn't quite launch the way I'd hoped it might, but this new idea is very different. Plus, what's wrong with working with Tyler Adams?"

"She's connected to a divisive figure in the media," Isa replied. "Her father is seriously the worst. He's very outspoken on everything anti-LGBTQ+, anti-liberal, anti-you name it and he has a shit ton of money that he funnels into politicians who back his stances. He's a powerhouse here in DC, and he uses his power for evil."

I frowned. Tyler hadn't given me a lot of information about her family background—in fact, she'd clammed up pretty quickly after the topic came up. "I can't imagine they are very close then. Either that, or he has no idea who she really is behind closed doors."

"Because she's a lesbian?" Isa asked, then waved her hand. "She's not out to the public, so I wouldn't be surprised if she keeps it from some of her family, too. But those of us who have listened in since the beginning have kind of suspected she might be. And, you basically just confirmed it for me."

I could feel the heat swelling in my cheeks. "I mean, I'm not trying to out her. That's her life. It's just a business relationship right now. I want to lease a space in her building to open a lesbian bar."

31

"She owns a building?" Isa tapped a finger against her lips. "Or her father owns a building?"

"Her father," I corrected as I felt the flicker of hope being extinguished in my gut. "Which I'm guessing now might be why I haven't heard back about my application. I can't imagine he'd sign off on a lesbian bar if those are his politics."

Isa shrugged her shoulders and went back to scrolling through her phone. "You never know. Maybe he's not as involved in the day-to-day stuff like that, but if he is, I can help you find a retail space for it. A lesbian bar in Virginia is your first business idea I can actually get behind."

"Hey!" I huffed, polishing off the last seltzer I'd been drinking. I stepped over to the fridge to grab another. "You loved the idea of my androgynous clothing line back in the day."

"Yeah, until I saw your skills as a fashion designer are nonexistent. Those designs flattered no one's body type." She was smiling at me, even though I knew her critiques were genuine.

I didn't take offense, because she wasn't wrong. Clothing design had turned out not to be a skill of mine. As well as sex toys. And edible panties. Subscription models in general. Even the prototype of my silicone, wearable butt enhancers had fallen flat. But none of that mattered now. A lesbian bar was going to meet all my ADHD skill sets—customer-driven, high energy, and just the right amount of rowdy to keep me from ever getting bored.

"So, are you going to handle all the PR shit for the bar in exchange for free drinks?" A girl could hope. "Because clearly I'm going to need the help."

"A few drinks won't even come close to the amount I charge," Isa replied. She wasn't lying either, because I knew she was one of the most sought-after in the city. "But we can work it into the family discount rate. Have you created social pages for the bar yet? Gotten some interest going for the concept? What about investors? What's the bar's name going to be?"

"Uh...I'll email you over the business plan." The business plan I hadn't finished yet. I had some stuff sketched up, but it was a far cry from ready to go. So, time to change topics. "What about you? What's going on at work?"

Isa let out a heavy exhale. "Well, we are about to take on a sports team in DC if everything goes according to my plan. I can't say which one, but think ice."

Well, that was an easy solve.

"And it is just nonstop crisis after crisis," Isa continued. "We're still in the preliminary interview stage and haven't even scored the account yet, but I swear to God, there isn't a Friday and Saturday night that goes by that one of the players hasn't stuck his dick somewhere he shouldn't have."

I grimaced. "Thank the good Lord I've never liked dick."

"That was at least one full therapy session of mine recently. Me just crying over the fact that I wish I liked women, but I prefer men and their stupid floppy penises." Isa shook her head and let out a sigh. "Why does my body betray me like this?"

I laughed and tossed the empty seltzer can that had been sitting in front of her into the trash then went and grabbed her a second from the fridge. "My sympathy goes out to you."

She let out a last deep exhale and then stood up from her seat. "Okay, I'm going to go christen your new toilet."

"Have fun with that." I pointed her down the hall to my bathroom and she headed off.

I picked up my phone and glanced at my missed notifications. I had received a text message from a number I didn't have saved.

Can you stop by later today?

Intrigued, I swiped on the message and typed out a reply. *Who is this?*

The response was almost instant. *Sorry. Tyler. It's about your application.*

That sounded both ominous and promising at the same time. I asked her for a time and we arranged to meet up in two hours.

Isa was returning from the bathroom just as I put my phone down on the countertop. "Good Lord, what did you do while I was gone? It was like three minutes."

I immediately felt flushed. "What? What do you mean?"

Isa gestured toward my face with her index finger waving. "You look all red and gooey-eyed. Who were you texting?"

"No one!" I held up my empty hands like that was proof, despite the fact that she'd seen me on my phone when she had walked in. "It's probably from the alcohol in the seltzer. Heats my blood up, you know?"

"Asian glow affects me, not you." Isa narrowed her eyes at me, and I could tell she wasn't buying any of it. "I'm going to go after this one. I've got to bail a client out of jail."

"Out of jail?" I made a mental note that public relations was also not a fit for me or my skill set. "Christ, your job is intense."

She waved it off like it was nothing. "He deserves to sit there for a little longer, believe me. In the meantime, tell me about the bar concept. I'm kind of excited for this one!"

I gave Isa a slightly shorter recap of the description I'd given Tyler about my ideas for the bar, and Isa was all hands on deck immediately. She'd already begun texting contacts and making plans for ways to market it before she headed out.

The conversation had reinvigorated my enthusiasm for the entire concept, though, and I felt like I was almost bouncing on the sidewalk as I walked toward Tyler's building later that evening. I had convinced myself that it had to be good news—

why else would she want me to come in person unless there was something I should sign?

I got to her building quickly and took the elevator up to the top level, debating whether to knock on her apartment door or the manager's office door.

I settled on both and then just waited to see which opened.

"Hey," Tyler's voice hit me as softly as perfume as the door to her penthouse opened. "Thanks for coming on such late notice."

"No worries. This is actually perfect, because I was going to reach out in the morning if I hadn't heard back by then." I walked past her into the penthouse as she gestured for me to do, letting her close the door behind me. "I'm really hoping this means you have good news for me."

Tyler led me to her kitchen island where a stack of papers was sitting, and I couldn't help myself from noticing that she wasn't in business attire. In fact, it looked like I'd just woken her up from a nap, including the slightly mussed look to her hair like it hadn't seen a brush today. She was wearing a skintight white tank top that showed a sliver of midriff before the top of her also-white lounge pants. Everything about her screamed angelic and yet the way she chewed on her bottom lip only brought devilish thoughts to my mind.

"It's not bad news," Tyler began, glancing toward the paperwork and then back at me. She wasn't wearing any makeup, and her eyes looked smaller than the last time I'd seen her, but somehow just as bright, and I still didn't want to look away. "But there are some contingencies I want to discuss. Do you want to sit down?"

I took a seat on the barstool against the island that she gestured toward.

"You're not really convincing me on the whole *good news*

front if I have to sit down for it," I joked, kind of hoping she'd assure me otherwise.

She didn't.

"I have wine in the fridge. Do you want a glass?" Tyler completely avoided my gaze and walked over to a cabinet by the fridge, pulling out two wineglasses instead.

Okay, so definitely not good news...unless this wasn't about business at all. I couldn't see the papers from where I was sitting, so I didn't even know if those were meant for me. Had she called me over here to talk business? Or was this a booty call? Color me intrigued.

I let my tongue slide across my lower lip, wetting it slowly as she watched me. The way her body stiffened in response and her eyes immediately darkened as she watched me was even more intriguing. "Uh, sure. I'll have a glass of wine with you."

Or more.

Chapter Five

"I told you that your application was going to be a hard sell to my father," Tyler began as she poured some white wine into two glasses and slid one toward me.

She put the bottle back in the fridge as she sidestepped around her sleeping chihuahua in his doggy bed and took the other glass to the barstool next to mine, sliding on close enough that our knees touched.

"Right..." That certainly wasn't making me more optimistic on the business front, but I also couldn't stop thinking about the fact that her knee was against my thigh and my skin literally felt like it was on fire despite the thick layer of my denim jeans between us. "Cheers to that."

She gave me a wry smile but tapped her wineglass to mine and we both took a more than hearty sip. "Well, I really like your idea, and it's a hell of a lot better than the other applications I've received for that spot."

Intrigued, I sipped my wine. "What were the others?"

"A tanning salon, a cat bakery, and an attorney firm." She listed them off one at a time with her fingers in the air.

"Hold on," I interjected. "When you say cat bakery, do you mean like baking treats *for* cats or baking cats?"

"Honestly, the application didn't make that clear," Tyler said, a grin crossing her face.

The air lightened between us as I laughed and shook my head. "Christ, you better not let Larry near them. He basically looks like a cat."

Tyler playfully touched my knee, as if to push me away but without any actual force. I would be absolutely okay if she did that again. And maybe a third time. "Excuse you. Larry is a beautiful, robust dog, thank you very much."

"Robust?" I laughed loudly at that characterization, my head dipping backward before I glanced over at her chihuahua watching us from the floor. "Larry is another dog's sneeze at best. We should go visit the animal shelter and check out the golden retrievers or labradors—those are *dog* dogs."

"*Anyway*," she continued, waving her hand to dismiss my remarks. "I want you to get that spot. I think your bar will help a lot of people, and I want to be involved in making that happen."

I lifted my brows. "You want to be involved?"

"As a property manager," she quickly clarified, but the rosy-red sheen that popped up on her cheeks told me she wanted something more. "Not that I wouldn't be interested in more, but my father—his ideas, his beliefs—will get in the way of this application. So, I think we have to brainstorm how to convince him. I think we have to make it something he can't say no to."

I mean, that made sense to me. I wasn't above a little kiss-ass to get what I wanted. "What's something he can't say no to?"

Tyler took another sip of her wine, longer this time, before she leveled her gaze at me. "Me."

"Okay..." I replied skeptically, because I had no idea where she was going with this or how that would help me. "Are you saying you're going to vouch for me to him?"

"That won't be enough in just a professional sense." She was still not making eye contact with me as her finger traced around the rim of her wineglass. "He'll tell me it's a business lesson and I just have to do what he says. I have to appeal to him as his daughter—not his property manager."

Her father-daughter dynamic was clearly even more complicated than mine, because I was completely turned in circles by this conversation. "I'm going to need a map to follow whatever this journey is you're taking me on."

Tyler laughed, this time lifting her gaze to finally meet mine. "Are you dating anyone right now?"

So, we were just throwing out the map idea entirely, apparently.

"Uh, no..." I replied. "Why?"

A sly grin crossed Tyler's face as she sat up a little taller and focused on me. If I'd thought her eyes were captivating before, they shone on an entirely new level when she was feeling naughty—which her expression clearly told me she was.

"What do you think about dating me?" she asked.

I hadn't expected that question, and the U-Haul part of me was like *absolutely, let's do this*, but the practical part of me was already running out of this penthouse like my jeans were on fire. "Uh..."

"Not for real," she quickly clarified, putting a hand up between us. "But if we can convince my father that we're together, I think he'll give you the space out of his love for me. No matter how antiquated his beliefs may be, he wants me to be happy first and foremost."

I pressed my thigh against her leg just a bit harder, feeling my breath coming faster as I tried to picture the reveal—our arms linked together as we walked into his office. It felt exhilarating in a way I couldn't really pinpoint—not the deceit of it all, but just the fact that I'd be playing that role. Even if it wasn't real, I could feel the pull in my gut telling me to step into it.

Into her.

"This feels out of the norm for you," I finally admitted after a few moments of silence slipped between us, this time biting the edge of my bottom lip and then slowly releasing it. "You struck me as the play-by-the-rules type when we first met."

"I usually am a strict rule follower." She lifted her chin defiantly and shrugged one shoulder. The top she was wearing slid lower on her shoulder, and I couldn't—wouldn't—avert my eyes. "But..."

She paused, and I missed her eyes on me. I missed her leg pressed against mine, and despite how insane her idea was, I couldn't distract myself from the blaze slowly etching its way across my skin in scorching flames.

I placed my wineglass down on the counter and leaned my upper body in a bit closer to hers. "But what, Tyler?"

"Maybe I want to explore another side of me." Her voice suddenly had a huskier, whispered quality to it that I'd never heard before, and her eyes were back on my lips again.

I took the wineglass out of her hand next and placed it down on the counter by mine. "Tell me about this other side of yours."

Maybe she forgot her words, or maybe there aren't any words that would accurately describe the sizzling tension hanging in the air between her body and mine, but Tyler didn't say anything.

Instead, she leaned in, closing the space between us and pressing her lips to mine. For a second, my body froze, and I heard my own breath hitch at the suddenness of it all. I'd pictured this before—woken up a few times over the last week to this dream with my hand between my legs—but actually living it was entirely better than I could have imagined.

My stiffness melted away in nanoseconds as my hand lifted to her cheek and hooked around the back of her neck. I pulled her closer to me and deepened our kiss. Her tongue slid across mine, and she was off her stool and climbing into my lap.

I held her against me as I explored her softness against the tip of my tongue or between a small nibble of my teeth. She moaned into my mouth when I did that, and my arms slid around her back, anchoring her tighter to me.

I don't know how much time went by—if it was only a second, or if we were kissing for an hour—but when Tyler began rocking her body against me, I felt ready to explode.

"Tyler," I gasped between breaths and presses of our lips together. "Where's your bedroom?"

She slid off my lap quickly, and I immediately felt the cruel, cold air she left behind. She grabbed my hand, however, and pulled me off the stool and in the direction of a hallway to the right of the kitchen.

I followed her like a lovesick puppy, and I wasn't even remotely ashamed of my unabashed desire in that moment. Whatever this woman wanted to do, I was going to say yes.

Signed, sealed, delivered—tonight's decision had been made.

The door at the end of the hallway was open and inside was a king-sized bed with dark burgundy blankets and sheets covering the entire thing like a fluffy red cloud. The only light turned on was on the nightstand, and the bulb was a warm color that made the entire room look soft and hazy, and I didn't have the ability to focus on what else was around us as Tyler stood at the end of the bed and turned to face me.

In one swift and yet agonizingly slow motion, she gripped the bottom hem of her sleeveless shirt and lifted it over her head, then tossed it to the floor. She wasn't wearing a bra and my mouth went dry at the way her nipples stood at attention and the pointed, fullness of her breasts.

"Break the rules with me," she said breathily.

I didn't need to be asked twice. My shirt followed suit, joining hers on the floor and my hands found the top of her linen pants and began sliding them down her legs. She undid the top button of my jeans, and I helped her wiggle them the rest of the way off. Her underwear was delicate—a blush pink lace that I decided not to remove.

I wanted to touch that lace, and I wanted her to feel the lace between us until we couldn't stand to have anything between us anymore.

"Get on the bed," I instructed, my voice more demanding than normal.

Who was I kidding? This *was* my normal.

She licked her lips and slid backward onto the bed until she was in the center of the dark wine-colored sheets. I crawled after her like a parched woman in the desert crawling toward a pool of water and praying it wasn't a mirage.

Our lips met again as I pressed my body down on top of hers, my hand sliding between our bodies to cup her right breast. It fit perfectly in the palm of my hand and my thumb grazed across her nipple, noting the way her body shook beneath me at that contact. My lips disconnected from hers, and I left a trail of kisses down her jawline, her neck, her collarbone, and finally, her breasts.

My tongue slid in a circle around one nipple before pulling it into my mouth and sucking on her.

Tyler cried out, and her back arched, bringing her even closer to me. "Yasmeen..."

The way my name sounded on her lips only fueled the fire in my core. I switched to her other breast for a moment, tenderly giving it the attention I'd given the first, before kissing down her rib cage and across her stomach. The hem of her lace underwear beckoned me and I ran my tongue across the length from one pelvic bone to the other.

"Wait..." Her breath stuttered and she pushed up just enough to close her legs to her knees, the bottom half of her legs still divided on either side of me. "I just—don't judge me, okay?"

I furrowed my brows and lifted my gaze to meet hers. "Judge you for what?"

She sat up further and traced a hand across her inner thigh, directing my attention to the small pink etches across the skin. "It was a long time ago. Being a teenager was hard for me. It just...it makes me self-conscious sometimes because most people don't know it's there. Then I'm hooking up with someone and suddenly...you can't *not* see it."

The light was dim in the bedroom, but there was no mistaking the beaded, self-inflicted scars in careful, small lines that started just below the crease of her leg and went another ten inches down toward her knee.

I reached out and ran the tip of my index finger across the bottom scar which was a bit darker than the top, and then leaned forward and placed a soft kiss against her inner thigh.

"You don't think it's hideous?" Tyler's voice was dripping in a vulnerability I didn't want to trample over, but if I was being honest, the only thing that bothered me about her scars was knowing the pain she must have been in to redirect it in this way. "I wish I'd been able to see a therapist back then, but my dad didn't believe in that kind of stuff. I haven't done it in over a decade now, I promise."

"Of course it's not hideous," I replied, then pointed to the scar at the top and moved my finger down across each one. "It's kind of beautiful if you think about it. Like a healing ladder, tracking your most painful moments until the moment you decided to stop. There's a story here—and it's one of growth and strength. Nothing can be hideous about that."

I didn't add that it was also touching that she trusted me enough to let me see this part of her. We barely knew each other, but something in this moment felt like I was seeing inside of her, and she was welcoming me in. It was overwhelming and terrifying and just intoxicating enough to make me want to know more.

"A ladder..." The words fell softly from her lips, like a whisper she was digesting in time. "I think I like that reframe."

"I think I like you." I slid back up her body until she was pressed back down against the mattress. "Do you want me to keep going?"

Consent is sexy, folx.

She nodded her head furtively and the dark heat had already returned to her pupils. I kissed the hemline of her lace panties one more time before making my way back to where I'd been before—and this time, she didn't stop me.

Thank fucking God.

Tyler's entire body shuddered now and she lifted her hips to meet me. Whatever inhibitions she'd had moments ago had shed between us. I pushed her back down onto the bed, grinning up at her. Her desire in this moment might be the sexiest thing I've ever seen. It was completely no-holds-barred, and she was opening for me like she'd been waiting for me the entire time.

"Put your hands on your breasts," I instructed her softly, despite the gravelly sound in my throat. "Play with your nipples."

She didn't hesitate to follow my instructions, and the moment she began, I placed my mouth against the lace that was covering her, and I sucked hard.

She gasped audibly, her body trembling against me as her hand continued to play with her breasts, my mouth and her core soaking the lace between us. I bit the lace between my teeth and dragged it up and down against her—just rough enough to make her feel it but lightly enough to not let her come yet.

I wanted more time.

"Oh, God, Yas...I can't...I need...oh, my God, I'm so close..." The words were tumbling out of her mouth now, and she was barely coherent, but this was a map I knew how to follow and I was going to show her how I mastered this trail.

My finger hooked around the wet lace now, pulling it to the side and allowing my tongue the first real contact with her. She nearly bounced off the bed, but my hand flat on her pelvis pinned her down. I licked the length of her, dipping inside and then finding her clit and ravaging anything she might be holding back.

Tyler cried out and this time I didn't let up. "I'm coming, Yas..."

Her entire body was shaking against me until I felt her sag into the mattress in defeat as her climax finished ripping through her. I slowed then, soft and gentle touches until her shaky body finally became still and her breath evened out.

I put the lace back and climbed up her body, lying to one side of her on the mattress and letting my hand rest on her stomach and trace small circles up and down her ribcage and sternum.

Tyler turned hazy, drooping eyes toward me and curled into my chest, tucking her head into my neck. "That was...that was incredible."

My arm circled her back, and I felt a tenderness well up in me that I hadn't before. I pulled her against me and kissed her cheek, then pushed a few loose strands of hair behind her ear. "I can't disagree."

Her hand slid down my chest, trailed my stomach, and slid into the top of my underwear. "I want to see you like that," she whispered into my neck.

I spread my legs to give her further access, and her fingers found my core like she'd been there before. She touched me quickly, easily, and after everything we'd just done, I was already at the precipice of my own climax.

Her finger dipped inside me while her thumb rubbed against my clit, and I could feel my body respond almost immediately. I groaned as I held her closer to me and pressed my hips against her hand. When it hit me, it was like a warm tidal wave that somehow felt excruciatingly powerful and gently intimate all at the same time.

I felt her kisses against my neck as I came on her hand, and when she finally pulled away, I found myself speechless as she trailed her fingers up her own body and to her lips. She sucked on the tips of her fingers to taste me, and I knew then and there that I needed her again.

I pushed her back down against the mattress and covered my body with hers, my lips on hers with a fierceness I didn't even know I had the energy for in that moment.

I wasn't going anywhere tonight except wherever she wanted to take me.

Chapter Six

The last woman I'd had sex with had a tattoo of Barnacle Boy from SpongeBob SquarePants on her ass, and that was honestly the first thing I thought of when I woke up and glanced over at Tyler asleep next to me.

She was hugging a pillow like it was her best friend, her mouth slightly ajar with the tiniest pool of drool slipping out, and her bare flat ass up in the air as her knee was propped up beneath her abdomen. No tattoos to be seen, but the morning sun from her bedroom windows added a golden glow to her usually pale complexion.

I'm not a one-night stand type of lesbian, but I do have a history of fast and serious. My average relationship spanned maybe three months—if I'm being generous—and was usually near the proposal or move-in stage before things imploded. Isa likes to call me a U-Haul lesbian, and that would probably be true if I had lived alone the last decade. However, living with Mila and Rachel meant that they'd veto my suggestions immediately anytime I wanted a new girlfriend to spend more than a few nights in a row at our place. They were like my self-sabotage antidote, and now that I was living on my own, I had all the freedom in the world to shit where I ate if I wanted to.

Not that that's what I was going to do with Tyler. But it didn't feel entirely impossible given how things had escalated in the few days we'd known each other.

Last night had been…I'm not even sure I knew how to describe it. It hadn't felt like just a random hook-up. It hadn't even felt like some weird business deal. It felt primal. It felt predetermined. It felt like her body had always been meant to be pressed against mine, and now as I watched her sleeping in the small puddle of her own saliva and the tangle of sheets we'd worn through throughout the night, I couldn't help but feel a throbbing in my chest that was somehow both unfamiliar and entirely familiar all at the same time.

And I was going to go into business with this woman.

I lifted my head and glanced around for my cell phone, remembering then that she and I still hadn't worked out the details on how this whole plan with her father was going to work out to begin with. Or whether or not she even wanted to do it. Or if I wanted to do it.

Do I want to do this?

I found my cell phone in a pile of my clothes on the floor by the bed and scooped it up, checking my missed text messages. There were multiple in a row from Isa.

I found some listings in Clarendon and Ballston that might fit your bar idea better than Tyler's place. Call me.

That had come in last night, and she'd followed it up thirty minutes later with another and two missed calls.

There's zero chance you're asleep right now.

I just checked your location, and I don't know where you are, but that is not your new address.

Yas, you better not be with Tyler right now.

Do you remember our entire conversation about not opening

a queer bar in a building owned by a prominently anti-queer White man?

After that onslaught of back-to-back messages, she had waited an hour and texted me one last time.

Call me in the morning when you're ready to do damage control.

I held the laugh in my chest so as not to wake up Tyler, but it was always funny to watch Isa spiral into her crisis-public-relations mode. If there were two ends to the spectrum, she and I were at the opposite from each other. Everything was deadly serious for her, and I firmly operated under the concept that forgiveness is always easier to obtain than permission, and no one gives a shit anyway.

I tapped Isa's name and shot off a quick text assuring her everything was fine, then went and clicked over to my other messages. One from my father asking me to return his call. Another from Mila with pictures of her daughter eating an ice cream cone upside down. And last, a message from a number I didn't have saved in my phone that came in around one o'clock in the morning and just said, *"u up?"* I wasn't even going to bother trying to figure out which of my past hook-ups that was from, and I deleted it immediately.

I was about to put my phone down when a notification from HER app slid down from the top of the screen telling me that someone had liked one of my photos. I clicked on it, and the dating app opened to the profile of a gorgeous woman posing on the steps of the Supreme Court looking fierce as hell. I recognized it immediately from the night Ruth Bader Ginsberg had died and everyone who cared about women's rights and was able-bodied within walking or driving distance gathered on the steps to mourn together.

I clicked *Like* on her photo as well.

49

"Seriously?" Tyler's voice still had that sleepy roughness to it, but there was also an undertone of aggression.

I glanced over at her and gave her a smile. "Good morning?"

"Yes, it's a lovely morning to wake up to the woman in my bed swiping on a dating app for other women." Tyler's sleepiness had faded into active irritation now.

She tossed the sheet off her naked body and maneuvered to the edge of the bed to stand up, but I grabbed her forearm and pulled her back down onto the mattress.

"Yas—" She groaned angrily but didn't fight me.

"Look," I began, lifting my phone up in front of both of us and then turning it off entirely. I tossed it to the end of the bed out of both of our reach. "I'm sorry. I swear it wasn't like that. I wasn't even thinking."

She was on her back on the bed as I leaned over her, so it was easy to see her roll her eyes with as much dramatic effect as I'd ever seen eyeballs do.

"Whatever." She refused to make eye contact with me, and I couldn't help but smile and let out a small laugh. "It's not funny, Yas!"

"I know," I replied, still laughing. "But, look—you're jealous. It's really cute."

"I am *not* jealous," she clarified, this time physically pulling away from me and wiggling her way off the bed. She walked over to her closet and grabbed a robe hanging on the back of the door, covering herself with it. "It's just a respect issue, you know?"

I leaned back in the bed, resting my neck on top of my arms behind my head. "Sure, definitely not jealous at all. I completely buy that."

She shot me an angry look, her nose scrunched up and her

lips turned into a frown that somehow made her look even less threatening. "I'm *not* jealous."

"Okay." I sat up and reached for my phone where I'd tossed it. "I guess I'll just go back to what I was doing then."

The flames in her eyes said more than she did as she stomped out of the room.

I sighed and pushed myself to the edge of the bed, grabbing at my clothes and allowing myself to take some time to get dressed before I chased after her.

Dating women was always so dramatic.

When I walked out into the kitchen where our wineglasses were still sitting from last night, I found Tyler chopping the tops off a bunch of strawberries with all the ferocity of a lion attacking a gazelle. It was like a berry massacre on the counter, and she'd nearly juiced half of them at this point.

"Those poor strawberries," I commented as I slid onto the stool I'd been sitting on last night. My previous glass of wine still had a few sips left in it, and I sniffed it and then downed the remainder. "Huh. Still good the next day."

She wrinkled her nose as she leveled her gaze at me. "You know, I was nominated for People's Choice Podcast of the Year last year."

Not the direction I'd expected this conversation to go. "Congratulations?"

"And I was class valedictorian of both my high school and my university," she continued, returning to smashing/cutting up the bowl of strawberries.

"Don't forget prom queen," I teased, tossing out a guess.

She paused and looked at me. "Actually, yes. I was prom queen twice in high school—including once at a school I didn't even go to. I was voted president of my college sorority, too."

I nodded along to her list; my lips set in a tight line. "Cool, cool."

"I am *not* someone who gets tossed to the side after a hookup like it was nothing." She'd finished cutting up the strawberries and was now popping them in her mouth, talking in between juicy fruity bites. "I am someone who is pursued, chased, begged for their attention. I am a fucking catch."

I placed my hand over my mouth to keep her from seeing me smile. *And she really wanted to pretend she wasn't jealous?* "Well, okay, Ms. Adams. I hear you loud and clear. You are a goddess, and I should be kissing your feet to thank you for giving me the exclusive privilege of tasting that Grade-A pussy."

Her cheeks tinged a darker pink than the strawberries. "That's not what I meant."

I stood and walked around the island, coming to a stop next to her and leaning back against the countertop. I reached into her bowl of strawberries and took one for myself.

"Last night you said you wanted to explore another side of yourself," I started, grabbing a second strawberry. I didn't miss the way her gaze followed my hand to my mouth and stayed there. "Maybe that other side of yourself is the one that doesn't get everything she wants just because she wants it."

"Now you're making me sound like a spoiled brat." Tyler huffed and placed the bowl down on the counter. "That's still not what I meant, and you know it."

"It's not what you meant, but it's what you said," I replied, picking up the bowl she'd just discarded and helping myself to the rest of the strawberries. "I don't beg for attention. I don't pursue. I don't chase. And, might I remind you, you invited me over here last night. You knew exactly what you wanted, and all I did was give it to you. You could start with saying thank you, you know."

Her mouth fell open, and her eyes could have pierced through me in that moment. Instead of letting her talk and

52

curse me out, I popped a strawberry in between her open lips. She swallowed it quickly, and I'm pretty sure that strawberry boiled in fury before it ever hit her stomach.

Good Lord, this was *fun*. It also felt a little harsh, but I'd committed to the role and there was no going back now. Even if a huge part of me didn't want to leave at all, and instead desired to just drag her right back to bed and let her thank me that way.

"I'll consider your business offer, Ms. Adams," I continued, trying to keep my own thoughts at bay. "If it's still on the table, that is. But this isn't the beginning of a love story, and I'm not someone that anyone gets to lay claim to. We are not dating. Nor are we going to start dating."

Something about that sentence didn't feel entirely true, but I was sticking to it anyway.

"Anywho, I should be going." I polished off the last strawberry and placed the bowl back down on the counter.

Without missing a beat, I took a step toward her and kissed her directly on the lips—the firm type that would linger just long enough to make her body go from rigid to leaning into me like *she* was begging *me* for more.

It took all my strength to not pick the *more* option.

Instead, I separated and stepped away from her, heading for the front door and completely ignoring the way her breath had hitched when I'd kissed her or the hard swallow in her throat. "In the meantime, you have my number if you're willing to meet me on my terms."

She was still staring after me, her mouth agape like she wanted to respond but didn't know what to say.

I love to leave a woman speechless.

Chapter Seven

"You have to lift your chin higher," I told my nonbinary friend Kari as I tweaked the angle of the lens videoing them. "It's too low in the second transition and looks fragmented."

I was standing behind a ring light stand with Kari's cell phone anchored in the center as they posed and danced in front of a blank wall and lip-synced to a Lizzo song.

All in the name of TikTok.

"Ugh," Kari let out a loud sigh and shook their shoulders out. "Okay, let me try again one more time with the suit, and then I'm going to do the glam side. Ready?"

I wasn't one to spend a ton of time on social media, and my platform of choice was usually Instagram. Anything else felt like a void that was too easy to be sucked into, but I was happy to support my friends who loved it. Kari had accumulated over two million followers doing transition videos from the masculine version of themselves to the female version—both of which were so equally, sexily, bangable that they had half of the Internet confused about their own sexuality.

My finger hovered over the record button. "Ready!"

Kari put their hand on the tie around their neck and lifted their chin just slightly higher. "Go!"

I pressed record, and Kari seductively stared down the camera as they slowly pulled at and loosened their tie, the collared shirt they were wearing coming unbuttoned at the top. They turned their head to the side quickly after a few seconds, and I knew that meant to hit stop recording.

"Got it! I think that lines up really well," I commented, replaying the video for myself. "Which glam are you going to do?"

"I'm thinking the redheaded wig and like a cropped cardigan—Catholic schoolgirl style," Kari mused as they came over and reviewed the footage with me. "Are pigtails too far?"

"Yes." I grimaced. "Don't do pigtails. That's creepy."

Kari handed the phone back to me and walked over to the wall of wigs in their studio apartment that was also host to an entire makeup table—lights and everything—and a wardrobe of outfits that they used for filming. Being a studio, that meant their kitchenette, toilet, and full-sized bed were against the other two walls. It was a tight squeeze, but prime Dupont real estate, so win some, lose some.

"So, Isa told me you're hooking up with someone famous," Kari started.

I dropped down on the purple velvet chaise against the far wall that was often a backdrop used in Kari's OnlyFans photos and kicked my feet up. "She *wishes* she was famous."

Kari was halfway through taking off their suit as they glanced over at me and lifted one brow. "Well, is she, or isn't she?"

I shrugged my shoulders like I couldn't care less. Except I did, of course. "I mean, she has a pretty big podcast, I guess. True crime stuff, so you know people eat that up."

"I can't listen to that shit," Kari replied, then glanced at me. "Don't tell her I said that. It's just too depressing, you know?"

"Real life tends to be like that," I agreed. "I have enough on my plate without glancing over my shoulder for the next great serial killer."

"By the way, Isa also told me about your bar idea. I'm totally down to do some marketing on my Instagram and TikTok for your new spot when you're ready," Kari added as they slid a checkered skirt up their legs and fastened it around their waist. "Can't guarantee I'll regularly trek out to Virginia to visit, though."

I laughed. "Frankly, I have no idea where it's going to be at this point. The next step is convincing my father that it's a solid business plan to use my trust on."

Kari's brow furrowed. "Can he block it?"

"I mean, not really, but he can make it harder since he's the executor of the trust. There are other ways around him if I have to." I propped my arm across my face, covering my eyes with the inner crook of my elbow. In doing that, I felt my Apple Watch on my wrist vibrate. I lifted my arm again to glance at the notification which was, of course, from my father. Maybe he had my phone bugged.

Let's discuss your email tonight over dinner. Le Diplomate at 6pm.

Shit. My father knew I wasn't going to turn down a free meal there, and it wasn't very far at all from Kari's place, so my reasons to say no were quickly dwindling. "He just texted me and wants to go over the business plan at dinner tonight."

Kari was now taking their hair down out of a tight bun and smoothing it across their shoulders. "Oh, you have to go. He always takes you to the most expensive places."

I rolled onto my side, facing them. "Yeah, because it's a

great substitute for actual emotional intimacy or vulnerability. Calamari and top-shelf liquor are close seconds."

Kari grinned and shook their head. "Maybe that's where you get it."

"Get what?" I balked. "I'm more emotionally available than anyone in my family."

"I mean, that might be true, but you're like the poster child for black-or-white thinking," Kari continued. "That's what my therapist would tell you."

Christ, everyone is in fucking therapy. "My therapist would tell your therapist that that is a carefully honed trauma response, and I'm doing fantastic."

Kari made a face like they didn't believe me, their brows lifted with a sly grin across their lips as they applied a thick layer of red lipstick. "Okay, *sure.* Let's ask your most recent ex what they think."

"Don't bring Gianna into this." I put up my hand and wagged my index finger in their direction. "She had sex with her roommate while I was literally sleeping in her bed in the next room. Now *that* is emotionally unavailable. And physically. And loyally. And just morally, for fuck's sake."

"Fair," Kari agreed. "But you know what I mean. You never even told her about your mom or introduced her to your family, even though she asked repeatedly."

"I met *her* family," I countered. "Her sister and I literally played pickleball together."

Kari motioned for me to come back over to the camera stand to continue filming now that they were in full feminine glam. "Exactly. You're all in for the other person and think that by doing that, they won't even notice that you haven't given anything of yourself. It's all about them."

"Some would call that selfless and a gifted lover," I joked, but Kari's words were hitting a chord somewhere in my gut. I stood and joined them behind the camera, ready to hit record again. "But I hear you."

Kari wiggled their brows at me and then teed up in the same position in which we'd left off. "Ready? Go."

I hit record, and we spent the next two hours filming several more TikTok videos and a few risqué but not fully nude OnlyFans videos. By the end, it was almost time to head out for dinner with my father.

A quick Lyft ride later, I was stepping out onto the sidewalk in front of the restaurant realizing that I should probably have asked Kari for something to wear that was a bit fancier. My tunic, belt, and leggings weren't too far off base though, so hopefully it would be fine since I'd added a few chunky accessories to jazz it up.

"Yasmeen," my father called out to me from where he was standing slightly to the side of the entrance. "You're late. As usual."

Damon Kiani was everything you'd expect from someone who owns a security firm. Towering over literally everyone at six foot six, he had the shoulders of a linebacker but the waist of a swimmer. His style was consistently business casual—slacks and fancy black shoes paired with a collared shirt or a tailored sweater, but absolutely never a tie.

He motioned for me to follow him into the restaurant and then began walking in that direction without so much as a greeting handshake, let alone an embrace.

Guess I'll just catch up. I picked up my speed and joined him at the host stand as he relayed our reservation information. The waitstaff took us back to our table and handed us menus—which I quickly set aside and looked for the wine list first.

"I'll order us a bottle," my father said, taking the wine list from my hands and making the decision for us as he announced to the server what we'd be having.

"And for you, miss?" The server had finished taking my father's food order—the New York strip steak, of course—and was now looking at me.

"Scallop Provençal," I said. "And a water."

He nodded and quickly left us alone.

My father adjusted the cloth napkin in his lap. "So, a bar?"

"Before you veto the entire thing, let me explain—" I began, putting my hand up toward him in premeditated defense.

He cut me off almost immediately. "I love it."

"What?" I lifted my eyes to his, waiting for the punchline. "Uh...what?"

He nodded stoically as if he didn't get the joke. "I looked over the business plan, and it's actually quite good. I have a few suggestions, of course." He pulled a stack of papers out of a briefcase by his feet that I hadn't even noticed he'd carried in with him. "I think it should be two businesses—the bar side as the money maker, obviously. But the salon side as a subsidiary nonprofit to offset the costs and taxes of the bar. Financially, it's a win-win, but I love the concept."

I took the stack of papers he was offering me and slowly glanced through the first few pages which included hand-written edits and notes in the margins from him. "Wow...I, uh, I don't know what to say. I thought you'd hate it and want me to come back to the security firm."

My father tilted his head to the side ever so slightly. "Yasmeen, I've always been supportive of you following your dreams."

He was? I could feel my heart swelling in my chest. *Was this fatherly pride?* I wanted to wrap myself up in his words like a warm hug he hadn't given me since God knows when.

But then he continued. "This just happens to be the first dream you've had that actually makes financial sense."

Cue the sound of air hissing out of a balloon.

"Right. Okay." I nodded my head and kept my eyes focused on the papers in my hands so he couldn't see the disappointed daughter hanging out in the fetal position behind my eyes. "So, then the next thing to do is secure a space and get a contractor engaged."

"I do have some concerns over the space you mentioned in your business plan, however," he added, holding out his wine-glass as the server had returned and was giving him a sampling from the bottle. He sniffed at it and swirled it around before taking a gulp. An approving nod, he placed the wineglass down on the table, and the server immediately began filling up both of our glasses. "The building is owned by lobbyist Walter Adams. He has consistently pushed against any legislation that's pro-LGBTQ advancement or equality, and so the idea that he'd allow a lesbian bar to open in his own building seems unlikely."

"But not impossible," I countered. This time, I placed the papers down and picked up my wineglass, taking a much larger than usual gulp. "After all, his daughter is gay."

My father's brows lifted. "Really? You know this?"

I had my suspicions after the other night, but I didn't say that part out loud. "Uh, yeah. She's not publicly out, but most people around town know that she is. She's also the building property manager."

"Hmm." He took another sip of his wine. "That's interesting."

We were both quiet then, and a minute or two later, the server was dropping our dinner plates off in front of us. The scent of the food wafting up toward my nose was intoxicating, and I immediately started salivating and grabbed for my fork.

"Isa sent me some other listings I can look at," I finally broke the silence after swallowing the first bite of my meal. "The draw to Adam's place, however, is the money saved on renovations and construction up front, since the plumbing and electric is already set up in that location for a hair salon. We could open both simultaneously, whereas anywhere else, we'd have to probably open the bar first and start the salon side later once construction could finish."

My father cut off a piece of steak and speared it with his fork. "That is a good point. Cost saving is going to be important, and doing both at once would be cheaper."

I continued, "And the parking around this place is much easier than other neighborhoods in Arlington. Street parking is free here, but it also has an underground parking lot that our guests could use free of charge."

"Free of charge to the guests, but what's your fee?" he asked.

I read off some numbers to him that I'd already done the research on, including guest parking and staff parking costs. We continued our meal while going through the rest of the logistics, and, honestly, by the end, I was beginning to feel like I could really do this.

Some part of me up until now had discounted all of it as just another whim, another entrepreneurial idea of mine that was destined to fail. That's kind of how I'd been treating it in my mind, but I *had* worked hard on the business plan, and I had done all my research into the concept over the past two weeks, as well as spoken with several other local business owners for advice and feedback now that had worked for them.

Sitting here, across from my father who was all business, I suddenly realized...I *do* know what I'm doing at least to start. I had more to learn, sure. But this concept could actually work, and I could legitimately make it happen.

Confidence surged through me like a tidal wave, and I sat up taller in my seat as I placed my fork down on my empty plate.

"So, we're doing this?" I asked my father.

He lifted his wineglass to me. "No. You're doing this, Yasmeen. I'm only here if you need me to be, but I have full confidence that this could take off and you're the person to make that happen."

Although he wasn't one for hugs or affection, that vote of confidence, right there, was all the fatherly validation I needed to ride high for at least another six months.

"Thanks, Dad," I replied as I lifted my glass to his, and the edges clinked together. "Here's to a successful launch of *The Dirty Derby*."

"We should probably revisit the name, though," he added.

I grinned because I just couldn't have it all, could I? "I'll think about it, but I think it would be fun to make it sound sporty—not that there's anything gayer than a derby in sports. But people will think it's just a sports bar, and then, bam, rainbows and fishnets everywhere."

My father shook his head with a grin. "Again, we'll need to discuss that part further."

I would have responded but my attention was pulled to my cell phone vibrating on the table in front of me with a new notification. Tyler's name popped up, and I could feel my insides squeezing with anticipation, but also maybe a little bit of dread? I kept my expression neutral as I lifted my phone to shield the screen view from my father then clicked on her text message.

Are you home right now?

I sucked in a hiss of air. Holy crap, Tyler was, apparently, the queen of last-minute booty calls, and I don't know what the hell was wrong with me but I was one hundred percent in.

No. At dinner in DC with my father. I'll be home in a half hour.

Three dots bubbled up from her side of the conversation, then a reply pinged through.

Perfect. See you then.

I don't remember when I'd sent her the invitation, but my skin felt prickly in a way that only excitement could bring. I put my phone back down on the table—the screen dark—and felt myself wiggling a bit in my seat in anticipation.

"So, should we grab the check?" I asked my father as he polished off the last of his glass of wine.

He eyed me suspiciously and then glanced down at my phone for just a moment before returning his gaze to mine. "No dessert? You always order dessert."

Guilty. But my mind was already focused on my next course waiting for me at home. "Uh, yeah...I'm pretty full. Probably better to skip dessert this time."

My father eyed me for a moment longer, then shrugged his shoulders. He indicated with a hand signal to our server that we were ready for the check, and the man scooted over almost immediately with it.

All paid up, my father walked me out to the sidewalk where he'd ordered an Uber for me to get home—something about a corporate account with Uber that was cheaper than sending me home in my preferred Lyft. Whatever. A free ride is a free ride. We said our goodbyes, and I was off, headed to my new home with a belly full of scallops and anticipation.

The only issue was...I had no idea which Tyler I was about to run into. The Tyler who writhed beneath my tongue and begged me to keep going or the Tyler who snipped at me and spoke down to me like I was nothing compared to her.

Either way, I was about to find out and I was ready for a fight.

Chapter Eight

When I stepped out of the Uber in front of my new place, I spotted Tyler immediately leaning against the railing on the top step by the front door. She was scrolling through her phone absentmindedly, which was normal, but what was *not* normal was what she was wearing. A sparkling silver sheath dress hung down her body perfectly curving around every part of her and then stopped just beneath her knees. She had a faux fur (I hope it was faux fur) stole around her back and upper arms, and her hair was swept up into a sleek high ponytail straight down her back.

"Um, did I miss a dress code memo or something?" I came to a stop at the bottom of the steps, trying my best to not rake my eyes across her body...but, damn, I'm only human.

She lifted her eyes to mine. "Actually, yes."

I hadn't noticed earlier, but there was a zipped-up garment bag hanging over the side of the railing. Tyler picked it up and slung it over her shoulder as I walked past her and unlocked the front door, letting us both inside.

"So, what's going on?" I turned to her after I'd placed my things down on a moving box to the side that was serving as a table for now. "Your text was vague as hell, and this—" I waved a hand up and down her body. "This outfit is only giving me more questions."

"If one of those questions is—how do I make this dress look so good?—then I can answer that." Tyler placed the garment bag down on the couch and then did a little spin to show off her outfit. She slid the faux fur (I hoped) stole off of her arms and placed it next to the garment bag. "If you still want the space, my father is hosting an event tonight and this would be our chance to begin the groundwork."

"Groundwork?" Why was this woman always four steps ahead of me in any conversation? Something about the way her brain worked was just off the median enough to make her fascinating instead of insane. But, still, maybe a little insane. "What are you talking about?"

"Dating. Being a couple? Convincing my father to lease you the space you want?" Her brows pushed together like she couldn't believe I wasn't following her train of thought. "I thought you said you still wanted it."

"I do..." I replied slowly as I walked over to the garment bag and picked it up with one hand while unzipping it with the other. Inside was an incredibly elegant black jumpsuit with silver streaks patterned across it that were only just noticeable, but somehow made the fabric look like it was in motion. "Is this for me to wear?"

"If you want," Tyler confirmed. "I figured if I was springing a last-minute event on you, I should come prepared in case you are still unpacking and all that."

She eyed the dozens of still fully packed and sealed moving boxes in the corner of my living room. I'd been walking past them for weeks now.

"Good call," I agreed, lifting the fabric from the bag and sliding out the jumpsuit. "It's beautiful."

"So, you're in?" Tyler shifted her weight to one foot, and I noticed the strappy heels she was wearing along with what looked like a recent pedicure. "Are we doing this or not?"

"Oh, I'm in." I motioned for her to follow me to my bedroom where I hung the jumpsuit up on a hook on the back of my closet door and started looking through my closet for a pair of heels to match.

Tyler sat on the bed, one leg crossed over the other as she watched me. "It's a cocktail reception for pro-gun lobbyists at Hotel Harrington."

My eyes cut to her immediately. "Jesus H. Christ."

She shrugged and looked down at her feet to avoid the clear judgment my facial expression was throwing her way. "I told you my father is...who he is."

"Okay, but let's be clear here..." I found a pair of shoes that would work and tossed them on the bed next to her, then walked over to my long dresser where my makeup was sprawled across the surface. I began putting on some hints of eyeshadow and covering any heaviness beneath my eyes. "You're asking a Black lesbian to go with you to your White father's pro-gun party and convince him to let me operate a queer bar on his property?"

"The worst that might happen is he could say no," Tyler tried to assure me.

I paused and gave her an *are-you-kidding-me* look. "Believe me, that is not even close to the worst thing that could happen."

Her cheeks tinged a darker pink color, and her voice squeaked out an octave higher. "Well, I'll be there with you. I won't leave your side, and my dad always has security detail watching me at events."

Security detail didn't make *me* feel more comfortable, but

somehow, I was still in. I finished applying a bit more makeup—going for a minimalistic look—and reminded myself of everything my father and I had spoken about earlier. This was important to me, and I could make this bar happen if I wanted to. And as much as I tried not to get too excited about, well, anything, the ship had already sailed on this one.

I was excited. Not just for myself and what I knew I could bring to the community, but I was excited for what this could mean for queer people in general. With less than twenty-five lesbian bars in the country, I could make this one the third in the Washington, DC area. We could single-handedly turn this entire geographic area into a safe haven for the queer community to come to from all around the country and encourage more queer folks to get involved in politics, to push for better and more equal rights for all of us. I could make Washington, DC into a gay mecca.

This could actually be something real and meaningful.

"Do we need to, uh, talk about the other night?" I asked, looking at her reflection in the mirror as I finished a swipe of gloss across my lips.

"I hope not," she replied almost instantly. She uncrossed her legs and then recrossed them in the other direction.

I lifted the jumpsuit off the velvet hanger it had been on and held it up to my body in front of the mirror. "I mean, not talking will probably make us an even more realistic couple—harboring our emotions deep down instead of communicating about them."

The smallest laugh bubbled from her, and I couldn't help but smile. Placing the jumpsuit down flat on the bed next to her, I reached for the bottom of my tunic and lifted it straight up and over my head, tossing it off to the side.

Tyler's gaze followed my tunic and then returned to my body as I wriggled out of my leggings in front of her. I didn't miss the way she pulled her bottom lip in between her front teeth and gently chewed on it.

"What?" I asked her, daring her to say what she was really thinking. God, I could sense my own core heating as I felt her eyes on me.

"Nothing." She quickly looked away, but her breath was coming faster, and I could see her chest rising and lowering quickly.

Liar.

"If you have something to say, just say it..." I coaxed, stepping closer to her.

She uncrossed her legs again, but her gaze still wouldn't meet mine. I didn't give her a chance to recross her knees, because I slipped my own leg in between instead.

"We're going to be late..." Her voice had a raspiness to it that sent shivers skittering across my skin.

Still only wearing a pair of cheekies and a matching push-up bra, I hooked a finger beneath her chin and lifted. When her eyes finally met mine, there was a sparkle to them that screamed heat, and I felt my own breath hitch in my throat.

"I'm not known for being on time," I said, lowering my volume to barely above a whisper before I leaned down completely and met her lips with mine.

A soft moan escaped her throat as our mouths collided, and I cupped her jaw in my hands. Her hands wandered to my hips and pulled me closer to her, and as my tongue dipped into her mouth, she slid one hand between my legs.

I stepped apart just enough to give her full access as her fingers slipped beneath the fabric and slid across me, finding the perfect moment to dip inside as my tongue swirled around hers.

I was the one groaning against her now as she stroked a flame into an inferno, and it didn't take long for her to bring me to the edge and toss me over with reckless abandon. My body exploded like it never had before, and it took every effort to find my breath again after several excruciating moments.

"If our lack of communication doesn't fool them, the way you're looking at me right now definitely would," she said with a sly grin as she let go of me.

I chuckled because normally I was the one with the comebacks like that, but she was clearly learning to keep pace with me. She kissed me once as she stood up, and I leaned in a little longer. My legs trembled from the recent climax, and I switched places with her on the bed as she stood and headed to the bathroom. I took a few more deep breaths before finally pulling the jumpsuit on and trying to acclimate myself.

By the time Tyler returned, I was buttoned up and ready to go, offering her only a smirk as acknowledgment of what had just happened between us.

Honestly, what *had* happened between us?

"You look great," she commented. "Should I order our Lyft, or do you need a few more minutes?"

"I'm ready," I confirmed as I slid a pair of silver hoop earrings into both ears and reapplied the gloss on my lips that had smeared off in the last few minutes.

I could see her in the mirror's reflection as she pulled out her phone and, I'm assuming, ordered the Lyft. "So, what am I supposed to call you?"

Tyler shrugged loosely. "Girlfriend is fine, right?"

"And how long have we been dating?" I asked. "We need to have the same story. How did we meet?"

"Uh...a month? Two? What's reasonable to feel serious enough?" she asked. "It's been a while since I've dated in general."

"I mean, I'm usually almost married at the three-month mark, so I don't think I know what's reasonable," I joked, knowing if any of my friends were here right now that they would absolutely sign on for that remark. "But, yeah, let's say two months. And we met at a yoga class—I couldn't stop looking at your butt as you went downward dog."

She grinned and shook her head. "I don't think we need that level of detail for my *father*, Yasmeen."

"Most people just call me Yas," I reminded her. "My girl-friend would know that."

"Noted." She glanced back down at her phone. "The Lyft is three minutes away."

"We met at yoga class and have been dating for two months," I repeated. "Is that going to feel real enough to make any sort of impact on your dad?"

She shrugged as she waved down the Lyft driver slowly idling down the street trying to find us. "Given that I haven't introduced him to anyone in like five years...I think it will. My last girlfriend was...well, that's a story for another time."

We climbed into the backseat of the Lyft, and Tyler confirmed our destination with the driver.

"I feel like your girlfriend should know some details about your ex," I reverted us back to the previous conversation as the car took off. "What was her name?"

Tyler side-eyed me for a moment, then exhaled. "Gissele. She was a dark period for me."

I frowned. "How so?"

"I call her my 'teen angst phase' even though I was in my twenties," Tyler explained, this time a sheepish smile spread across her face. "Everything about her life was messy and complicated and tangled up in something. I was just along for the ride, and it was all thrill-based."

I couldn't picture Tyler doing anything thrill-based, so it actually made me kind of glad to hear that she'd experienced some sort of period of that.

"But clearly, my family was not on board with that, and when they bailed her and me out of jail for being drunk in public, my father freaked the hell out. That was our entire romantic relationship—binge drinking and sex and the consequences of that." Tyler was looking out the window now, and I could just make out her reflection in the glass as I gazed toward her. "And now I have a permanent mark on my record. It was a huge thing for his political career—had to bring in a crisis public relations person and everything. Safe to say, Gissele wasn't welcome around anymore, and I needed a reality check that her lifestyle wasn't for me. So, I ended things."

"You ended things because she got you arrested?" I asked. I mean, I had ended things for less, so I didn't entirely blame her.

Tyler shook her head. "Not exactly. More so because that wasn't me. I'm by the book, and I like it that way. She was the type who dog-eared the pages of books. It was never going to work out."

I did not tell her that out of the few books I did have, most had folded corners somewhere in them.

"Okay, so it wasn't a personality or values match," I mused, trying to ignore the unsettled feeling in my gut. Why was I getting nervous at her description of her ex? It's not like I was out getting arrested for being drunk in public...ever. But I also wouldn't ever pretend to call myself a rule follower. "And then you haven't introduced the family to anyone since."

"Correct." Tyler repositioned her body so that she was angled toward me now, leaning her head against the backrest. Her gaze looked dreamy as she smiled at me. "You'll have to dazzle and wow him."

"I mean, I just have to not get you arrested is what it sounds like. Feels like a low bar."

Tyler laughed. "It makes no sense, does it?"

"What?" I asked.

71

"I'm sitting here saying I'm not a rule breaker, and that's why things ended with my ex, and yet I'm literally bringing a fake girlfriend to my father to convince him to allow you to lease that space." Tyler closed her eyes for a moment and inhaled. "Maybe I'm not as tightly bound to the rules as I thought."

I didn't respond to that, but her words did give me a small sliver of comfort. After all, this entire scheme had been her idea. If this wasn't like her, then why was she willing to do it at all? Even more so, why was she willing to do it for me?

Something stirred in my chest that I didn't want to focus on, so instead, I leaned forward and kissed her lips.

"Tonight is going to go great," I assured her, a low whisper this time.

She let out a small hum of breath before kissing me back. When we separated, she leaned her head on my shoulder for the rest of the ride, and I stared out the window as I considered what I was getting myself into.

And if I was ever going to be able to get out.

Chapter Nine

The conference room turned ballroom that was hosting Tyler's father's cocktail reception was decked out in gold and black...everything. If I'm being honest, it looked like a hybrid of a New Year's Eve celebration and a college graduation at best, but even I had to admit that the crowd was highbrow.

There was Secret Service scattered throughout, plus a private security detail, and if you weren't on the list, then you weren't getting in the door. In the time span it took Tyler and me to approach the entrance, at least four members of the press were turned away and stood there gloomily on their cell phones yelling at their editors and trying to find someone who could gain them entrance.

Tyler barely waved at the security stationed at the door of the ballroom, and they let her and me pass without even coming to a rolling stop.

I grabbed her hand as we entered, because my skin was already beginning to prickle with nerves, and something about the way Tyler strutted forward with confidence felt like safety.

She squeezed my hand and offered me an apologetic smile. "Do you want to get a drink first?"

"Maybe two," I replied, my eyes already darting around the room to find the bar.

Tyler laughed and pulled me in the direction of the far right wall where several different bars were set up to accommodate everyone.

She ordered for the both of us—two glasses of pinot noir—and handed one glass to me. "Here."

Tyler sipped on hers as I grimaced internally. I hated pinot noir for a lot more than the staining it left on my teeth. The taste was just not for me, but as I glanced around the room, everyone was drinking something red.

Seemed telling.

"I see my father in the corner over there," Tyler finally said, nodding her chin toward that area of the ballroom. "Let me know when you're ready to go say hi, and we can do introductions and all that."

A man stepped up to the bar next to us wearing an overly large cowboy hat with holstered revolvers prominently displayed on both of his hips.

"Uh, I'm ready now. Let's go." I inched away from the bar and gave Tyler a gentle push in the direction she'd been pointing. "Gotta face the music sometime."

Tyler didn't seem to notice my discomfort, but she took my hand and led me across the room with all the confidence of a WASP heiress in a crowd of pale pawns.

"He's the one talking to Senator McCarty." She gestured toward a small circle of men in intimate discourse.

I recognized the senator immediately from his most recent Twitter—*is it even called Twitter anymore?*—tirade and backlash about welfare recipients, but the man next to him was new to me.

So, this is the infamous Walter Adams.

Tyler's father was at least six inches shorter than she was, which made me wonder if she got her height from her mother. There was no doubt that she definitely got her eyes from her mother, because there was nothing crystal blue and deep about Walter's pebble black irises that felt sharp in an entirely feral sort of way. He had the same hair color as Tyler, however, although it was tinged white around the temples now.

I found myself wondering more about Tyler's mother as we stood outside the circle of men, waiting for an opportunity to break in and say hello. She'd told me a while ago that her mother's abandonment had been a crucial part of her childhood trauma, but seeing her father's beady eyes now...I couldn't help but wonder what other damage he'd done to give her such a high ACE score. Something about this man just didn't feel safe, even standing in front of him not knowing a thing about him.

We were almost in front of him now, and my stomach was in my chest.

"Tyler!" Walter finally spotted his daughter and waved for her to come closer, indicating for several men in front of him to move to the side. They immediately scuttled away like they'd just been chastised, and Tyler stepped forward into the circle like a fresh breath of air being let into a dark cellar. "Senator, you've met my daughter before, haven't you?"

Tyler pulled me up next to her, and Senator McCarty cast a furtive glance at our hands clasped together, then quickly looked away.

He pushed a formal smile onto his face and tipped his chin toward her. "Ms. Adams, lovely to see you again."

Tyler responded in kind and then gestured toward me. "Always a pleasure, Senator McCarty. Father, Senator, please meet Yasmeen Kiani, a small business owner from Arlington."

I put out my one free hand for a handshake, and both men

shook it with all the limpness of a wet noodle. "Nice to meet you, gentleman."

"What sort of business are you in, Ms. Kiani?" the senator addressed me before taking a sip of whatever dark liquor he was nursing. "I get out to Arlington occasionally, and it's always growing with new businesses and construction."

"Actually, Yasmeen is going to be leasing our Pike location to open a new food and beverage establishment," Tyler cut in for me before I could respond.

"Yes, a queer bar, actually," I quickly clarified, shooting Tyler a look. This might be her show and her arena, but there was zero chance I wasn't going to speak for my damn self. "We're hoping by adding a third queer bar to the Washington, DC area, when there are so few around the country, will allow the metro region to become a destination spot for queer folks around the country to come visit."

Tyler glanced sideways at me, and the nervousness on her face was not even remotely hidden. "Uh, yes. Because the financial aspect of bringing in that demographic will help small businesses and the local tourist economy to flourish in new ways."

Ooh, she was trying to soften the blow of my truth with finances.

Tyler's father blinked twice, then seemed to reboot into public speaker mode, patting Senator McCarty's back with a firm hand. "An incredible win for the tourism industry is something any politician can support. Right, Senator?"

"Local tourism has decreased since the pandemic," the senator churned out his words like a prewritten speech. "Anything the community can do to attract visitors and help our local businesses is certainly welcome."

I could practically feel how hard that was for him to say,

but I was impressed that he managed to force the words out of his mouth anyway.

"I'm going to grab another drink," the senator informed us before stepping away. "It was lovely to see you again, Ms. Adams."

I noted he didn't even acknowledge having met me, but I wasn't surprised.

Once he was gone, Tyler's father stepped closer to us and lowered his voice in that disapproving way parents do. "This seems like a lot of new information to provide me in front of a senator, Tyler."

I glanced at Tyler, and her expression had taken on that of innocent doe eyes.

"It was?" Her voice was even higher pitched now and sweeter than sweet tea. "I thought you'd be so excited, Daddy. I found a great applicant who can really make an impact on the area. I sent the lease application to your office a few days ago. Did you not...did you not have time to read it for me?"

Okay, damn. It's one thing to know there is family dysfunction, but it's another thing to watch the woman I've been fucking play her father like a goddamn fiddle right in front of me. I wasn't sure if I was horrified or turned on, or some obscene mixture of both.

"Yes, yes. I heard all about it, and it's waiting for me on my desk for Monday." Mr. Adams glanced toward me now. "I'm sure you understand, Ms. Kiani, that I'll need to review the application more thoroughly before anything is a done deal."

"Of course," I assured him, trying to adopt a similarly sweet tone to Tyler. "Tyler's gone on and on about your business prowess since we first started dating."

Two can play the brown-nosing game.

"Dating?" Her father's brows lifted, and he looked between

Tyler and me. "I didn't know you had started dating anyone, Ty."

She wrapped an arm around my shoulders and placed a pointed kiss on my cheek. "It's only been a few months, but I'm really happy, Daddy. I hope you can be just as happy for the both of us."

Walter Adams looked even more uncomfortable than the senator had a few moments ago. "Um, right. Yes. Of course, sweetheart. Anything that makes you happy makes me happy."

That didn't feel like a true statement, but I didn't say shit.

Not my circus, not my monkeys.

"So, a few months?" His gaze turned to me now. "How did you two meet?"

"Yoga class," I immediately replied, casting a silly grin toward Tyler because after all this, there was no way I wasn't going to stir the pot. "Every week, watching her bend over and stretch in downward dog—I mean, how couldn't a woman fall in love?"

Tyler's cheeks immediately darkened as she tried to keep a stony smile on her face.

"Love?" Mr. Adams now turned his focus to his daughter. "That sounds pretty serious, Ty."

"Uh, yes." She nodded, trying to keep her expression the same, even though I could see the daggers she was shooting at me. "It's been a bit of a whirlwind, I'll admit. But what is it you always said about Mom? When you know, you know."

Her father took a step backward at the mention of Tyler's mother, and I glanced between them, realizing that that had been some sort of power move between them that I didn't understand.

Okay, so I *really* had a lot more questions about her mother now. Why had her mother left? Where was she now? What was the leverage Tyler was wielding over her father right now?

"That's great," he replied, the smile on his mouth appearing just as forced as Tyler's. "And so, this bar...it's yours alone, Ms. Kiani?"

Tyler didn't give me a moment to answer. "Yes, but I'm going to be heavily involved in the entire thing. I'm thinking about investing, that's how good the business model is. I'm so excited about it, Daddy. You should see the plans we have already. The buzz is going to be huge."

His gaze flitted from mine to hers, then back to me. "I'll definitely have to look at these plans on Monday."

"If you need to," Tyler continued, her hand snaking around my back now and pulling me into her side. She placed another kiss on my temple, and I cozied into her like I was already an expert at this act. "But we really just need a signature to get started. I was just telling Yasmeen earlier in the car how great of a father you are because you'd support anything I am really excited about."

"She was," I agreed, nodding emphatically and offering him an appreciative smile. "And what a great thing to hear. Not a lot of families out there like that these days."

He was backed into a corner, and he knew it. "Yes, that is a founding principle of mine—valuing family, especially my daughter. She excels at everything she puts her mind to, you know. There's nothing she can't do."

I leaned into Tyler's side. "One of the things I love about her. She really is willing to do anything, and does it so well."

The tone I said that in was just innocent enough to sound dirty.

"Right..." He straightened his shoulders and looked at Tyler. "Well, I'll be eager to check out the proposal and application. Maybe we should meet on Monday, Ty? Go over it together?"

"I'd love that, Daddy. Want to come out to Virginia and see

the space in person?" Tyler tilted her head to the side slightly. "We can do lunch together—like a father-daughter date."

Good Lord, the fake sugar in her voice was going to give me cavities. My mind trailed back to the bits and pieces she'd told me about her childhood, and I could imagine just from watching this interaction that she'd spent a lifetime holding things in. Being someone who was so boldly out in every way— sexuality and personality—I couldn't imagine living behind so many masks.

It seemed like every day I was with Tyler, a new mask revealed itself.

"It's a date," he confirmed with an all-too-wholesome smile. "It was lovely to meet you, Ms. Kiani. I hope you both enjoy a few drinks and the performance we have planned later from a local jazz band. As you can imagine, I have to keep circulating the room and chatting up donors."

"Of course." I offered my hand to him, and he shook it. "I'm sure I'll see you again very soon—maybe at the grand opening?"

His smile was tight-lipped. "Maybe, but we'll surely have to have you over for a family dinner before then at some point."

"I would love that," I replied. Definitely a lie, but I'd do it if it meant I could get my bar...and her. "Have a great evening, sir."

Tyler gave her father a stiff hug, then he left the two of us alone. She turned to me with a wide grin and wiggled her brows. "Well, what do you think?"

I leveled my gaze at her. "I think your therapist needs a raise."

She rolled her eyes, but the smile didn't leave her face. "I'm serious. I think that went really well. He basically has no choice but to say yes now. The senator hearing all of that was icing on the cake."

"I guess we'll find out on Monday." I handed her my glass

of pinot noir. "But in the meantime, I'm going to need a drink that doesn't taste like metal berries."

She placed both of our glasses down on a catering tray nearby. "Why don't we just get out of here? We're not that far from As You Are—want to pop in there?"

"Tonight's karaoke night," I replied. "So abso-fucking-lutely."

"I kill at karaoke," Tyler informed me.

I tried not to snort when I laughed, but failed hard. "Yeah, I'm definitely going to have to see that to believe it."

She linked her arm around mine. "Guess my go-to song."

That one was easy. "Don't Stop Believin' by Journey, obviously!"

Tyler grinned. "Am I that predictable?"

"I don't know," I admitted. "Before tonight, I would have said yes. But now I just have a zillion more questions."

And I highly doubted she'd be providing me answers anytime soon.

Chapter Ten

"I'm not going to ask you for your autograph," Isa informed Tyler the moment we all sat down at brunch at El Centro in Georgetown the next morning. She sat across from Tyler and Rachel sat across from me, and neither of them knew that my open-toed sandal was running up the back of Tyler's calf or that she and I had spent most of the previous night wrapped around one another. "But, if you ever wanted to give me a tour of your podcast studio, I wouldn't say no."

Tyler grinned as she laid out her menu on the table in front of her and scanned the selection of tacos and huevos rancheros. "Hard for me to say no to anything after a bottomless brunch."

I shot Tyler a wicked grin, wiggling my brows, then looking around the restaurant for our server. "Oh, we should definitely get our first round of mimosas then."

Rachel rolled her eyes. "We get it. You guys are dating."

"We're not dating," I responded almost immediately to Rachel's assumption. "Tyler is merely helping me get this new business up and running."

Tyler cleared her throat, but I noticed that her gaze was

focused so hard on her menu, it was almost like she was going to bore a hole through it. Had I spoken too quickly?

"Yes, we're just friends, of sorts," Tyler added on, finally lifting her head to scan the room, completely avoiding eye contact with everyone at the table. "Who is our server?"

"I think that's her," Isa pointed to a woman taking orders at the next table. "I'm sure she'll be over shortly. But in the meantime, where are we at with this business plan?"

"And have you talked to your dad yet about this?" Rachel added, her always cautious viewpoint staring me down now.

"Dad's on board," I confirmed, which bought me a relieved nod from Rachel. "And tomorrow is when Tyler will get her father to finish signing off on everything. I've got a contractor ready to get started, and it's looking like maybe two to three weeks of work before we could be ready to open."

"Meaning a Pride Month opening?" Isa asked. "Is there going to be a theme, or something significant about the opening date? Some event to really make it hit big? We really need to nail down a marketing strategy for the entire thing in advance. Did you call any of the referrals I sent you?"

"I will, after tomorrow," I assured Isa.

The server made her way to us, and I paused my defensive explanation as she took our first round of food and drink orders. Bottomless brunch in Washington, DC truly means bottomless —if we're not stumbling out of here in two hours with our heels in our hands, then we haven't done brunch justice.

"I'm waiting to get the official green light on the application," I continued after the server had left. Our glasses of water were now full, and I took a big sip from mine. "There's still a chance he could say no or back out."

"He's not going to," Tyler assured me, placing her hand on top of mine. "After last night, he can't. Not only did a senator hear the plan, but he thinks we're a couple. If there's one thing I can trust about our relationship, he'll try and buy my affection long before we actually sit down and have real, meaningful conversations."

I looked at our joined hands for a moment longer than I meant to and realized Isa and Rachel were doing the same thing.

Isa cleared her throat. "Damn. I wish I had a father who wanted to buy my affection."

"Your father is literally the nicest person alive and showers you with unconditional love," I reminded Isa, because I'd spent many a night and weekend with her Filipino family.

"Yeah, but love doesn't pay the rent," Isa joked in reply, even though I knew that there was absolutely nothing she wouldn't do for her family. If I thought *my* family was too involved in each other's business, Isa's family took the cake on that one entirely.

"So why does he buy your affection?" Rachel asked, her expression deadpanned as she watched Tyler over the rim of her glass of water. She swallowed her sip and then continued. "Was he a deadbeat dad or something? Where's your mom?"

Tyler's entire body stiffened, and I sent the tip of my shoe into Rachel's shin as a sign to shut the fuck up.

"Christ, Rachel," Isa scoffed. "You just met the poor woman. Who opens with a therapy question like that?"

I knew it wouldn't be long until the verbal punches began between Isa and Rachel—these two were the definition of frenemies.

Rachel shrugged, her voice defensive. "I'm just curious!"

"No, it's fine," Tyler assured her, even though I could see none of the tension had left her body, and her back was rigid straight against the chair. "He's been my primary parent most of my life. My mother left when I was young. For all I know, she might be dead or whatever."

"Oh, shit. That sucks." Rachel put her glass down on the table. "You know, Yas is in the Dead Parent Club, too. I might be, I don't know. Never knew my dad."

My toe to her shin again. "Rachel, for fuck's sake."

I would love Rachel like a sister until my dying breath, but she wasn't known for her delicateness or tact. In fact, she was kind of like a blonde bull in a china shop completely unaware of the shattered porcelain and crystal in her wake.

"Ow!" Rachel winced and pulled her legs away from me. "Stop kicking me. It's not like it's a secret!"

The server dropped off four champagne flutes and a full pitcher of mimosas for us to split.

I grabbed it quickly and filled my glass then Tyler's. "If you wanted to leave this brunch right now, I'd totally understand."

Tyler laughed and shook her head before sipping on her drink. "No, I'm having fun. You guys are...you're honest. It's refreshing. There's not a lot of that in the circles I travel in."

"I think she's talking about her dad now," Rachel added, lifting her empty glass for me to fill.

I poured her mimosa to the very top of the rim. "Drink the fuck up. Just chug that one, and I'll pour you a second right now."

"Wait, me first!" Isa held up her glass as well, and I filled it with a normal amount for her. "But then, yeah, maybe just hand the whole pitcher to Rachel and stick a straw in it."

Tyler laughed and held up her glass. "Let's make a toast."

"I honestly can't think of a single thing to toast right now except my complete horror and embarrassment at how today is going," I said before downing half my mimosa and refilling it. "But, sure, let's cheers."

"To new friends," Isa said, lifting her glass.

"To new businesses," Tyler said as she elbowed me to join in.

"To *successful* new businesses," I tagged on to hers, clinking the edge of my glass to both her and Isa.

Rachel added her glass next to Isa's. "And to the Dead Parents Club!"

I exhaled dramatically. "Oh, here we go."

Both Isa and I groaned and lowered our glasses, but Tyler clinked hers even harder against Rachel's, and a small amount of orange booze slipped over the edge as they both laughed.

Great, now they were colluding.

"Lighten up, Yas," Tyler teased me, leaning into my side and bumping her shoulder into mine. "It's brunch. Drink up and let it all slide off your shoulders—tomorrow's the start of a whole new life for you."

I shot her a grateful smile. "I feel like I shouldn't get my hopes up until I see everything signed on the dotted line."

"Too late," Isa replied. "The excitement and hope are all over your face. I don't even remember seeing this level of enthusiasm with the edible anal beads."

"The what?" Tyler looked from Isa to me. "Did she say edible anal beads?"

"Edible panties and G-strings," I quickly clarified. "Not anal beads."

"Okay, but I still think that's an untapped market," Isa joked, polishing off her first mimosa and pouring her second.

"Probably untapped for a good reason," Rachel added. Finally, she was talking sense.

"I think we've been in the spotlight enough today," I said, trying to steer the conversation in a different direction far, far away from Tyler and me, or even the bar business. "What's going on with you two? Any recent love interests? Anything happening at work?"

"We've got a big case at work that's been taking up all of my time." Rachel leaned back in her chair as a food runner dropped off our first round of small plates in front of us. "But we did just hire a new paralegal who is ridiculously attractive, so that's been a fun distraction."

Isa rolled her eyes as she took a bite of her taco, then spoke with a half-full mouth. "Now *that* is a public relations nightmare about to happen. You're the attorney. You can't date the paralegals."

"Who said anything about dating?" Rachel grinned and ate a bite of fruit from her plate. "I'm just talking about enjoying the new scenery around the office."

"This type of talk is how I stay so busily employed," Isa huffed under her breath before finally speaking louder and directing her attention toward Tyler and me. "But, in other news, I have actually started seeing someone."

"Blake?" I asked, remembering the guy she'd shown me recently on her phone.

She looked at me like she had no idea who I was talking about. "Who? No, not Blake. That was like two guys ago."

"Sorry, it's so hard to keep track," I joked, already halfway done with my small plate of huevos rancheros. *God, the food here is delicious.* I filled my mimosa glass a third time and offered more to Tyler as well.

"Ha ha," Isa sounded out sarcastically. "Eduardo and I met on Hinge, so you know it's actually legit."

"As opposed to what?" Tyler asked.

Isa shrugged. "I don't know, like Tinder or OkCupid or something like that."

"What's he do?" I asked—because this was Washington, DC, and that was always the first question we asked everyone.

"He's on the management staff for the Washington Capitals," she answered quickly, this time looking down at her plate. "Great guy. Free ice hockey tickets whenever we want them."

I narrowed my eyes and pointed an accusatory finger at her.

"So you got the Capitals' account, then? Or is this a business mixed with pleasure kind of thing?"

"That would be a cool account to have." Tyler glanced at me and then looked at Isa. "Is it crisis management, public relations, or marketing that you do?"

"A little bit of everything," Isa confirmed. "And, honestly, I don't know that we're even going to get the full five-year contract on that account yet. This is totally unrelated and nothing to do with that."

"The lies!" Rachel laughed emphatically as she polished off her glass. "You're one hundred percent dating him to secure this account."

I shoved a large bite into my mouth so I could avoid being part of this conversation.

Isa shot Rachel an angry look. "Rachel, I would *never*. I mean, how would I even know I'd match with him? Or where he worked?"

"Was it in his bio?" Rachel pried further.

Isa was blustering now. "I can't remember. I barely look at those things, you know."

Another round of small plates was delivered to our table and the empty plates cleared away. The waitress was close behind and took our orders for more rounds of food, as well as dropping off another pitcher of mimosa for us all.

"Even I have to call bullshit on that one," I finally interjected. "Don't break the poor man's heart for a business deal."

"You're one to talk." Isa was now pointing between Tyler and me, and shit, this was exactly why I should have stayed out of that conversation entirely.

"Me?" Tyler's eyes widened as the bite of food that had been on the way to her mouth was now suspended in the air in front of her. "No one is breaking my heart, I can promise you that."

Don't ask me why the first thought in my mind when she said that was *challenge accepted.*

"This is strictly business and friendship," I repeated. "No one's heart is getting involved here."

Both Isa and Rachel rolled their eyes at the two of us.

"I'm serious!" I added. "Other body parts, maybe. But no hearts."

Tyler jutted her elbow into my side. "Jesus, Yas."

Her cheeks were tinged red again, and the freckles across her nose looked darker which only reminded me of when she was last writhing beneath me. Okay, I definitely needed to slow down on the mimosas before I crossed from tipsy-sociable to drunk-horny.

I gave her a wink anyway and let my hand drop below the table, finding her thigh and giving it a gentle squeeze. "I'm just teasing."

"No, she's not," Rachel called me out as she chewed on a large bite of churro.

"*Anyway.*" I picked up my glass of water and chugged at least half of it. "When are we going to meet Eduardo?"

"I love Caps games," Tyler added. "My father has a box, so if you guys ever want to go, we can. Sometimes I can even wrangle a press pass to get back to the locker rooms."

"A press pass?" Isa's brows lifted so high that they nearly touched her hairline. "Wait, how do you do that?"

"Podcast perks." Tyler took another bite of her food and washed it down with her remaining mimosa, which I quickly refilled for her. "It depends on who you talk to over there though—and their age. If they're over thirty-five, then good luck convincing them that podcasts are news sources at all."

"That's us," Isa joked, now jabbing an elbow toward Rachel. "But I actually do listen to your podcast religiously.

Not to sound like a weird stalker or anything. I'm even in your fan Facebook group."

"That *does* sound like a weird stalker," Rachel quipped.

Isa waved her off. "It's just, the way you tell stories is very engaging. You really make me think about the cases from a different lens, you know?"

"Thanks," Tyler replied. "That's kind of the goal, so it's nice to hear."

"I do have a question though," Isa continued, waving her fork toward Tyler as she continued eating. "People in your Facebook group speculate all the time about your sexuality, but you never address it on the pod."

Tyler swallowed the food in her mouth and took a long sip of her mimosa before answering. "Well, people are always going to talk. That's just the nature of any public-facing position."

"Right," Isa agreed. "But, why not just come out? It could be really meaningful for the queer community to have you as a public face or spokesperson—particularly given who your father is."

"No one *has* to come out for other people," I interjected, feeling a little defensive of Tyler. "I know you're thinking from a marketing mind, Isa, but someone's sexuality isn't content fodder for their job unless they want it to be."

I squeezed Tyler's thigh again, this time letting my fingers stroke down the inside. She gave me an appreciative smile before turning back to look at Isa.

"I understand your point, though," Tyler assured her. "No harm done. It's just, my relationship with my father is complicated. His stances publicly are not always what line up with his beliefs at home. He *does* support me, despite how uncomfortable my sexuality makes him. Which, yeah, I get that doesn't make much sense. It doesn't make much sense to me either. But he has always been really honest with me about where he's at and what he feels, and I have to appreciate that about him— even if I don't always like the answers he lands on. He struggles with the dynamic as much as I do, and I can't discount his experience."

I hadn't really considered how complicated it must be to have a father like Walter Adams, but as Tyler described their relationship dynamic, I felt a sad weight on my chest for the both of them. Despite my father's frustrations with my employment history, his love and adoration and support for who I am as a person, and who I love has never once been a question. I've never had to even worry about not being fully accepted, or being able to openly be myself, and that's a luxury that I know a lot of queer people don't have.

Isa seemed quieter after that response. "I can't imagine how difficult navigating that must be."

Tyler didn't respond, and instead took another bite of her food. Rachel did the same, and the table fell into silence for a few moments as we all focused on our food and probably reflected on the relationships we had with our own parents.

"Time for another round?" Tyler asked, breaking the silence as the waitress came over again.

Tension seemed to ease around the table as we perused the menu for more food to order, my eyes immediately being pulled to the churros.

Rachel grinned and lifted her flute in the air. "Fill' er up!"

It wasn't even noon yet, but I had a feeling today was going to be interesting...

Chapter Eleven

It's a blessing that I don't have an office I have to be at every Monday at nine o'clock, because otherwise I would have been calling out late today. Yesterday's brunch lasted until dinner, and the aftereffects were still clinging to my dopamine-depleted brain today.

Hello, hangxiety.

"Are we really doing this today?" Tyler groaned from the other side of the bed where her naked body was still splayed across the sheets after last night.

I rolled onto my back as well and stared up at the ceiling, which wasn't staying as still as I would have liked it to. The textures of the stucco decor in the paint were rolling around my eyes like a ship at sea, and I silently cursed myself for the previous day's liquid indulgence.

"Do what?"

"We have a meeting at noon with my father, remember?" Tyler turned to her side to face me now, propping her head up in her hand as her elbow jutted against the mattress.

I groaned and closed my eyes. "That's at noon. We can worry about that later."

"It's eleven fifteen," she countered.

Despite my eyes being closed, she must have grabbed at the sheets covering me because I felt the woosh of the fabric run from my skin and a chill take its place.

"It's what?" I asked again, curling into a ball to try to retrieve my warmth.

"We have to be at my father's office in forty-five minutes," Tyler said.

I shook my head but just managed to wedge it further into the pillows in my protest at daylight. "Never going to happen."

She was already out of bed, however, and it didn't appear she gave two shits about my hangover. "Up and at 'em!"

"How are you *not* hung over?" I asked, scrambling to find the sheets and blankets and abscond away into them again.

Tyler smacked her right hand against her upper left arm where there was a small tan patch adhered to her skin. "Hangover patch. I put it on yesterday before brunch. Works like a charm. Plus, I scheduled us for an intravenous hydration boost later today to replenish."

Absolutely not was I getting an IV for a hangover. "All of those are a scam. They aren't even FDA-approved. There's no oversight on them at all."

My logic didn't seem to change her mind. "And yet, I'm out of bed and you're turtling."

"It's called 'cocooning,'" I clarified, but finally pulled myself out from the warmth of my bed.

Cocooning in bed was a valid and healthy coping skill, and I wouldn't be convinced otherwise.

Pushing myself up to a standing position, I took inventory of Tyler's bedroom around me. The clothes we'd been wearing yesterday were strewn about in random places across the floor and on furniture, and there was an open bottle of coconut oil on the nightstand.

Okay, so we had some fun last night. The bits and pieces of last night were returning to my memory—all of which had me as the aggressor of the evening. I had absolutely thrown myself at Tyler. And shamelessly, at that.

"I don't have time to go home and change." My feet hit the fuzzy carpet as I came to the realization that I'd probably have to wear yesterday's wrinkled outfit to this business meeting with her father.

He'd spot my *walk of shame* a mile away.

"You can borrow something of mine," Tyler replied.

I squinted at her. "Won't he know that it's yours?"

She shook her head, and the flash of hurt that crossed her face was wiped away just as quickly as it appeared. "No. He won't notice. Go look in the closet for something you like."

I stayed quiet after that, watching her puttering around the bedroom and bathroom for a few minutes instead. She'd changed into half a pantsuit and was flat ironing her hair in the bathroom mirror before I finally made my way over to her closet and scanned through the racks.

Christ, designer tags are still on half this shit.

"Have you even worn all of these?" I called out, fingering the material on a silver blazer. "Most of these look brand new."

"Some of them," she called back. "People tend to send me stuff out of nowhere. They want me to be photographed in it, ya know? It's them trying to promote their own brands. It's not about me."

That seemed to be a common theme in her life, but I didn't say that out loud. The whole rule-follower aspect of her made it easy to see why she'd struggled during her teenage years—why she probably still did—I couldn't imagine having to keep so much inside like she did.

It felt like a special treat that I had any sort of insight into her real self at all, and my chest felt a warmth as I considered what a privilege that probably really was. It felt like we'd come a long way in a short period of time, and I didn't even know what that meant, but I knew I didn't dislike it.

I picked a pair of black trousers that fit me pretty snugly— unlike Tyler, I actually had an ass. I did some squats and lunges to try to get them to fit a bit better, but they were still pretty tight around my derriere. We might be similar sizes, but my ass was double the flat pancake Tyler had going on back there. Not that I didn't like her pancake booty. Believe me when I say I'd lick syrup off those flapjacks all day long. I'm all for embracing the body you've got.

I found a silk black tank top in her dresser drawer to wear under the silver blazer, and then assessed myself in the bathroom mirror behind where Tyler was still straightening her hair.

"You look great," she commented, even though I still felt like I could fall over at any moment due to the champagne rolling around in my guts like it owned the place. "That top is perfect on you, actually. You should keep it."

I was pulling the price tag off the armpit as she said that and glanced up to look at her reflection. "You don't have to ask me twice, but only the blazer."

She placed the flat iron down on the counter and turned it off, then fluffed her fingers through her hair as it lay flat against her shoulders and chest. "You don't like the pants?"

"I'm about to bust out of these pants," I clarified, turning my lower half and popping out one hip. "My ass does not fit in these. There's a good chance when I sit down, I will rip a hole right down the back."

A smirk lifted the corners of her lips. "I mean, it's not a bad look, though. As long as you stay standing. Very tight and accentuating all the most important features."

Okay then.

"Well, well, well...someone is being extra flirtatious this morning." I grinned at her reflection and let my hands wander across her back until they found a resting spot on her hips. I placed my lips against the top of her shoulder blade and kissed a soft trail up her neck to her hairline.

"I'm surprised you still have any energy left in you after last night," she teased, but the way she jutted her butt back into my hips told me she knew exactly what she was trying to do.

I wiggled my eyebrows at her in my reflection in the mirror as one of my hands left her hip and slid to the front of her pants. My hand slid inside the waistband and then the top of the thin cotton undies I'd watched her slide on earlier.

Tyler loosened her stance and stepped one leg out further to allow me more access. "We're going to be late..."

Her objection was barely above a murmur as my fingers found her core and began coaxing her toward climax.

"We'll get there," I replied, my mouth near her ear and my voice lower than before.

Her back was pressed against my chest as her head fell against my shoulder, and I kissed the soft spot on her neck below her ear. She groaned, and I hummed, letting the vibration in my chest tell her how much I was enjoying feeling her clench and tremble against my fingers.

I could see the expression on her face in the mirror in front of us—her eyes closed, and her mouth parted just enough to let out small gasps every few seconds as I changed my movements. These were the few moments I saw that look of carefree abandon on her face. The rest of the time, everything about Tyler was guarded and held close like a secret. But she didn't really have any secrets—rather, her entire existence was a secret of sorts. Like she lived under the veil of expectations of others, and everything that made her who she was, actually was more of an afterthought.

But right here, right now, with my hand against her and my fingers sliding inside her as she began to climax against me... nothing was held back. She was bucking against my hand as I gripped my other hand around her waist and held her up, her knees already buckling as the wave of pleasure begins to subside.

When we were finished, she leaned against the bathroom counter to catch her breath as I washed my hands and then borrowed some of her lip gloss. She didn't have anything I needed for my hair, but I combed my fingers through some of the springy curls until I was pleased with the outcome.

"My father's car is probably out front already," Tyler mentioned as she pushed herself back up to a standing position and did the same hair and lip check in the mirror. "Are we ready?"

I nodded and crossed my fingers between us. "Let's go open a lesbian bar."

Tyler grinned and dropped a small peck on my cheek before we both headed out of her penthouse and down the elevator to the lobby. Sure enough, a black Town Car was waiting at the curb out front, and a driver in a professional suit and cap stepped out to open the door for us.

"This is fancy," I commented.

Tyler slid into the back seat of the car first. "It's just protocol."

"It's still fancy." I slid in after her.

She was quiet now, and I recognized that the mood had shifted for her. After we'd buckled ourselves in, I reached my hand across the space between us and took hers. She let me, and we just held hands quietly for the rest of the drive until we reached her father's office.

An elevator ride and an awkward moment of standing in front of the receptionist as he finished a phone call later, we were ushered into a large office that was set up like it was part conference room, part lounge, and then someone had thrown a desk in the corner.

"Come in, come in," Walter Adams called out to the two of us as we stepped inside.

Tyler's face immediately split into an extra happy beam as she walked toward him with open arms. They embraced like two polite strangers might, with a small pat on the back and a quick step apart.

"Thanks for sitting down with us, Dad. I know how busy your schedule is." Tyler was motioning for me to sit in the chair next to her as we congregated at a conference table that had several stacks of paper sitting on it, including what I recognized immediately as my business proposal and potential lease.

"Of course, sweetheart." He sat diagonally from us around the table and picked up a fountain pen that was sitting on the pad of paper in front of him. "Let's get right into it. I read over the proposal and lease terms this morning."

I sat down slowly, mindful of not letting my ass vacate the seams of these pants.

"Everything is pretty standard," I quipped, trying to ease the tingle of nerves that was beginning to bubble in my stomach. "I really appreciate your leniency with the rate. It'll be really helpful for us to be able to give more back in the nonprofit side of things when we're keeping our overhead lower like that."

Walter nodded his head, but it was curt and stiff. "We're going to have to increase by three percent annually, of course."

"Of course," I replied, because that was standard on most retail leases.

"I have some concerns," he continued, and I braced for the bad news with a tight Kegel. "Starting with, the neighborhood business association is going to have to approve of any new business opening there. The quarterly meeting is next Thursday, and you're both going to have to go advocate for the business or we won't be able to proceed forward."

Tyler glanced sideways at me, like this was the first time she'd heard of this. "Really? I don't remember having that stipulation with previous businesses in that space."

Her father shrugged his shoulders like it wasn't up to him. "It's the new bylaws. They put them in place at the end of the last fiscal year. I'm ready to move forward on allowing the lease as long as they are on board, but I think it might be an uphill battle. That corner there really values quiet surroundings, and they are probably not going to like the idea of a rowdy bar coming in and changing that."

"We're not going to be rowdy," I countered, almost feeling a little offended at that comment. Even though, of course we were going to be rowdy. "We can certainly respect any neighborhood quiet hours if needed."

"Great." Walter gave me a thin-lipped smile that didn't meet his beady eyes that shifted away from me, like he couldn't look me directly in the eye. "Explain that to the neighborhood association, and then I'm sure it'll all go through just fine."

"Thanks for your support, Dad." Tyler reached a hand over and placed it on her father's forearm. "It means a lot to me that you're helping Yasmeen do this."

Yeah, that really is kind of surprising. I'd expected a bit more pushback in this meeting, but he was acting like he would be our mascot if we asked.

"Well, I hope to see you both coming around more," Walter

added, this time looking between Tyler and me with a slightly uncomfortable smile. "It's been a while since you've let me meet someone you're dating, Ty."

Tyler turned to me with a grin across her face. "She's something special."

Walter focused on me then. "Is that right, Yasmeen? You're treating my daughter well, I'm sure?"

I leaned to the side and placed my arm across her shoulders, pulling her against me. "Nothing I wouldn't do for my girl."

I completed the show with a kiss on her cheek, not missing the stoniness in her father's expression as I did so. *What the hell is going on between these two?* I'd thought my family was complicated, but after the last few minutes with Tyler and her father, I was beginning to think I might have the easy version. Everything here felt performative, like the acceptance and support only went so deep.

"Let me know how Thursday goes and what else I can do to help you both," Walter said, this time standing up and offering his hand toward me.

"We absolutely will," I agreed, shaking his hand. "Thursday will be a cinch, I'm sure."

Tyler didn't seem too certain, but she hugged her father anyway and then took my hand as we walked out of the office.

"Such a cute couple," the receptionist called over his headset as he waved us goodbye.

I waved back then we both stepped onto the elevator. As soon as the doors closed, I glanced at Tyler. "Does your dad know his receptionist is gay?"

She laughed. "Absolutely not. Daniel keeps a stock photo from HomeGoods of a random straight family on his desk just to keep up the ruse."

This whole place was the upside fucking down.

100

Chapter Twelve

"Tyler, your dad has the hook-up," Isa commented as we all walked into the box her father owned for the season above the Washington Capitals ice hockey rink. "This is an incredible view."

Tyler laced her fingers with mine and leaned into my side. "Thanks. There are plenty of snacks over on the side table and a fully stocked bar. Everyone help yourselves to whatever you want."

Me, Tyler, Kari, Rachel, Isa, Eduardo, and my friend Samira were all filing into the box that still had more than enough room to invite ten more people if we'd wanted to, which in fact, we had.

Between Tyler's friends and mine, it was going to be a meet-and-greet for everyone important in our lives—not including family or Mila and Ari, who were in New York right now. But Lukas, Ari's stepson, was already here. He was currently pouring himself shots while on TikTok Live and answering questions from his fans. He annoyed the living shit out of me, but Mila and Ari loved him and insisted I invite him out to more things so this was his pity invite for the year.

Ari's brother, Aston, was also here with his fiancée—I would be a bridesmaid next year in the wedding and was looking forward to it—and his mother, Nomi. Inviting Nomi meant, of course, that I had also invited Chicky and her new husband, Reverend Steve Wilson. I'd also been a bridesmaid in that wedding, and I had never seen a bigger wedding in my life or ever seen anyone make out so hardcore at the altar before. Nomi had actually been Chicky's maid of honor because she and Mila had had a fight about floral arrangements, but they'd worked it out eventually.

Families are complicated, man.

"Do you think everyone will get along?" Tyler whispered to me as we walked over to the bar area.

I grabbed us both a can of hard seltzer and opened the top for her. "They seem to be so far. You have to introduce me to your friends. Who is that talking to Lukas?"

"Who's Lukas?" Tyler asked.

I pointed him out and quickly filled her in on his weird role in our life and friend group. He was taking a selfie with someone with the ice rink in the background.

"That's Riley, my producer." Tyler pointed to the beautiful trans woman smiling next to Lukas in the photograph. "She works for the company that owns my podcast and makes every episode perfection. I honestly don't know how she does it."

I gave her a courteous smile and nod as Tyler waved to her. "I definitely need to meet her. What about that guy by the door?"

Tyler followed my gaze to where a short, plump man was deep in conversation with Rachel and Isa. Eduardo was standing partially behind Isa like he was trying to get a word into the conversation but she wasn't giving him an inch.

"That's Sanchez," Tyler explained. "He leases the retail space next to yours."

"The bike shop?" Where the bar was going to be situated was also next to a bike repair and sales shop that was pretty popular in town. "That's cool that you guys are friends."

"Sanchez is more than a friend," she added.

I glanced at her with one brow raised, but she laughed.

"I mean, he also helps fill in for me as assistant property manager when I'm busy or out of town. He gets a slight reduction on his lease because of that. It's really helpful, because it's such a huge building, and I just can't do it all on my own."

That made a lot of sense, but I don't know why I'd never thought to ask much about her property manager duties before. "Oh. Wait, why can't I get a discount on my rent to help with that? I'll help, too."

She rolled her eyes at me. "You're a hard enough sell at full price, Yas."

"Gee, thanks." I laughed. "Come on. Let's go meet everyone."

We spent the entire first period just going around and making introductions. Thankfully, everyone seemed to be getting along and mingling easily. The drinks were flowing, which probably helped with that, but I was counting my lucky stars either way.

"I scored a press pass," Tyler whispered in my ear after we'd made the rounds and talked to everyone. "Want to sneak out with me, and I'll give you a tour?"

I grinned and nodded, because that sounded like a hella good time.

She took my hand, and we casually slipped out the door into the hallway. Aside from a random person walking to or from the bathrooms, it was pretty empty since the game was currently going and everyone was in the stands. I followed her through the maze of concrete hallways until we came to an *Employees Only* marked door, which Tyler waltzed through like she had every right to. Another hallway down, we passed a security guard who barely acknowledged us after Tyler waved her press pass at him.

And then we were in the empty locker room.

"For some reason, I thought it would be bigger," I mused as I walked around the benches. "Like Ted Lasso's locker room or something."

"It's never like the movies," she commented, taking a seat on one of the benches in front of marked lockers.

"Nothing ever is," I said with a sigh.

She reached out a hand to me, and I took it, letting her lead me to sit on the bench next to me. Our fingers were interlocked and resting on her knee, and we were just quiet for a moment.

"Our friends all get along," she mused after a quiet moment. "You've met my dad. You're moving into my building."

When she laid it all out like that, it began to make me feel nervous, but I pushed the butterflies down. "And to think we didn't even know each other last month."

"I kind of like where this is going," she continued. "I don't know how you feel about everything, and I know this wasn't really meant to be anything. It doesn't really feel like a business tactic anymore though, unless that's all we want it to be."

We weren't looking at one another, rather just sitting quietly next to each other. "It's a little bit more than just business," I admitted. "I was actually thinking that maybe you should meet my family. Make things fair, you know?"

She looked at me now, surprise etched on her face. "Yeah?"

"Yeah. My dad wants to meet you since he's been helping with the business planning side of things, and I think you'd get along with my brother and sister really well." I beamed whenever I talked about my family. I couldn't help it, but the feeling of love and warmth overflowed my heart anytime I thought about them. "I mean, no pressure or anything. It doesn't have to mean anything. Business-related, you know?"

She didn't respond immediately to that. "I'd like to meet them, and I also think I'd like to be more involved in the bar if you're looking for that. Maybe from an investor standpoint? I could plug the opening on the podcast."

That might actually be really helpful, but I didn't give a firm yes or no in that moment. "We should definitely talk about that."

A player walked into the locker room and was lifting his shirt up over his head when he paused as he saw us sitting there. "Uh, hello?"

"Sorry!" Tyler jumped up from the bench, pulling me along with her. "We'll get out of your way."

I laughed as we scurried out of the locker rooms and wove our way back up to where we were supposed to be in the box with our friends.

"You're going to get your press pass revoked," I teased her. We tried to slip back into the room as seamlessly as possible. Half of our friends were watching the game, and the other half were engaged in lively conversation, so it actually was pretty easy to go unnoticed.

Tyler interlaced her fingers with mine as we held hands, and things just felt...nice. Even though things between us had been subjected to a bit of a rocky start, the physical connection between us had been undeniable from day one. But now it felt like it was more than just the way my body reacted whenever I looked at her. There was definitely something deeper happening here, and as much as part of me wanted to run the other direction, another part of me just couldn't let go of her hand.

Chapter Thirteen

"So, we're not lying to your family? Just mine?" Tyler asked as we walked up the porch steps to my childhood home that Sunday afternoon.

"Unlike your dad, my family is already aware that I'm the family fuck-up and doesn't hold it against me," I replied, but then thought about it for a moment longer. "Actually, they *are* always up my butt about it, but still...it's not a secret. Either way, I don't want to lie about us or anything like that to them. They'd know right away."

I barely had my hand on the doorknob when it swung open, and my sister Nia was standing in the opening.

"Please tell me you brought the sauce," Nia immediately fired off a question before all else.

I opened my tote bag and pulled out a glass bottle of barbecue sauce from our favorite barbecue restaurant in Atlanta called Anna's BBQ that I had picked up earlier this year at Atlanta Pride—literally my favorite month of the year. Anna's BBQ was a little behind the times in all ways technology, so shipping it to us wasn't an option. Now, everyone in my family made it a point to stop by and get some to go if they were ever in Atlanta.

"Hello to you, too," I responded as she took it from me. "This is Tyler, by the way."

Nia finally seemed to register that someone was standing next to me. Her eyes scanned Tyler with every bit of judgment you'd expect from an older sister.

"Nice to meet you, Tyler." Nia extended her hand, and her tone turned from urgent to cordial. "Yas did mention she was bringing a guest, but she kept us all in the dark on who. How do you two know each other?"

Tyler's face had gone full white-girl-panic, so I put my hand on her forearm and hugged her closer to me.

"Tyler and I have been getting close lately, and now, she is also a business partner," I informed my sister. "You guys are going to need to get to know her because she's an angel investor in my new project."

That had been a new development that we'd firmed up yesterday after the game, and I was excited about the doors it opened for us. Tyler was only going to come in at eight percent, so I was absolutely still the majority owner. However, her contribution would allow us to promote the bar on her podcast, utilize her resources, and add some "celesbian" fame to the bar's background.

Nia ushered both of us inside the familiar entry way to my childhood home. "The bar?"

I didn't get a chance to answer before Demetrius walked in with his arms spread wide. "Hey, baby sister."

He caught me up in a bear hug that lifted me right off my feet. "We get it—you have muscles. Put me down!"

At least he had the sense to do what I told him with a big grin across his face. Tall and broad, he had the body of a linebacker and was overly confident about it for my liking, but whatever. "Haven't seen you around the office in a while. Do you still work for us?"

Demetrius worked full-time for my father at Kiani Security, where he was currently training to take over for the Vice President of Operations at the end of the fiscal year. I loved D, but there wasn't a creative bone in his body, so following in our father's footsteps had just come natural to him. He had played football in high school and college—just like Dad—and now was stepping into Dad's career.

He was a therapist's wet dream, I'm sure.

"Hell no. I quit last year," I reminded him. To be fair, I'd been back and forth at the company anytime I needed a routine paycheck, it was hard to keep track. "I'm starting my own business now."

Demetrius's best friend, Nicole, walked in behind him and gave me a tight hug. "Hey, Yas!"

Nicole was at every family function to the point that I basically considered them a sibling—they were nonbinary, so I was always careful to use appropriate pronouns. Neither of the two would admit to it, and God knows no one in my family would ask, but there was definitely something between them and Demetrius. I was just waiting until they one day finally decided to come clean and admit they were a couple—or maybe my brother was actually stupid enough to not realize what a catch Nicole was yet.

Whatever—not my monkeys, not my circus.

"What do you mean? What business?" Demetrius continued. "Does Dad know about this one?"

"I'm opening up a lesbian bar." I pulled Tyler up next to me and gestured toward her. "Demetrius, Nicole—this is Tyler, my close friend and investor."

Close friend really didn't feel like it covered it at this point, but I wasn't about to give my family the same performance we'd given her dad.

"Oh, my goodness!" Nicole gasped, their hands flying to their chest. "The Deviant Devotee!"

"The what?" Demetrius glanced at Nicole, then at Tyler.

"Uh, she's referencing my podcast," Tyler clarified. "I have a podcast called The Deviant Devotee."

Nicole playfully whacked my brother's arm. "D, I literally talk about it all the time. Remember the episode on copycat killer of The Vampire of Hanover who'd bite his victim's necks like the original killer did? That was game changing. The pod went viral after that one."

I made a mental note to ask Nicole for the Cliff's Notes version of the podcast because I still hadn't gotten around to listening to it, and that was absolutely going to come back to bite me in the ass at some point.

"Can we stop crowding the entry and everyone head to the kitchen?" Nia pointed toward the doorway that led to a small hallway and then our open plan kitchen, dining, and living room area that had always been the center of our home when we were growing up.

Some things never changed.

My father was seated in the worn leather La-Z-Boy recliner that was pointed toward the wall-mounted television above the fireplace. Back in my time living here, we'd had the big, old-school, boxy television on a stand in the corner, but my father was all about the latest technology. New iPhone hits the market? My father had it before the public could even buy it. Practically every single thing in this house was now run by a remote or a voice command, but the nearly thirty-year-old recliner had never once been served an eviction notice.

Nia was already back at her usual spot in front of the stove where she was using the sauce I'd brought her to coat a rack of ribs.

"Dad, do you know about Yas's new business?" Demetrius dropped onto the deep-seated couch that jutted up against my father's chair. "She said she's opening a bar."

He glanced sideways toward us for a millisecond before turning his attention back to the game on the television. "I know."

Tyler and I settled in at the counter-height chairs against the kitchen island where an open bottle of red wine and a few clean glasses were calling my name. I poured us both a glass and took a quick sip before reengaging with the raucousness that was my family.

"He already went over the whole business plan with me, D," I informed my brother, my tone slightly haughtier than I intended. For some reason, I always felt the need to defend myself around him. "It's solid."

"Half hair salon, half bar. The concept has legs," my father agreed but then turned the volume up on the television.

Nicole joined Tyler and me at the kitchen counter, and I poured them a glass of wine as well. "Don't mind your brother. You know how he can get."

"I know I have to put up with him because we're related, but I have no idea why you do," I joked. I'd probably warned Nicole a hundred times to head for the hills, but for whatever reason, they had yet to give up on my brother. I mean, I guess he wasn't all terrible.

Actually, he wasn't terrible at all, but he did have very strong opinions on how I should be living my life and that wasn't the vibe.

"What's your role in the bar then, Tyler?" Nia asked as she licked a spot of sauce off the back of her hand.

"Mostly promotional and financial," Tyler answered as she

clutched her fingers around the stem of her wineglass like it was life support. "I'm just really excited about the concept and what need it's trying to meet in the community."

"What need is that?" Demetrius added himself to our conversation from where he was still seated on the couch across the room. "People who want the rim of their cocktails lined with hair clippings?"

I shot him an irritated look. "Ha. Ha. Haaaaaaaaa."

I let the last part drag out as my voice deadpanned my annoyance with him.

"There will be a clear divide—door and everything— between the hair section and the bar section. We've already okayed it with the county, and there are other places already doing something similar, like Scissors and Scotch."

"Ooh, I like that place," Nicole said. "They do a great undercut."

Tyler eyed Nicole with what seemed like a new sense of appreciation. "I've been strongly considering getting one of those, but I'm still too chicken."

Nicole turned around and lifted the back of their long hair, revealing a geometric undercut design underneath. "Highly recommend. Especially in the summer here in DC. This whole place is built on a swamp, you know."

I grimaced, not looking forward to that right around the corner. "It's true. The humidity in July and August is truly disgusting."

Tyler had a few more questions for Nicole about getting an undercut, so I floated my way over to Nia by the stove while the two of them kiki'd.

"So, Tyler, huh?" Nia cast me a quick side eye before handing me a spoon and instructing me to mix up the potato salad. "Things good there?"

I pushed the serving spoon into the bowl and began stirring

in a sloppy, chunky fashion. "I mean, yeah. Why wouldn't they be?"

Nia added some salt to the bowl I was stirring. "I mean, like...*good* good?"

"We're figuring it out," I replied, continuing to dodge the question because honestly, I didn't have a fully complete answer yet. Also, Nia and I didn't go into details too often. We were close—hell, she was probably the closest person in my life. She was like a mom to me, but she respected my space and never pushed for information unless I wanted to give it.

My sister shrugged. "Just that you haven't brought someone home since Angie that summer after college—"

I lifted the spoon out of the bowl and held it up between my sister and me. "We do not say that name in my presence."

Nia chuckled and put her hands up in defense. "I'm just saying. This feels like a big deal—bringing Tyler here? Having her meet all of us?"

"It's not like all that," I reiterated. "We're friends right now. And business partners."

She was as relentless as a dog with a bone. "So, you two haven't hooked up at all?"

I paused stirring, because Nia rarely asked me about my sex life. "Uh...I mean, *friends* can mean a lot of things these days."

Nia snorted and shook her head, then took the bowl of potato salad from me and handed me a head of iceberg lettuce. "Here. Tear this up for the salad."

I did as she instructed—per usual—and smacked the core of the head against the edge of the counter, then pried it out with my fingers before tearing the leaves apart and depositing it into a ceramic serving bowl.

Nia was tossing in halved grape tomatoes, chopped-up green peppers, and slivers of red onion as we worked in harmony. "If y'all were to be more than friends, I don't think that would be terrible, you know."

My knees almost gave out from under me, and I turned to stare at my older sister in disbelief. Could this actually be the rare older sister approval I'd always heard of but just skirted shy of for the last thirty years?

"What?"

She didn't respond right away but glanced behind us where Tyler was now feeling Nicole's undercut and commenting on how soft it was.

"I mean, she seems like good people." Nia handed me a bottle of olive oil and another bottle of balsamic vinegar. "You need good people in your life, Yas. You've worked hard, and you've got a fire in you that can't be replicated. It's special."

I began to toss the salad with dressing as I listened. When Nia gave praise, it was meaningful. There wasn't a doubt that she was speaking from her gut, and the raw honesty of the moment was making me feel choked up.

"Thanks, Nia."

"Do you think she'd let me come listen to her record an episode of her podcast sometime?" Nia added, a sly grin now spreading across her fan.

I gasped audibly. "No! Don't tell me you're a fan."

"Listening to podcasts really passes the time during the workday," Nia replied. "She's got a really great voice, too. Super soothing and somehow edgy, like it keeps you coming back."

That, I couldn't disagree with. "She *does* have an amazing voice. I just never took you for a podcast person."

She took the salad from me when I was done tossing it. "Have you listened to it?"

"I'm going to." Seriously, I really was. "But...thanks. That means a lot to me that you're on board."

"Of course," Nia replied. "But speaking of being on board with things, I need your help with Dad."

And there it was.

I groaned loud enough to express my annoyance. "What kind of help?"

Nia placed a hand on her hip. "I want him to join a ROMEO group in the area. He's been really lonely lately, and I think it'll be good for him to get out with more people his age."

The corners of my lips pulled down in a frown. "What the hell is a ROMEO group?"

"Really Old Men Eating Out."

I blinked once...then twice. "I'm sorry...what?"

"ROMEO," Nia repeated. "It stands for Really Old Men Eating Out. It's a national old men's social group where they get together for lunch once a week."

"Ooooh," I said, the pieces clicking into place. "Eating out as in eating out at a restaurant."

Nia furrowed her brows. "Obviously. What else would it mean?"

"I thought you were trying to get Dad some ass."

Nia's expression turned to one of revulsion. "Jesus Christ, Yasmeen. Get your mind out of the gutter."

"Do you think I want to be thinking of Dad eating out?" I countered. "That image right there is a full therapy session, and I'm sending you the bill."

She laughed and shook her head. "I'm serious though. He needs to get out there more and make friends. Talk it up at dinner in front of him."

"Fine," I agreed, even though I still wasn't sure I was on board with the concept. They should at least consider changing the name, for frick's sake.

"Yas!" Nicole waved me back over to where they were standing with Tyler. They had their hands in Tyler's long, straight hair and were pulling it to one side. "What do you think if Tyler shaves off this side and half of the back, then does a striped design in it?"

"You'd look great no matter how your hair is," I replied, letting my eyes hold Tyler's gaze for a moment. "But I have no complaints with the way your hair is right now, either."

A light pink hue spread across Tyler's cheeks, and I was wondering if she was thinking about my fingers sliding through her hair and pulling her toward me with a gentle tug.

I was definitely thinking about that.

"Hey, do you want a tour?" I asked Tyler. "This is actually my childhood home, so all the skeletons are here."

Tyler grinned. "I'd love that."

I grabbed her hand and pulled her away from the living room and toward the hallway with the stairwell at one end and the laundry room at the other. I pointed out a few pictures on the wall, a guest bathroom, and a scratch on the bottom of the baseboard from when my brother and I had tried to play hockey in the house when we were teenagers. We scaled the stairs to the second floor next, and I gave her a quick peek into my siblings' rooms, my father's room, and then we stopped in front of the door to my room at the far end of the upstairs hallway.

"This is your room?" Tyler asked as she stepped through the doorway and surveyed the walls lined with peeling pop star posters and collages from magazine clippings that hadn't aged well. Tyler pointed to the largest one in the corner. "Usher? Really?"

"You don't have to be straight to want to get it on to 'You Make Me Wanna'..." I countered. "His sound is straight fire."

Tyler grinned as she sat on the top of my old twin-sized mattress with the fuchsia-colored bedspread. "I don't disagree. I learned to masturbate to "Nice and Slow.""

My jaw dropped as my mouth fell open. "Well...damn."

She pushed a bit further onto the bed, then leaned back onto her elbows. "You ever hooked up with someone in this bed?"

The answer to that was absolutely yes, but I'm no fool.

"Never." I glanced toward the hallway and quickly closed the door to give us some privacy. "But we could change that right now."

"Bullshit," Tyler called me out on my lie. "How thin are these walls?"

"Thick enough that I've never been caught," I replied, not that my father was home much to monitor me when I was a teenager. As a single father, he'd been working almost around the clock to support the three of us children. I appreciated the hell out of that, but it also meant that there was a lot of growing up quickly and fending for myself.

"Quick." Tyler's single word was a command.

I lifted one brow as I sauntered toward her. "Yes, ma'am."

My lips found hers quickly as I pressed her down into the mattress and covered her body with my own. She groaned against my mouth, and my entire body lit up in response.

"Tell me what you want," I whispered between nibbles of her lips down to the flesh of her neck as I traced my tongue across her jawline.

Tyler didn't hesitate to grab my right hand and push it between her legs. It took all my restraint to go slowly, but I pressed my palm flat against her stomach and slid it underneath the waistband of her jeans. She grabbed the top button and zipper and loosened it for me as I slipped beneath the lacy fabric of her underwear until I found the spot I knew would make her body react. It did. The moment I touched her, her back arched away from the bed, and she exhaled against my lips like she'd been broken open.

It didn't take long for me to work her to the edge of her

fervor, and I slid my middle finger deeper inside as I felt her fall over the edge, her body trembling against me in heavy pants and shivers. I didn't let up until she stilled, trying to catch her breath.

"Turn around," she whispered to me once she found her voice and scooted herself up into a seated position.

I did as instructed and sat on the mattress with my back to her chest. She pulled me tighter against her, clutching me in a hug as her arm wrapped around to my front. There wasn't even a moment of hesitation on her part, as she seemed to know exactly what I wanted.

The way our bodies connected felt like old flames who'd never been apart. She knew me in a way few other women had, and I had been around long enough to know what a rarity that was. Our connection was more than physical, of course, but in this realm, we knocked it out of the freaking park.

With every strum of her finger, I pushed my back harder against her, somehow wanting to be closer than we already were. It wasn't possible, but I had to try. A moan escaped my lips that absolutely could not be silenced—and was much louder than I intended.

Tyler moved her other hand to my mouth and gently, but very firmly, pressed her palm against my lips, silencing me. "Shh. We have to be quiet."

I was panting at that point, and something about her forcing me to be quieter was only spurring me closer and closer to the edge of climax. My groan was now vibrations against her hand, and I slid down on the bed as my body gave way to the complete ecstasy of the moment.

She slowed but didn't fully come to a stop until my body was no longer trembling. Only then did she release the hand from over my mouth, leaving kisses on the side of my neck as a parting gift.

"Come on." Tyler slid her leg around me and stood up off the bed. "Your family is going to start suspecting something if we're up here much longer."

I literally could not care less in that moment, but I grinned and took her hand, following her downstairs.

Chapter Fourteen

"**A**re you ready for this?" Tyler turned her head to me as we came to a pause in front of the heavy wooden doors that led into the large conference room where the Pike Neighborhood Association met every quarter.

"Do not quote any Taylor Swift lines tonight, Tyler," I warned her, already as she sang her question at me in the tune of one of Gaylor Swift's songs. "We have to be very professional."

She wasn't having any of my shit tonight. "Uh, out of the two of us, I'm the consummate professional. That's literally my entire vibe—stoic professional."

I grinned. "Not in bed, it's not."

She pointed at me with one long index finger. "See?"

I put both of my hands up in defense. "Okay, I see your point. But I'm not worried. We're going to kick their ass tonight."

Tyler smiled, but it didn't reach her eyes. She gripped the messenger bag at her side that had all of our talking points and presentation pieces in it.

My fingers slid between hers, and I gave her a squeeze. "Seriously. We've got this."

The smile tinged her irises now, and she nodded her head. "Let's do this."

I nodded. "Let's do this."

And so, we fucking did this.

But here's what I wasn't told in advance. When a neighborhood association only meets once a quarter, people come with shit to say—which, first of all, why? I swear I thought we'd be the only people in the audience, but there's a line, and then a panel of...I don't know. Board members? Elders? Kings and Queens of the Pike? Whoever they were, they had the final say over every matter presented at the lone microphone in the center aisle facing them. Half the time, they didn't give an answer at all, but would say that the issue would be tabled for a vote at another time. The other half of the time, they took the vote right then and there in front of all of us, and they were not quiet about it. There were no hushed whispers as they came to a decision, but rather people just stood witness to being talked about openly until they were given a yay or nay on whatever they were proposing.

All of that would have been fine, or, well, at least tolerable. However, no one warned me that we would be well into hour three of this meeting, and our number still hasn't been called. Three hours of Tyler elbowing me in the side to wake me up anytime my head started to lull backward as I couldn't possibly take another moment of this monotonous soundtrack.

How the hell people had this much to talk about on one street was unbelievable.

"It's our turn!" Tyler's whispered warning came paired with a bang of her knee against mine. "Get up."

I snorted out half a snore that had been about to escape my

lips as the dream world called me. My head jolted upright. "What?"

"It's *our* turn," she repeated, now hissing as she was standing and motioning toward the center aisle.

I jumped to my feet and somehow beat her there. We walked to the microphone side-by-side, and she passed me a stack of index cards while she held a clipboard stuffed full of looseleaf paper. I glanced briefly at the index cards but her handwriting was color-coded in gel pen and had hearts dotting every "I," so I immediately discarded them to my back pocket.

"Good evening, ladies and gentlemen," I began, giving purposeful, and awkward, eye contact to each person on the panel in front of us. "My partner and I are from *The Dirty Derby* and—"

Tyler's elbow hit my side again, and she cut me off. "We're still workshopping the name."

Are we, though?

"Anyway," I continued, dodging the side eye she was giving me. "We're leasing the retail space at the corner of Walter Reed Drive and Columbia Pike and turning it into a lesbian and queer bar that will also have a pro bono hair salon in the back. We just need a few signatures to confirm the neighborhood association is on board with this, and we'll be out of your hair. I'm sure all you wonderful civil servants are ready to be home with your families—a glass of wine is waiting for you, am I right?"

One of the women on the panel chuckled lightly, and I could see she was already thinking about whether she was going to have a red or white.

The man sitting in the center didn't seem as amused. "You're opening a bar?"

"I've actually got our proposal and business plan here." Tyler stepped up to the long table the members were sitting at and began distributing paper packets to each one. "As you can see, we're already in the process of getting our liquor license, remodeling will all be completed by local neighborhood construction businesses, and we're even partnering with A-SPAN to offer one day a month of free haircuts for the underhoused."

Everyone just called it A-SPAN because it actually stood for Arlington Street People's Assistance Network, and there was no one alive who wanted to say that sentence out loud. Thankfully, they were changing their name soon.

"What are you going to do about noise compliance after hours? There are a lot of high rises and similar residences within earshot of that location." The man in the center wasn't even bothering to read the papers that Tyler had handed him. "We owe it to our neighbors to keep quiet hours and not have raucous activity happening directly below their windows."

"We're across the street from a theater that has been oper-ating for years and is very familiar with moving large crowds in and out at night without being a major disturbance." Tyler shut his concerns down without hesitation, and the look on his face told me that didn't happen often. Damn, this woman had balls. "And we're contracting with Arlington Police to hire off-duty officers for overtime on Thursday, Friday, and Saturday evenings to assist with traffic and security."

He didn't seem the least bit swayed but did stay quiet for a few minutes as other members on the panel asked about events, parking, and other relevant matters. Both Tyler and I answered each and every question fully, and I swear to God, this felt better than winning at pickleball. I was knocking this shit out of the park, and it was doing everything to stroke my confidence in being a near-future business owner.

"I'm concerned about the demographic a place like this would attract," the man sitting center stage said after the woman to his right had finished her question about litter and maintenance of the sidewalks in front of the bar. "This neighborhood has a long history of upstanding citizens. The unruly type that would frequent that type of establishment could send the wrong message. Not to mention the pro bono aspect to it would probably bring vagrants sniffing around more often and sleeping on the benches in the park down the street. We have to consider the safety of our neighbors and children in allowing that type of exposure."

Tyler didn't respond immediately, so I stepped closer to the microphone. "Can you clarify what you mean when you say 'that type of exposure'?"

I knew exactly what he meant.

He began to fidget in his seat and looked away, like the answer might be written on the wall behind me. "I'm not saying anything negative. I'm just pointing out that it caters to a crowd that isn't exactly family-friendly."

Not family-friendly? He meant to say "gay."

"Actually, we plan to do plenty of family-friendly and dry events during the day, especially to give queer teens a place where they can feel at home and accepted if they don't have that elsewhere." I took Tyler's hand in mine, interlacing our fingers. "My girlfriend and I can't wait to be able to bring a safe space to queer folx all over Northern Virginia to find community, love, and, maybe, a good drink. If you're over twenty-one, of course."

His gaze dropped to our hands, and the discomfort was visible in his expression. "We'll have to vote on this, you understand. It's a big decision."

"We understand," Tyler replied, her diplomatic tone back in full force even though she was clutching my fingers so tight I thought they might fall off. "Are there any other questions we can answer to help assuage any concerns?"

"I think we've heard enough." He turned to the other members on the panel and proposed a vote, someone seconded taking a vote, and then they polled each member individually for a *yay* or a *nay*. Literally while we were standing right there watching them, and they avoided making eye contact with us at all costs.

"Well, that decides it, then." The man turned back to face us and adjusted the lapels on his suit jacket. "Three in favor and two opposed. Your proposal is provisionally approved for a one-year term, but it will need to be revisited in the next fiscal year and pass the county requirements and inspections before granted. We'll also be holding another vote next meeting to determine guidelines on noise compliance, security, parking constraints, and traffic control that you will be required to follow."

Tyler somehow squeezed my hand even tighter, and her voice cracked with a high-pitched squeak. "Thank you, sir."

"Thank you to everyone who supported our proposal," I followed up, because the two opposing votes had been the man in the center and a smaller balding man to the right side, and I was not thankful for either of them. He picked up on my nuance immediately, raising a single brow in protest. "We really appreciate your faith in us and can't wait to show you what an asset *The Dirty Derby* will be to this neighborhood."

"Again, we're still workshopping the name," Tyler added. "Thank you so much for your time."

She was pulling me away from the microphone, and I knew she didn't want to risk me saying anything else.

Fair.

We passed through the double doors and back out into the hallway where one or two people were lingering, looking half asleep and like they were waiting for someone inside to be done so they could go home.

The moment we got on the elevator and the doors closed, Tyler and I turned to each other and let out juvenile squeals.

"We're approved!" she said, punching her fists in the air.

I clapped my hands and did a little body roll and wiggle. "We're going to be business owners! We're going to be bar owners!"

"Queer bar owners—just lesbians everywhere as far as the eye can see," she teased, stepping closer to me and hooking a finger in one of the belt loops on my jeans. "Imagine the possibilities."

I snorted out a laugh. "Are you trying to make me jealous, Ms. Adams? Because that is not going to work. I'm more than fine with us bringing some guests home to join us."

Her eyes widened like she'd never considered the possibility before but was not entirely opposed. "Oh..."

"That's not a no," I joked before placing a kiss against her lips.

She grinned, kissing me back before the elevator doors opened, and we both stepped out onto the lower ground floor. "You know, you called me your girlfriend in there."

I didn't meet her gaze when she said that but just offered a noncommittal shrug. My stomach suddenly felt like it was flipping over in my abdomen, and something inside me just wanted to walk back every word I'd ever said. Now that the business was a definite—the bar was absolutely happening—everything between us romantically suddenly felt über serious. I'd been here before—rushing into things was my forte, and messing around with someone I worked with had never benefited me in the past. I had promised myself I wasn't going to keep repeating that cycle. Yet, here I was.

"Well, yeah," I said, trying to find my words. "We said we'd pretend for your dad, and he's probably going to hear about this vote and stuff. Better to keep the ruse going, you know?"

She didn't respond to that, and the way she pushed open the glass door, with a little too much force, before we exited onto the sidewalk told me everything she was feeling.

Shit.

"Tyler," I called after her, but she didn't turn around. My cell phone began to vibrate in my pocket, and I fished it out as I followed her toward the car. I doubted she'd leave me behind—no matter how mad she was—because we had carpooled there.

The number on my cell phone screen wasn't one I recognized, but I decided to answer it anyway. "Hello?"

"I'm trying to reach Yasmeen Kiani," the voice on the other end of the line said. "You're listed as the tenant of this retail space."

I felt my gut clench in anticipation. "What retail space?"

He listed off the address of the bar. "Ma'am, I hate to tell you this but we've had a pipe burst in the ceiling while we were working on updating the hair washing sinks in the back. You'd better get down here, because we're going to need someone who is authorized to make decisions on budgetary alterations."

I groaned audibly, not caring that he could hear my frustration. "I'll be right there. Give me ten minutes. Thanks."

Shoving the phone back in my pocket after hanging up, I picked up my speed and jogged a little faster after Tyler. "Hey, Tyler! We have to go to the bar!"

She paused her stride for half a second, long enough for me to catch up. "Why?"

I exhaled loudly, trying to catch my breath after chasing her down. I really needed to consider restarting my gym membership. "Contractor just called. There's a burst pipe in the back room."

She looked as frustrated as I felt. "I'll drive."

Chapter Fifteen

I expected maybe some water-stained drywall and the need for a small wet vacuum or pile of towels to sop up any little pools the burst pipe had created. But, no, that was not the situation Tyler and I walked into when I arrived at the bar.

"We're going to have to redo all of the paneling on the ceiling," the main contractor explained to me as he pointed to the giant open gaps in the ceiling to the industrial piping above. "The water damage will leave them all stained and have potential for mold, so best to swap it out entirely."

There was still a drizzle of water coming out of one of the pipes and falling neatly into a bucket someone must have set up before we got here. It seemed a bit pointless since we were also currently standing in at least an inch of water that had pooled to the center of the room—I hadn't realized until right now that the floor wasn't level in the back room, which I guess comes in handy for a flood.

"How quickly can your guys get all the water out so we don't have to replace the flooring, too?" I asked.

He looked at me like I'd lost my mind. "Ma'am, we're headed home. We normally never work past five o'clock so the fact that we're here late into the night already has my men riled up."

"Oh. Right. Of course." I glanced at the time on my phone, and it was a little after eight o'clock at night. "So, tomorrow morning?"

"We'll be back Monday morning," he clarified. "We're scheduled somewhere else tomorrow and we are off for the weekend. We've got the measurements we need for the new material though, so we'll be in bright and early to start replacing everything."

"But what about the water?" I pointed down at our feet and the wet floor all around us. "Who's going to clean that up?"

He didn't even look up from his electronic tablet or offer so much as a shrug. "Try a plumber."

With that impressive piece of advice, he left me standing in the backroom as he and his men packed their stuff and exited the store front.

"Yasmeen?" Tyler called out for me as she stepped into the back room. "Do we know that everyone is leaving? Why is everyone leaving?"

My hands were now perched on my hips as I surveyed the mess. "They're not plumbers."

"What?" Her brow pulled tight as she looked at me, then she gestured to the pool of water. "They're not cleaning this up? Wait, who is going to clean this up."

I handed her a stained white towel and a squeegee mop. Then I walked over to the one wet vacuum that had thankfully been in the back storage room. "We are."

Her expression looked like she was waiting for the punchline.

"I'm serious. We're cleaning this up. We can't leave it like this, or we'll have to redo the flooring, and the smell from standing water will be impossible to get out of the place, not to mention the mold we'll get," I explained. "I'll work the vacuum, and you push as much water as you can to the center, getting the edges as dry as you can until I can get it all up."

Tyler's mouth fell open. "Oh my god, you're serious. Yasmeen, this is a lot of water. It will literally take us all night."

"I think we'll be lucky if we get it all done in one night," I mused, but she didn't appreciate that answer.

There was a tenacity building in me that wasn't going anywhere. I'd failed at business too many times to just walk away now when the going got tough. This is absolutely the last way I wanted to spend my night tonight, but I'd never felt a sense of calling or conviction like I'd felt for this space and this bar. I was going to put in the elbow grease to make it everything I dreamed, but I also knew that Tyler hadn't agreed to that level of hard work.

I turned to her. "Listen, if you don't want to, you can go home. This is my place, and I'm going to take care of it. You don't have to worry about it. I promise, it's really okay. Head on home."

She propped the squeegee mop up against the wall, turned, and then walked out of the back room leaving me alone with my flood.

Well, damn. I couldn't blame her, but still. What the hell?

I looked down at the wet vacuum and began fiddling with the hose, trying to figure out where the on switch was or how to use this thing.

To my surprise, Tyler walked back in a few moments later, and her hair was now tied back in a sleek ponytail, the jacket she'd been wearing gone. "I'm not going to leave you here to do this by yourself. It'll be faster if we work together. As long as we can get the standing water out tonight, we can do the actual clean up and sanitizing part over the weekend."

I smiled at her, genuinely grateful. "Do you know how to turn on a wet vacuum?"

She eyed me for a moment and then handed the squeegee mop to me. "Here. Take this, and let's switch."

For whatever reason, she knew exactly how to work the little machine and was hosing up water faster than I could keep pushing it toward her. Every five minutes or so, the tank would get full, and we'd both have to wheel the incredibly heavy machine out to the curb and pour the water down the rain gutter, then wheel it back inside to refill.

Again, and again, and again.

Around two o'clock in the morning, most of the water was gone and we were in the process of setting up large floor fans to try to dry the rest of the residual moisture up over the next few days.

"I need to sit down for a minute," I told Tyler as I popped a squat right in the middle of the front room—the place was still unfurnished, and my clothes were already sweaty and dirty, so I didn't really care at that point.

She followed my lead and let out a tired sigh as she found a spot on the floor next to me, leaning back on her hands propped up behind her.

Both of us were silent for a few minutes, just trying to recapture our strength. This entire evening had been one of the weirdest nights of my life—from the neighborhood meeting to the moment of tension we'd had after to then working together to fix a potential disaster—none of that had been on my bingo card.

"Tonight has been unexpected," Tyler said out loud, echoing my thoughts. "I desperately need a shower and bed."

I glanced sideways at her, a small grin already pulling on my lips. "You know, a great way to save water is..."

My voice trailed off as she turned to look at me, and I wiggled my brows at her instead of finishing that sentence.

"I'm exhausted." She laughed and shook her head. "Plus, I'm still mad at you."

"For what?" I put on my most innocent face and shrugged, like I had no idea what she was talking about. "I didn't burst the pipes."

"Are we really not dating?" Her knees were pulled up to her chest now as she was watching for my reaction.

I was fiddling with a stray nail on the floor next to me. "I mean, what even *is* dating these days?"

"Yasmeen." She wasn't letting this one go.

"Okay, obviously we are dating." I finally uttered the words out loud. I wasn't trying to be obtuse, and clearly Tyler and I had crossed the more-than-friends line multiple times, both fictionally and in reality. "Do we need more of a label than that?"

"I do," Tyler responded. "This isn't something I do often. I'm not a casual dater or into the hook-up scene. No issue with anyone who does that, but it's not my vibe."

"You're not the sharing type," I joked, discomfort rattling around in my rib cage as I dodged the seriousness in her tone. "You've made that very clear."

She smiled. "Only Child Syndrome."

We let a moment of quiet pass between us until one of the fans suddenly stopped working. I got up to mess with it, switching it to a different outlet to get it working again.

Tyler was standing at the half-constructed bar when I returned. Her eyes were heavy, and she had her purse over her shoulder. "Ready to go?"

I guess we were continuing this conversation later.

I interlocked my fingers with hers, and we head out the entrance, securing all the doors and locks behind us. We didn't discuss where we were going, but we naturally just headed around the retail space and through the residential entrance to the apartments above. A slow elevator ride later, and we were stepping out at her penthouse. Larry, her chihuahua, rushed us the moment we walked in and spun circles around Tyler's legs. The bastard barely glanced at me, but I was fine with his ambivalence because the feeling was mutual.

"I'm going to take him out really quick," she said. "Towels are in the linen closet in the bathroom if you want to shower."

"A shower sounds perfect," I replied, heading in the direction of her room as she leashed up her furry demon.

The towels were exactly where she'd indicated, and I pulled out a plush white towel that had to cost more than the sheets on my bed right now. I'd literally never felt something this soft, and I carefully placed it next to the glass shower door for later.

Tyler's bathroom was modern and marble, and her shower stall was large enough to host a small party if she wanted to. The tile work inside was exquisite white and gray with a rain showerhead directly centered on the ceiling in the middle of the shower and then multiple other showerheads on the side walls pointing in.

I began turning each one on and I swear to God, they got hot right away. Listen, that might seem like a weird thing to fawn over, but ninety percent of apartments in this area are a thousand-year-old former military housing, and their pipes haven't been updated since the original construction. It takes the bathtub at my new apartment a minimum of seven minutes to get lukewarm, and if I have the audacity to want to shower during personal hygiene rush hours when everyone else in the building is also doing that…forget it. Or if I try to run a load of wash in the laundry at the same time? Hot water is off the table.

But this? This was bliss.

I shed my clothes, quickly peeling them off my sticky body and stepping into the warm sprays. After a thorough rinse, I inspected the row of bottles on a small inset shelf on the back wall.

Gypsy Water Gel Douche.

Hermès Eau d'orange verte Gel Douche.

I didn't even know Hermès did body wash and I didn't want to know how much it probably cost. Also, why are all the rich people soaps called douches? I shuffled through a few more bottles before I finally found a bottle of Dove Sensitive Skin Body Wash in the back row.

Finally, something normal.

I was in the middle of lathering myself up when the door to the shower stall opened, and Tyler popped her head in.

"Room for one more?" she asked, one brow raised in a teasing manner.

I reached out for her, and she took my hand and stepped in, already completely naked.

"There's room for more than even us in here," I joked. "I thought you were exhausted?"

"I can rally." She smirked at me as she let the water run over her body and hair and turned her face into the spray. "This shower is my favorite part of the entire place."

She reached for one of the gel douche bottles, but I grabbed it first.

"Can I help?"

Tyler sucked in her bottom lip, biting it gently as she nodded. She turned her back to me and slid her hair to one side.

I squeezed a small handful of Hermès into my palm and then rubbed my hands together. I started at the base of her neck rubbing it into her skin, and I have to give Hermès credit because not only did it smell incredible, but it lathered like liquid silk and now I understood the price tag. I let my hands slide down her sides, rounding over her hips and then turning her body to face me.

She dipped her head back into the stream of water, letting it soak her hair as she lifted her arms and ran her fingers through the wet strands. The way she moved, her breasts lifted, and I took the opportunity to lather soap across her collarbone and down to her chest, spending extra time on her breasts as my thumbs slid across her nipples in unison.

Tyler groaned, leaning toward me as the water washed the soap away, and I dropped my lips to each pert bud, pulling her nipple into my mouth and sucking gently.

Her hands dropped down and found either side of my face, lifting me higher until her lips were on mine. We embraced under the water, our tongues exploring each other's mouths achingly slow until we finally pulled apart again. I finished lathering the rest of her body with soap as her hands explored my body at the same time.

There was a fervor in the way she was touching me, like she couldn't stop—and I didn't want her to.

When her hand found the space between my legs, it suddenly felt like the water was no longer touching me but rather evaporating the moment it hit my skin. She slid inside me and curved her finger in just the right way that I nearly collapsed when my orgasm hit me like a runaway freight train.

Tyler wrapped her free arm around my waist, supporting me to continue standing as the waves of pleasure rattled through my bones. Her grin was one of pride, and I liked seeing this side of her when it came to our physical intimacy. She knew what she wanted, and she wasn't the least bit shy about it.

When I felt like I could move unassisted again, I returned the favor, but this time with her back pressed against the shower wall and one of her knees hooked over my shoulder as I kneeled in front of her. The scars on her inner thighs occasionally collected beads of water, but every time her body shook with the orchestration of my tongue, the beads slid away and fell to the shower floor.

I made my way back up her body, and we kissed until the water began to feel cold and she shivered against me. "Come on. Let's get to bed."

She nodded and immediately yawned at the thought. "It's probably almost morning by now."

We toweled off, and I borrowed some of her pajamas to stay warm, then we both crawled into bed. I was barely under the covers when Larry jumped up on the bed and began circling at our feet, trying to make his own little dog nest. I didn't have the energy to nudge him away, instead turning to her and laying my head on her shoulder.

Her breathing was already slowing, and she was close to sleep, but I wrapped my arm across her stomach and gave her a small squeeze.

"Hey, Tyler?"

She didn't open her eyes. "Hmm?"

I bit my lip, contemplating what I wanted to say even though I knew it was insane and sleep was pulling at me so fast I wasn't even sure I'd get it all out. "I think I'd be okay with being your girlfriend."

Her chest rumbled beneath me with a light laugh. "I'll have to think about it."

"Oh, okay," I joked, my tone all sarcasm. "You do that and just get back to me when you decide."

She turned her body, pushing me onto my side and wrapping her arms around me as well. Her eyes were hooded with sleep, but her smile felt like a warm blanket wrapping around me.

"Good night, girlfriend," she whispered, and I let my eyes close.

Chapter Sixteen

I *have a girlfriend.*

In fact, I've actually had a girlfriend for over two weeks now, and that sentence still sounded crazy to me every time it rolled through my head. It wasn't that I didn't want to be with Tyler—I absolutely did—but I hadn't expected a serious commitment in the relationship department anytime soon. Not with how hard I was focusing on bringing the business to a place where it would be ready to open.

The burst pipe had set us back, which was actually quite devastating. I'd been hoping we'd be able to coincide our opening with DC Pride Weekend, but with the additional repairs and construction time, we were not going to make that deadline. Instead, we were looking at squeaking out an opening by the end of June instead, possibly early July.

Not the end of the world, and Isa still had me running ragged with marketing and PR work around Pride Month to get people in the area aware of the upcoming opening. DC Pride, Arlington Pride, Alexandria Pride, Prince William County Pride...everywhere around here had their own celebration, and

I was there with flyers and a team of friends making sure everyone knew that our bar was coming.

The Dirty Derby was no longer the name, however. Sad face.

Tyler had been pushing hard for a name that better represented what we wanted to do with this space, embracing queerness and acceptance of all people—and then she also added that it should make a nod to me. Well, that was hard to argue, because anything named after me was destined for good luck.

And so *KiKi: Cuts & Cocktails* was born.

Ki standing in for my last name, Kiani, and *kiki* being a slang phrase that meant casually kicking it back—so it worked on multiple levels. I already had a cocktail menu that was ready to slay with drink names like Amaretto Aftercare, Hard (Seltzer) Limits, and Tequila Therapy.

"I don't think this plug is working," Isa said to me as she gently put the neon sign she had been holding back down on the ground. She gestured to an outlet by the front window of the bar with the sign's electrical cord trailing from it. "I can't get it to light up the sign."

I walked over and tried unplugging it and plugging it back in myself as if my singular touch would yield different results. "Yeah, this one must be broken."

"I mean, I just told you that, Yas," Isa replied, shaking her head as she headed over to the long bar across the back wall—thankfully, construction was complete on that entire section, and we'd already begun racking bottles up on the shelves. "I'm taking an interior decorator break since...you know, I'm *not* an interior decorator."

Making a mental note to call an electrician about that outlet, I followed Isa over to the bar. "I really appreciate all your help getting things set up. We have a long way to go, but the end of the month is going to be here sooner than we realize."

Isa pulled out her phone and began scrolling as she sat herself in one of our new bar stools. "Speaking of, we need to finalize the content calendar for your social media leading up to the opening. Did you get my email with the proposed images and captions?"

I joined her at the next stool. "Yeah, but the hashtags and keywords part had me confused."

"Let me worry about those," Isa said with a wave of her hand. "The interns on our marketing team are geniuses at all of that—Gen Z knows what they're doing when it comes to cultivating a social media presence."

"Okay, but what about the videos?" I asked. "Kari's helping me make some TikTok videos, but we're barely getting any traction. I think our last video had two hundred views and that was it."

"The TikTok algorithm is a beast," Isa confirmed. "Again, we'll work on all of that. You just need to get me content— videos of before/after renovations, you talking about the business, Tyler doing like literally anything, and then whatever else you think a consumer would want to see. Maybe a few cocktail recipe videos or a behind-the-bar-scenes video?"

I nodded, because I'd already started working on that. As an elder millennial, I had grown up on AOL chat rooms and MySpace coding. If it wasn't in my Top 8, then I didn't know shit about it. I'd had a lot of extra time the last few years, however, with both my last business failing and a pandemic trapping me inside for several years so I'd tried to brush up on all things social media in that time frame.

"Oh, and one last request," Isa added, this time placing her phone down on the bar top.

I looked at her because Isa not holding that damn device was a rare moment. "What?"

She leaned back in her seat and crossed one of her knees over the other. "I think you and Tyler need to go public."

My eyes probably looked like they were bugging out of my face, but I quickly reinserted them into my skull. "Public with what?"

Isa tilted her head to the side and gave me a no-nonsense look. "You two are clearly dating, *and* she's an investor in this place. Her podcast fame will bring people in the door. In fact, I think you should ask her to consider hosting a live podcast recording on opening weekend that is a ticketed event only. People will be blowing up the website trying to snag one, and we'll keep it small enough to feel exclusive but big enough to make a splash. People will then crowd in on the off hours just to get a glimpse of her or even just to say they were there."

A live recording event on opening weekend actually didn't sound like a terrible idea, and I was pretty sure Tyler would be on board with that one.

I nodded. "So just announce her as an investor? I'll ask her if she wants to, but she did already agree to give it a free advertising spot on the podcast this month and next. I don't want to ask too much more."

"Not just her being an investor," Isa continued. "Announcing her being your girlfriend. She *is* your girlfriend, isn't she?"

"We, uh—" I cleared my throat. "We did recently decide to put labels on things."

Isa wiggled her brows, and her mouth split wide into a grin like the Cheshire Cat. "That would literally be perfect, because then Kiki could get an exclusive on the news."

"Tyler isn't really *out* out," I reminded her. "You should know that. You're the one who listens to her podcast."

"She's not *not* out, though," Isa countered. "It's like the worst kept secret—everyone knows, and she just hasn't confirmed. You could be her confirmation! Kiki could be the epicenter of all of it. The Devotees would be all over it with support."

It was still weird to think that my girlfriend had a fan club, but I couldn't blame them. And I had finally listened to one full episode of her podcast—thank you very much—it was pretty good. Still, I wasn't about to sit around and listen to hours more, but it wasn't due to her. Podcasts just weren't my thing. Like, why aren't we dancing and singing? If I'm listening to something on my Air Pods, it's music and I'm vibing with the beat, not a White woman telling me about murder. Life is short, y'all. No shade on the true crime peeps, but give me a romcom story line and a dance beat and I'm in my element.

"I will ask her what she thinks," I agreed. "But that's all I can promise."

Isa put her hands up defensively. "That's all I ask. Ooh, I've got tea for you, by the way."

I lifted a singular brow. "Spill."

She grinned and clasped her hands. "I met someone."

"Yeah, I know. Eduardo." I frowned because hadn't we just had this conversation and gotten Caps tickets out of the entire thing?

"What? No, Eduardo was apparently married. He left that entire part out of his Hinge bio," Isa said with a loud sigh.

I should have seen that one coming, yet I was still somehow surprised.

I loved Isa—seriously, I did. She was an incredible friend, and I was trying to remind myself of that right now instead of judging her. She was wicked smart and ridiculously silly, and her loyalty was blood-deep. Literally.

"He's a firefighter," Isa continued, ignoring my concern.

"This new guy, I mean. And not *just* a firefighter. He's Mister DC July."

Oh, okay. "In the sexy man calendar?"

I wasn't a purveyor of the end product, but I could appreciate a great physique like anyone else.

Isa nodded. "They don't give July to the throwaways. That's the sexiest month of the year!"

"I mean, debatable, but okay." We're ranking sexiness of months now? Don't count me in for that. "Let me see a picture."

She fiddled with her phone for a moment then pointed the screen toward me. Sure enough, the male specimen who donned center stage was a cishet woman's dream man. There was something familiar about him though...a sparkle in his eyes maybe? His lashes were longer than I'd have expected, and I could swear I'd seen him somewhere before.

"He's hot. And I think I've met him," I commented. "But I cannot remember where."

Isa pulled the phone back protectively. "Normally I'd be jealous, but since you're gay as hell, I'll push past my own insecurities."

"You do that," I teased, my eyes rolling hard at her. "But, listen, I'll ask Tyler about the podcast. I wouldn't hold out hope though. I don't want her doing anything that might make her feel uncomfortable. Things are still...they're new, you know?"

"I know, I know." Isa waved her hands again. "I don't want to mess up things between the two of you. I just can't turn off my PR brain."

I grinned. "I know that all too well about you."

She shot me an annoyed look. "I'm going to choose to take that as a compliment."

"It is," I confirmed. "You're the most impressive businesswoman I know. I wish I had half the prowess you do."

If Isa was a peacock, this is the moment she'd have fluffed out all her feathers and taken a proud walk around the bar. But reality was, that was the truth. I'd always struggled on the business front, and Kiki was the first time I'd ever felt a true conviction behind my actions. But Isa went into every project like it was her kin, and I admired the hell out of her dedication to her work.

Isa pointed toward my phone that was sitting on the bar in between us. "Well, then. What are you waiting for? Give Tyler a call."

"What? Right now?" I balked at the idea.

She wasn't done though, and her idea only took flight from there. "Wait, isn't she upstairs? She lives in the building, right?"

I hadn't told Isa that information, so it was weird that she knew but also...kind of normal for Isa. "I mean, yeah...she has the penthouse."

She nodded like it was obvious. "Of course she does. Go up there!"

"Right now?" Tyler had spent last night at my apartment for the first time, because obviously we spent a lot more time at hers since it was a million times fancier than my bare-bones situation. However, I liked my place and didn't need all the accoutrements that she required. "She's probably busy. I can't just drop by unannounced."

Isa's brow lifted, and she let her gaze rake over me with judgy abandon. "Oh, so you're not *there* yet, huh?"

Rude. "What *there* are you talking about?"

"The kind of level of comfort where you can stop by each other's places without warning. You're still in the ask-permission phase of dating," Isa explained nonchalantly as if she wasn't issuing me a challenge with every single word that came out of her mouth. "That's fine. Maybe you two will get there some day."

"I mean, we might be there," I countered, even though I had no factual basis to assert that claim. "I'm sure she'd be fine if I stopped by unannounced."

Isa gave me a daring look. "Cool. Well, go ask then. I'll hold down the fort until you get back."

"Okay then," I agreed, already walking toward the door as if I actually had the balls to follow through on the check my mouth was writing. "I'll be back soon then. Or maybe I won't. Who knows? Things might get busy."

Isa rolled her eyes. "Well, if you get distracted by her bedsheets, just text me a response, and I'll close up for you."

"Don't wait up," I teased, already half the way to the door.

She laughed. "Promises, promises!"

Chapter Seventeen

Larry knew I was there before I even got the chance to knock.

The demon dog was barking nonstop from the other side of the door as I raised my fist to knock against Tyler's penthouse entry. I banged a solid three clangs anyway, then stepped back and waited.

"Hey?" Tyler opened the door with a fast swing and gave me a puzzled look. She was wearing the shortest shorts I'd ever seen in my life and a tight tank top that made it very obvious she wasn't wearing a bra. "I wasn't expecting you."

Damn it, Isa.

"Uh, yeah." I shuffled my feet slightly, readjusting the hem of my shirt and trying not to look directly at her nipples pressing against the fabric of her shirt. "I was downstairs and just had an idea I wanted to run by you."

"Sure." She held the door open wider and motioned for me. "Come in, come in."

"So, Kiki needs to make a splash with its opening, right?" I said as I waltzed past her and headed toward the giant white sectional couch in her living room area. I took a seat on one of the chaise sections and stretched my legs out like I belonged there. That was the key to social anxiety—pretend you didn't have it. Fake it till you make it is a very valid coping mechanism.

Larry jumped onto the other end of the couch and just sat there, staring at me. I'd never seen a dog mean-mug someone before, but Larry had it down to an art form.

"Right. We definitely need the press," Tyler agreed, following me but not taking a seat just yet. She stood across from me, her arms by her sides. "Meaning...what?"

I spread my hands in an arch, my palms out. "Live podcast recording."

She blinked, then tilted her head to the side. "Of *The Deviant Devotee?*"

"No, of *Y'all Gay*, obviously. I just spoke with Ali Clayton, and she's in." I did actually like that podcast—one of the very few I'd ever actually entertained—but every word out of my mouth just then had been fabricated. I thought that was obvious from my sarcastic tone, but...

"Wait...really? I love Ali Clayton," Tyler began, clearly getting amped up at the very idea. "Are you serious?"

Swing and a miss. "No. Of course I was referring to your podcast. I mean, you're an investor, and we're together...it just makes sense, you know?"

She seemed to physically freeze for a moment, like she was trying to transition the idea with everything I was saying. "Like a marketing thing? Or like a personal thing? Are we revealing me being an investor? Or me being your girlfriend?"

"Not if you don't want us to." I sat up quickly on the chaise and bent one of my legs to push it beneath my torso. "I mean... it's free advertising. We should consider it."

"Yeah." Tyler took a few steps forward and sat on the edge

of the chaise, still keeping a good amount of distance between us. "And...?"

She was waiting for me to be honest. Les be honest, though, I didn't like asking for help.

I stared at her for a moment longer, then let out a deep sigh and dropped my head back onto the couch cushion. "Isa thinks we should come out as a couple on your podcast as part of the reveal for the bar—stir up gossip around the whole thing to bring more people out."

She didn't respond immediately, and I purposely didn't look at her to gauge her reaction. Honestly, if she looked horrified or even slightly worried, I wasn't sure I could handle it without feeling personally rejected. It had been a long time since I'd dated someone who wasn't completely out, and this feeling of fear and insecurity is exactly why.

I feel sympathy for the situation—believe me. I get the desire to stay in the closet and the benefit that can have for a lot of people and situations. But being out is the best thing I ever did for my mental health, and when I even had to semi-conform back to my closeted self, it can feel hella triggering.

"Is that what you want?" Tyler finally answered. "Or is that just what Isa wants?"

I lifted my head now, finally taking her expression in. I'd expected concern or disgust, but what I saw instead was unmistakably fear. "What?"

She looked down at her hands, fidgeting with her fingers. "Do *you* want to be public?"

"I mean, I'm not the one with a public following or fan base," I hedged my words, unsure exactly what answer she was looking for. "I'm completely out. There isn't anyone in my life that doesn't know I'm as lesbian as they come."

She glanced up at me beneath her long eyelashes. "I'm mostly out," she countered. "Maybe not publicly on social media or the podcast, but everyone in my personal life knows. It's not like it's a secret."

I felt like we were playing semantics now. "But it's not confirmed, and I know your career is important to you. I don't know what the ramifications would be on the podcast of coming out."

Tyler waved one hand like it was nothing. "Everyone has already guessed. It's like the top search engine result if you look up my name."

I couldn't imagine being in that type of position where everyone wanted to know my sexuality all the time. Just the idea of it felt...limiting. Like she was being boiled down to just one part of herself instead of embraced as her whole being.

Still, I wasn't sure where that left us or what she was aiming at. "So..."

"So, let's do it." Tyler shrugged. "Let's do a live recording opening weekend at Kiki. We can sell tickets to make it exclusive and then have an open outdoor area for walk-in traffic."

"Really?" My brows perked up. "The line would be around the block to get in."

Tyler grinned as she crawled closer to me on the couch. "That's the point, right?"

I nodded. "And...and us?"

Why the hell was I so nervous about her response? I mean, she was the one who convinced *me* to be her girlfriend. When the heck had I turned into a simp who was waiting for any moment of validation from the woman I was fucking? Yet, here we were. And her validation was all I wanted right now.

"Let's announce it," she replied, pausing next to me as she swung her legs around the couch to be right up against me. Her hand dropped onto my leg, and her fingers trailed from my ankle up to just above my knee. "We can do a whole show about us and the bar. It won't have a crime element, obviously, but the human element sells. It will get traffic, especially among the fan base."

My shoulders dropped as the tension eased out of me. "Shit. Really?"

She shrugged again, this time leaning in closer and letting her lips brush against my jaw in a way that made my insides coil in the best possible squeeze. "Of course. Are you surprised?"

No. Yes. No. Well, yes. "Uh..."

Tyler laughed, and her head tilted back when she did so. That meant she moved further away from me—which I definitely didn't love—but the way her neck stretched made me want to lick the entire length of it, and I didn't hate that. "You look like you saw the Ghost of Commitment Future."

My tongue slid out across my bottom lip. "Honestly? I think I expected you to say no."

She slid against the couch cushion next to me, aligning her body with mine and leaning her head against my shoulder. "Really? Why?"

That was a good question.

"I honestly don't know," I admitted, although the rule-follower side of her and her complicated familial relationship certainly came to mind. "I think it's mostly based on my own preconceptions. But...honestly? If I really think about it, I...uh... I guess I didn't think you'd publicly acknowledge being in a relationship with me...specifically, me."

Tyler looked as shocked as I felt about the admission. Where had that even come from? Insecurity was not my brand, but the words had flown out of me with a truth I couldn't deny.

"Yasmeen, I'm the one who wanted us to put a label on things."

That was definitely true.

She continued. "Of course I want to go public with you."

"This is clearly a topic I'm going to have to discuss further with my therapist," I admitted. "Because I don't really know where that came from. But when Isa was proposing the idea downstairs, I was just so sure that you wouldn't want to risk the podcast for the bar...or for me."

"Well, your feelings are valid. I'm sorry that was something you were concerned about, but the truth is..." Tyler leaned her body into mine and whispered a kiss against my cheek, her lips barely brushing mine. "I'm not risking the podcast for you or the bar. The podcast stands on its own."

"Oh, well that makes me feel better," I said, my tone laced with sarcasm.

Because, no, it did not make me feel better.

"Yasmeen, we don't," she continued. Her lips connected with my cheek now and I turned to face her, letting our kiss become real as her mouth touched mine. "We don't stand on our own."

Her mouth brushed mine, and I moved in for a kiss just as she pulled back. God, I was hungry for her. My body was already igniting just from the sheer proximity. "We don't?"

She shook her head, then leaned back into me. "This? This isn't automatic."

My tongue slid across her bottom lip, and I nipped softly at her. "What do you mean?"

I couldn't *not* kiss her right now. I had to taste her the closer she got to me. If that wasn't automatic, I didn't know what was.

"We are a choice." Her voice was hushed now, barely above a whisper. "There's nothing accidental about you or me. I want you with every intention of the word. This isn't a phase; it isn't even a moment."

We aren't just a moment.

Her words rang around inside my skull like a bell being slammed around by Quasimodo jumping on the pendulum.

Once last year, Rachel had taken a Buzzfeed quiz about who was her ideal soulmate, and Quasimodo had been her future husband-to-be. Weird, since she was gay as hell, but I would never let her forget that a Buzzfeed quiz considered her dream partner to be a hunchback. That's what true friendship is. Accountability and reality.

But enough with my ADHD thought train.

I returned my focus to Tyler.

"You and I are a choice I want to make every day," Tyler continued.

My lips passed by hers in a swipe—a promise, but not a guarantee. "We are?"

My sentence was barely a gasp, but she consumed every breath of it.

Her words were an exhale, and I felt my muscles unclench with every syllable. "Yasmeen, what are you afraid of?"

Her question reverberated in my ribcage like an echo.

"Saying that I want this and then you saying you don't." The words rolled out of my mouth before my filter could turn them off. "That's what I'm afraid of. I'm afraid even though you asked me for all of this, I want it more than you do."

I couldn't believe that I'd actually admitted to that, but I had. We were just going full honesty tonight, and I couldn't seem to reign it in. Hell, I couldn't believe I actually felt that way, but the words came out of my face hole so quickly it was impossible to deny them.

"Well, this is a new take," Tyler replied gently. "I hadn't considered before that *you'd* feel insecure about our label."

I bit my lip. "Yeah, I'm not loving this version of me right now."

Tyler frowned. "Honestly, I'm relieved. You always seem to have everything together and are so sure of yourself. It's actually really nice to see behind the curtain and know there's a real person under all that bravado."

"Very few people get to see behind the curtain," I teased, pulling her closer to me.

Tyler lifted the bottom hem of my shirt, sliding her hand across my stomach. "This curtain?"

I leaned into her touch, letting her push me into the couch cushions as her body moved over mine. "Mmhm..."

She kissed me slowly, like taste-testing the perfect glass of wine. My eyes fluttered closed as I found myself completely engaged with the physical sensations of her hand sliding against my skin. Then her body was sliding down mine, and her hand gripped at the waistband of my jeans. With quick dexterity, she undid the button and pulled at the zipper, and I wiggled my hips to help as she pulled the denim completely down and off my legs. She tossed the pants onto the floor behind us, and Larry immediately jumped off the couch and made a nest in my discarded jeans.

I couldn't think about the dog right now, though, because Tyler's lips were placing careful kisses across my collarbone and then down the side of my chest, seeming to bypass my breasts on purpose. My back arched as I aimed to bring her closer to my nipples, but she continued to make her way further south. I groaned lightly, but she just looked up at me with a devilish grin on her face, and I knew she was torturing me on purpose.

Her fingers hooked the fabric of my panties and slid them off as she settled herself between my legs. I could feel her breath against me first, and my entire body shivered with anticipation.

Finally, she traced a circle over me with the tip of her tongue, and I felt like someone had just hooked me up to a live wire of electricity. When her lips closed over the most sensitive part of me, she sucked just enough to give me a preview of what was to come before pulling away again.

Now I groaned loudly.

"I'll be right back," Tyler said, this time pushing up onto her feet and heading out of the living room.

I propped up on my elbows and looked after her. "What?"

"I'll be right back!" she shouted, but then disappeared into the bedroom.

"Don't mind me," I called after her. "I'll just sit here, clam out like an all you can eat seafood buffet."

Tyler laughed as she reappeared a moment later. "Patience is not your virtue."

"But orgasms are," I countered.

She held her hand up, and in her palm rested a small red, oval-shaped device in the palm of her hand. "Good thing I brought reinforcements."

I lifted one brow, intrigued. "Complaint rescinded."

Tyler settled herself back between my legs, and I heard a small buzzing noise as I dropped my elbows and lay back on the couch cushions. She placed the stimulator against my inner thigh at first, and I felt the soft pull at my skin as it vibrated and suctioned against me. The sensation moved up my thigh, and Tyler's fingers slid across my core, spreading me for better access.

When she placed it against my clit, I nearly bucked right off the couch but she placed her palm flat against my lower stomach to hold me down. The tension twisting in my core mixed with the pressure of her hand against me felt like the perfect combination and I was off to the races.

My hips moved of their own accord and she lifted her hand to allow me more movement. With the device still in place and pulling at me like it was begging me to unravel, Tyler's fingers swirled around my entrance. She pressed one finger inside first, and I clenched around her like I wasn't going to let go. When she added a second finger, I could feel the precipice approaching fast, and knew I was about to go overboard.

"It's so fucking sexy to see you like this," Tyler's voice was a throaty whisper and she didn't stop her fingers as her mouth kissed my inner thigh and her teeth left soft nips against my skin.

The combination of her voice, her teeth, her fingers, the device...I couldn't stop it any longer. My body tensed like a bomb, and when the explosion came, I felt wholly splintered with pleasure and purpose and waves of passion.

"Tyler!" I cried out her name, because holy fucking shit, how could I not? And my words only made her apply more pressure as she took me for everything I had to offer. It seemed to go on forever, like I was just perpetually falling into an abyss, and the pleasure and terror were one and the same. Maybe it was only seconds, maybe it was minutes—I didn't fucking know, or care—but my body pushed itself to the edge of what I even knew was possible.

When I finally went limp beneath her, she slowed her movements and softened her touch. The device was gone now, and she was instead gently caressing me with feather soft pressure to help me come back to reality.

"That was..." I let out a long exhale. "Incredible. You are incredible."

She dropped down onto the couch next to me, curling into my side. I hugged my arms around her shoulders and kissed her temple.

"Are you staying the night tonight?" she asked.

I nodded, because I was absolutely going nowhere after that. "Sure. Let me text Isa to close up for me though."

I could already picture Isa laughing and saying *I told you so.*

Chapter Eighteen

DC Pride is the best place to come out—as a couple or
a new bar.

I'd been able to secure KiKi a spot in the Capital
Pride Parade, and we were prepping in the staging area as we
waited for the entire thing to start. Technically, it should have
started already, but for some reason, we were all still standing
around in the blazing sun, sweating our asses off. People were
handing out bottles of water like currency, and I had a full
cooler on wheels stuffed to the brim with alcohol-infused popsicles that was making me the most popular person on this block.

"You guys are so freaking cute," Kari said as they rubbed a
paste of silver glitter up and down their arms with a large
makeup brush. "Do you want some glitter?"

Tyler had her arm around my waist, and I was leaning into
her. This was the first time all of my friends—and soon, all of
Washington, DC—was going to see us make a public appear-
ance together. She was wearing a bright gold body suit donning
her podcast's logo on the front with the tiniest gold skirt that

barely covered her ass cheeks—I didn't mind one bit. Around her neck and over her shoulders was a sheer metallic gold cape that was attached by small bands to each of her wrists. When it blew in the wind behind her while she was walking, it looked like giant wings. Pairing that with the gold crown she had on her head and Tyler looked like a queer goddess gracing us all with her presence.

"Sure, I'd love some," Tyler agreed as she stretched her arms out for my friend to paint with glitter. "Do you have gold?"

"I do!" Kari replied, opening their bag and pulling out a separate pouch and brush. "I also have ruby red and blue if you want."

Tyler shook her head. "Just gold."

Kari was wearing a T-shirt with our new bar logo on it—KiKi in huge rainbow block letters with a silhouette of two women dancing in between the letters. They'd cut up the T-shirt to remove the sleeves and had tied the waist into a knot, which only made the look better. Their hair was buzzed short on the sides with more length on top, dyed a bright orange color with flecks of other colors throughout.

I'd kept things simple—the T-shirt and jean shorts and a rolled-up Stoli vodka rainbow bandana around my hair. I also had a battery-powered fan attached to a lanyard around my neck, and Kari had already donned my arms and legs with glitter earlier in the day.

Several of the future bartenders and servers that we'd hired in advance were also here with us, all wearing some version of our logo-ed shirt that everyone had taken the liberty of customizing for themselves. One of the bartenders had her one-year-old in a stroller, and the kid was waving a pride flag like it was the best day of his little life. We also had two hairdressers on staff and both had come in full drag, which I loved but I don't know how their makeup wasn't melting in this sun.

"Who's going to hold the sign?" I asked the group, raising my voice loud enough to be heard by everyone. "We need at least two people, then can trade on and off throughout the parade."

Two of the bartenders volunteered to take the first shift, each one grabbing the opposite ends of the metal pole that was horizontal between them with a banner draping down from it with the KiKi logo and website for everyone in attendance to see.

Tyler grabbed a popsicle from the cooler—each one branded with the KiKi website and logo. She ripped it open and chugged it—or whatever the version of chugging partially melted ice is.

"Ready?" I laughed. "You look nervous."

"I'm not nervous, I'm melting," she countered. "I've got like four layers of SPF 70 on, and I still think I'm going to be a lobster by the end of this."

I'd made sure to put some extra sunscreen on my tattoos, but otherwise wasn't as concerned as my melanin-starved girlfriend. A good SPF 30 did the job.

"Guys!" Isa came bounding up to us in what could only be described as a gallop. "The opening is completely sold out."

"What?" My eyes widened. "The live recording?"

She was bouncing up and down on the balls of her feet, and there was a shot cup on a string of beads around her neck that had clearly already been used a few times today. "The entire thing! There is even a waitlist and people are requesting a live virtual option as well."

Even though we'd made the event exclusive and small on purpose—after all, I could only fit so many people into the space at a time without getting in trouble with the fire marshal

—I still hadn't expected it to sell out. Particularly since we just posted it this morning on Instagram, and nowhere else. "We should definitely do a virtual ticket."

"Already on it," Isa agreed. "My team is setting it up now and adding it to the Eventbrite link."

Tyler squeezed my hand. "Oh my god, Yas. This is so exciting! This is going to be big."

"Huge!" Isa added. "KiKi is getting national press. I even got in touch with someone at The Lesbian Bar Project, and they want to interview you."

"Me?" I balked. "Holy shit."

Isa nodded. "Yup. I'm meeting up with the firefighter tonight, but I'll get it scheduled first thing tomorrow once the hangover wears off."

"The firefighter is still around?" I teased.

She shot me a look. "You never know. Maybe this one is a keeper."

The crowd around us was beginning to move, and one of the bartenders called out, letting us know that the parade had started. Our group was behind a gym on an elevated float and in front of a tequila truck and mobile bar.

"Are you ready for this?" I leaned closer to Tyler, speaking only loud enough for her to hear.

She turned to look at me, her eyes sparkling in the sun and a wide smile across her face. "We've got this, Yas."

Hand in hand, Tyler and I walked behind the KiKi sign as I pulled the cooler along with us. Once we got to the main part of the walk, we began handing out popsicles and flyers to everyone along the sidelines.

"Oh, my god, it's Tyler Adams!" someone in the crowd screamed as Tyler waved. The cheers and shoutouts only got louder and wilder as we walked.

"Tyler Adams! Over here! Smile for us!"

"I'm a Devotee! Tyler! Tyler!"

"I'd die for you, Tyler!"

"Tyler, let me touch you! I'll never wash my hand again!"

Jesus fucking Christ, people were thirsty as hell. I mean, I get it. She's gorgeous, but what the hell. Get it together.

"You have fangirls," I commented to her with a laugh. "Thank God there's a metal fence barrier up, or they'd storm you."

Tyler laughed and lifted her hands so that her sheer gold cape waved behind her. "People are just having fun."

We held hands on and off while we walked and had to stop several times to take selfies with people—well, Tyler was taking selfies with people. I was just forcing myself into the pictures and throwing up peace signs like I belonged there.

But that was the whole point of today—get people on social media speculating about who was holding Tyler's hand, and then we'd confirm our relationship at the live podcast recording on opening weekend. Isa insisted that the slow build of hype and rumors was the key to making a big splash, and at this point, I trusted anything Isa advised. About marketing, at least.

We were about three-quarters of the way through the parade route when Isa grabbed Tyler's arm and held up her phone screen to her. "Tyler, you're nominated for an Ambie!"

"What?" Tyler was the one looking shocked now.

I was just confused. "What's an Ambie?"

"The Podcast Academy Awards for Excellence in Audio," Isa answered my question, but she wasn't looking at me. She was leaning over her phone pointing to the screen as Tyler scrolled through the list of nominations. "They just dropped the list today!"

"Oh my god! *The Deviant Devotee* is nominated!" Tyler was jumping up and down now, then she turned to me and threw her arms around my neck. "An Ambie! Yasmeen, I might win an Ambie!"

I wrapped her in a hug and lifted her off her feet, twirling her around. A photographer from Metro Weekly and the Washington Blade—shoutout to local icon Ward and his incredible eyebrows—rode past us and circled back to snap some photos of our embrace.

"So proud of you, babe!" I placed her feet back down on the ground, and I cupped her face with my hands as I kissed her smack dab on the lips.

I could hear excitement in the crowd, and out of the corner of my eyes I saw literally everyone around us holding up their cell phone, probably taking pictures or videos of our moment. I didn't care; just closed my eyes and leaned into it.

Tyler kissed me back with the same fervor, and when we finally pulled apart, her eyes were glistening like she was near tears.

"Are you happy?" I asked, giving her another peck.

Tyler nodded and took my hand as we kept walking so we didn't fall behind in the parade route. "Yas, I'm really happy."

I squeezed her hand. "Good, you deserve it. You've worked so hard."

"But I'm not *just* happy," she continued.

I glanced sideways at her but she kept her gaze centered in front of us.

She continued, "I think I could really be falling in love."

Now she did turn to look at me, and my mouth fell open slightly as I considered what she was saying.

"I think I'm falling in love with you, Yas."

I looked away from her, keeping my gaze in front of us at the back of the gym float. "Wow. That's...that's amazing, Tyler."

That's amazing? That was definitely not the response she

was looking for, but my brain felt like someone had taken an eraser to it. The words just weren't coming. Love—*in love?* That was a word I had thrown around a few times, or a lot of times, actually. I said it pretty easily and had probably told at least six or seven women I'd dated at this point that I was in love with them.

But something inside of me refused to let the words roll off my tongue right now...with Tyler, specifically.

"Uh...yeah." Tyler's hand went limp in mine, and then she pulled it away entirely, walking over to the crowds on the side and passing out flyers.

I watched her take a few selfies with fans as we kept moving, coming up on the end of the parade route sooner than I'd expected.

Tyler kept her distance from me, which was easy to do with the crowds and everyone moving in different directions as people dispersed at the end. One of the bartenders helped me roll up our sign and secure it in a wheeled wagon we'd gotten from Costco to carry all our stuff—mainly the eight packs of bottled water we needed to survive the afternoon. The cooler of popsicles was empty by now, and there was only a small stack of flyers leftover.

Isa rolled up on me without missing a beat. "Why do you look like you just saw a ghost?"

"I do not." I straightened my back, and my hands were on my hips. "It's just hot outside."

She narrowed her eyes, surveying me with the interrogative skills of someone on SEAL Team Six. "Whatever you did, you need to fix it."

I put my hands up defensively. "Why do you automatically assume I did something?"

She wasn't convinced. "Yasmeen."

Groaning, I dropped my hands to my sides. "Tyler said

she's in love with me—or falling in love with me. I don't know. Either way, I replied with 'that's amazing' and then nothing."

Isa rolled her eyes so hard that her head literally tilted backward. "Okay, okay. So that's bad. Pretty bad. She's pissed."

There was certainly no mistaking that. "Yup."

"So, what's the issue? Do you not love her?" Isa's brain was already diving straight into problem-solving mode. "Because I've seen you fall in love no less than four times in the last few years, so I know you're not scared of that word."

"I'm *not* scared of that word," I agreed. "I think I just...I think I might actually mean it this time."

Isa gave me a slow blink that then became a small smile. She spoke in a singsong voice. "Tyler and Yasmeen sitting in a tree, k-i-s-s-i-n-g. First comes love, then comes marriage, then comes baby in a baby carriage!"

"Slow your ovaries," I cautioned, putting my hands up. "No one is getting impregnated over here. I'm not Mila."

"Ooh, did I tell you they are planning on going for baby number two?" Isa grinned. "Love is just all around us right now. It's beautiful. Although I think I have to break up with my firefighter."

I was laughing now. "What? Why? You just said you were all smitten."

"He's hiding something from me. I can feel it in my bones." She waved a hand between us. "But that's not the point right now. The point is, you need to go tell Tyler how you actually feel and apologize for not saying it back earlier."

My lungs expanded as I inhaled deeply. "Okay, yeah. I'm going to do it. I'm going to tell her that I love her, too."

Isa pushed my shoulders, shoving me gently in the direction of where Tyler was standing talking to a group of women who were all wearing shirts with her podcast logo on them.

I put one foot in front of the other and was less than five

feet from her when I felt my phone vibrate in my jean shorts pocket. I paused for just a moment, pulling it out and glancing at the screen. It was a new email notification, and the subject line made my heart drop into my stomach.

Notice: Business License Revoked for Case #678: KiKi Cuts and Cocktails.

Chapter Nineteen

"Yas, go!" Isa came up behind me and kept trying to push me toward Tyler. "You can do this!"

I turned around to face her instead. "Isa, look."

She glanced down at my phone and swiped on the email notification. We both leaned over the screen and read the entire thing together.

To Ms. Yasmeen Kiani,

This letter is to inform you that the Columbia Pike Neighborhood Association has filed a complaint with Arlington County regarding your upcoming opening of a food and beverage establishment. Our goal is to find a resolution that is beneficial to all parties before moving forward with a new business opening. Your provisional license is currently suspended, pending further investigation. Please contact our investigator listed below on Monday morning to set up an appointment to go over the business plans and areas of concern.

Thank you,
Arlington County

"How can they do that?" Isa looked as shocked as I felt. "You are literally opening in two weeks. We just passed out hundreds of flyers with the opening date on it—and we have a sold out opening show!"

Every word out of her mouth was only making me more anxious about the entire situation. Because, yes, we were absolutely screwed if this was true.

"I don't know," I said. "They had approved everything. Even at the meeting, they said we were good to go. I mean, not everyone on the board was excited about it, but we got the majority vote."

"It was provisional, but this still doesn't make sense. Something had to have changed." Isa pulled her phone out of her pocket. "I'm going to start making some calls."

I felt completely numb when Tyler walked up to me.

"Are you okay?" She frowned, searching my face.

I didn't even have the energy to respond, and instead just handed her my phone so that she could read the email for herself. I watched quietly as her eyes scanned back and forth and then went wide.

"What!" She gasped. "They can't do that!"

"They did," I replied, taking my phone back. "Something had to have happened. I don't get it."

"Should I call my dad?" Tyler asked.

Walter Adams wasn't exactly the person I thought would save us in this situation. Hell, for all I knew, he was the one who had put us in it to begin with.

"*Your* dad?" I shook my head. "It would be in his political best interests for this bar to never open in the first place—especially with your name attached to it."

165

She took a step back, and a look of hurt crossed her expression. "I know he's not the biggest fan, but he wouldn't do anything to hurt me, Yas. He knows how much this means to me—because he knows how much *you* mean to me."

Frustration was beginning to rage boil in my gut, and I could feel the tension spreading across my limbs. I'd been so close—so freaking close—to my dream, and everything had been perfect this time. I'd failed at business more times than most, but *this* was supposed to be my saving grace. KiKi wasn't just another entrepreneurial whim. My entire soul was in this bar and the mission it was aiming to further, the help it was going to provide people, and the safe haven I wanted it to be.

"Tyler, you can't be that naive. Yeah, he's your dad, but he's a lobbyist whose income is dependent on who and what he backs—a queer bar isn't going to get a nod of approval from Senator McCarty or any of the shit he lobbies for." I could hear the little voice in my head telling me to shut up, yet, my mouth kept moving. "You can't keep pretending like he supports you being gay when his entire career is aimed at limiting and removing your rights. He might tolerate your queerness, but he doesn't support who you are, and you know that."

She swallowed hard, her gaze dropping to look down at her feet. The golden crown on her head fell slightly to the side.

"Wow." Her single response was flat in tone. "I guess it's good to know how you really feel."

"Tyler..." I didn't really have anything to follow that up with.

"You know, your family isn't perfect either." Tyler lifted her chin, and her words were soft in tone but felt as heavy as a weighted blanket. "This is the first thing you've done that your dad has supported at all. Period. My dad isn't perfect, but he has championed everything I've done since I was born. I never had to question that."

Shit. Now I really didn't have anything to follow up with. We were miles into Battle of the Dads territory, and neither one of us was going to win that one.

Tyler looked down at her feet again, then slowly shook her head. "I am going to head home. It's hot, and today's been a lot."

I stayed quiet. Honestly, I didn't want to convince her to stay. I just wanted to burst into flames and punch a weighted bag repeatedly. "Okay."

There was no goodbye or embrace. Instead, Tyler just turned on her heels and walked away from me.

And I let her.

"It's not good," Isa said, walking back to me with her phone still in her hand and pressed against her ear. She'd completely missed the exchange between Tyler and me and I wasn't about to fill her in on it. "I'm still trying to get more information, but three people on the board who voted in your favor have changed their minds. They held a special vote privately again, and this time, you didn't get the majority."

I frowned. "They can do a special vote without even telling us?"

Isa nodded. "It's in the bylaws. If there is concern for the integrity of the neighborhood, they can revisit previous votes."

"Now we're an integrity concern, too?" *What the hell was happening?* This was absolutely ridiculous and felt targeted.

"Where did Tyler go?" Isa asked, changing the topic as she glanced around. "We should ask her if she can get her father to help."

I swallowed hard. "Uh, I think that ship might have sailed."

Isa narrowed her eyes at me...again. "I can't leave you alone for two minutes without you self-sabotaging something."

Okay, if Isa was telling me that, then I really needed to take a look at myself because I felt completely unhinged. Like, I wasn't even in charge of what I was doing anymore.

I was on autopilot and the system was set to self-destruct.

"Let's get back to KiKi and strategize," Isa continued. "In reality, we might have to consider changing venues. I'll have my assistant send us a full list of open retail spots in Arlington, Virginia by the time we get there so we can review."

Moving locations would be an incredible amount of money out of my pocket. We were already more than halfway done with renovations on the current space, and having to redo those efforts in a new location would double the start-up costs. Not to mention all our business information, legal paperwork, and marketing had been done with that specific address. That would be a bit easier to change but an absolute time-sucking headache for me.

"I can't." My feet literally wouldn't move on the pavement.

Isa turned back to look at me. "What?"

"I can't strategize right now," I repeated. "Tomorrow. I'll meet you at KiKi first thing tomorrow morning, and we'll hit the ground running figuring all of this shit out. But not tonight. I have to...I have to go."

She looked slightly concerned, but the trust on her face reminded me why I appreciated her friendship so much. "Okay. I'll see you tomorrow, Yas. We're going to figure this out."

I attempted the smallest of smiles and nodded my head. "See you tomorrow."

It wasn't lost on me that Isa had nothing to gain personally or financially by working so hard to help me make KiKi a reality, and that she was using her time and connections to benefit me. I was beginning to realize that her friendship meant a lot more to me than I had ever realized. When Mila had gotten married and had a baby, Rachel and I had both drifted apart a little bit, and I had been very cognizant of the hole both women had left behind.

But Isa had stepped in and filled it seamlessly—not in a way that replaced Mila, no one could do that. And, of course, Rachel was still a part of my life as often as she'd let me. But Isa brought an excitement and security to friendship that felt like an antidote to a nameless period of deep loss in my life.

By the time I arrived on my sister's doorstep in Oxon Hill, Maryland less than thirty minutes later, tears were streaming down my face, and my contemplative Lyft ride over had me completely lost in my feelings.

Nia opened the front door to her three-bedroom, three-bathroom house that she'd gotten for the same price as a studio in Washington, DC. It was unbelievable how much the landscape could change even in such a short distance, but I'd always been so proud of her for saving up her own money from her job to buy this piece of property all on her own.

My older sister took one look at me and frowned. "Oh, Lord. Get inside."

Shoulders slumped, I walked past her into the foyer and made my way right to her living room. Nia lived alone except for her long-haired gray male cat with white paws and a black nose that looked like a giant dust bunny and was currently sitting on the arm of her couch. I ignored him and threw myself onto the cushions.

"I don't want to talk about it," I said in the most dramatic fashion I could muster as I buried my face in the couch cushions.

I let out a growl-scream-type sound into the fabric then flopped over onto my back and kicked my feet up on the coffee table in front of me. Nia's house was a walking advertisement for Home Goods, and as many times as I'd told her a house could only have so many *live, laugh, love* signs, she wanted no part of my opinion on it.

Nia had followed me more slowly and apparently took a detour to the kitchen because when she sat in the armchair across from me, she suddenly had a large mug of coffee in her hand. "I just brewed a pot. Want any?"

I closed my eyes and crossed my hands over my chest like I was in my own coffin. "Is it Folgers?"

"Maxwell House."

A loud wail left my mouth. "Could today get any worse?"

Nia laughed. "Listen, I'm glad you're here. I need some help."

"Can I do it while not moving from this spot?" I came over to her house for help, and of course she's got me helping her instead. "My legs are broken after the parade."

"That's fine. I only need your hands."

A loud metallic clanging sound made me open my eyes really quick, and I saw Nia scooting a giant five-gallon water jug in front of me. The entire thing was filled with pennies, however. Not water.

"What the hell is this?" I sat up now and peered over the edge of the couch and into the jug. "Did you rob a bank or something?"

Nia shook her head as she took the seat next to me and reached into the jug. "No, I collect these and then go through them every year to find the coins of value."

She extracted a penny that looked pretty dirty. "See, this one says 1985. It's worth nothing. I mean, it's worth a penny, but nothing more. We'll put those ones in rolls."

She handed me a stack of coin-rolling papers. "If you find one that's from before 1982, put it to the side because that's worth at least two and a quarter penny. They are mostly copper, but the ones they make since then are majority zinc and nobody wants that."

I lifted my gaze to Nia's face and just blinked a few times. "You are a coin collector?"

Had I ever even met my sister before? How did I not know she did this? There were thousands of pennies here—literally.

"Of course not," she countered, extracting the next coin. "I sell them for a profit. It's my side hustle."

"At two and a quarter penny for an hour of sorting?" I reached in and grabbed a handful of coins and flattened them in my palm. "That is the worst side hustle I've ever seen in my life."

Nia shrugged. "That's rich coming from you."

She had a point.

For the next thirty minutes, we sat quietly and just sorted through pennies. I actually found one penny that was from 1980, and although I'd never admit it, that was quite thrilling. I could kind of understand why my sister liked doing this—not that I'd ever do this unprompted on my own.

But still...I found one!

"Do you want to keep it?" my sister asked.

I palmed the dirty penny and rolled it over into my other hand. "Are you sure? It's worth a whole two cents."

"That's one way to look at it," Nia replied, taking the coin from me and holding it up between her thumb and index finger. "Another way to look at it is that it's worth double its value. That's pretty impressive for something that's been through so much wear and tear. Even after all these years, not only did it hold on to its worth, but it doubled it."

I grinned slowly, but I could feel the weight on my chest lightening ever so much. "Is this a big sister teaching moment?"

She shrugged and handed the old penny back to me. "You asked for my two cents."

I laughed.

There was a whole period in my twenties where I pitied myself for not growing up with my mother in my life. Losing her so young, I'd never even gotten the chance to know her, and that had been a hard pill to swallow when I'd seen friends at college go home to their parents or call their mothers or anything like that.

It wasn't until I was about to turn thirty and my sister was already forty-one years old that I'd realized a lot of what I'd been grieving missing out on had been in my life, just in the form of Nia, my big sister. It wasn't her role to be my mother, and she never should have had to fill those shoes. But she had. She mothered me my entire life, and I never said thank you. She never asked me to.

I glanced around her empty house as she kept sorting more pennies, wondering if her giving up so much of her life to take care of me meant that she'd lost the chance to pursue her own. I hoped that wasn't the case, and that if she still wanted to find a partner one day, she would. I knew if I asked her, she'd cut her eyes at me and tell me I was being stupid.

So instead, I just leaned my shoulder into hers and pressed in slightly. "Thanks for the penny, Nia. I think I'll keep it."

She nodded, but didn't look at me. "The guest room is set up if you want to stay the night. I'm making smothered pork chops for dinner."

My brows perked up at that. "With your white sauce?"

"Yup."

Signed, sealed, delivered. "I guess I can stay."

Nia handed me another fistful of pennies. "Keep sorting. We have a lot to get through if we're going to finish tonight."

There was zero chance we were getting through five gallons worth of pennies tonight, but I kept sorting anyway. It was every bit the distraction, and somehow also the reminder, that I needed today.

Tomorrow, I'd go back to the bar and figure out how to move forward with Isa. I'd apologize to Tyler and maybe send a fruit basket or something to her dad—whatever she wanted. This bar was going to happen somehow, even if we hit road bumps like this licensure issue. I'd hit bumps in the road before and let them steer me off track, but not this time.

Because in the end, Nia was right. I was someone who didn't just hold on to my worth after all this time—I doubled it.

Chapter Twenty

I fucking knew it.

"It could be a coincidence," Isa stammered as she leaned her elbows against the bar top and watched my reaction. I should have known when she first handed me her phone with a look of hesitation on her face that I was about to see something I didn't like, and holy heck, was that true. "The chair of the Pike Neighborhood Association probably golfed with a lot of different people—not just Tyler's dad."

I squinted my eyes at the Facebook photo posted publicly on the association's page of the chair with his arm around Walter Adams' shoulders this past weekend playing a round of golf at Washington Golf & Country Club together. They were announcing the sale of another property on Columbia Pike to Walter Adams and how his goal was to revitalize the neighborhood with his influx of cash and renovations.

He bought a dry cleaner attached to a mini-mart, and they were turning it into office space for the association so that they could "really dig into the work," and a stationary store for the chair's wife.

"This is definitely bribery, right? Like he absolutely bought their votes—with a fucking building," I said, looking up at Isa and placing my phone down on the bar top.

Isa shrugged. "We can't prove that it's related at all."

But of course it was. There was zero chance I was buying this all as some sort of tangential occurrence. Walter Adams didn't want his daughter's name attached to a queer bar—or queer anything—but he wasn't going to be the one to dash her hopes. Instead, he'd pay someone else to do it. It literally read like a privileged stereotype.

"Has Tyler seen this?" I mean, it completely proved I was right, but this felt like the hollowest win ever. "Because she'll connect the dots if she does. She has to."

"Your relationship dynamics—or dysfunction—are not my concern right now," Isa replied. "We need to move forward with a new location, because the current one isn't happening."

I groaned, closing my eyes and dropping my head backward. "I really don't know how I'll be able to do that financially. We've already put a lot of money into this place, and we're set to open in literally two weeks. This is actually insane."

Isa held up a file folder that had been sitting in front of her. "That actually brings me to the good news. Tyler's building is offering to recoup the renovation costs so you can walk away with a clean slate. It won't save us time, and we'll have to find someplace that is move-in ready if we even have a remote chance of a soft launch in a few weeks, but at least we won't be out everything you've already spent."

My eyes widened. "Wait...really? He's going to refund us everything?"

She nodded. "All the way down to the application fee."

"So, what's the catch?" Old Beady Eyed Adams was not out here trying to do me any favors, so I knew without a doubt that this gesture was coming with heavy strings. "What does he want in exchange for that?"

Isa slid her finger down the front of the paper and stopped on a line in the middle of the sheet. "The new location needs to be at least one mile away from this space—for non-compete purposes. They plan to give the space to another bar since it's outfitted already that way and don't want them to have competition from the jump."

Stupid, but I honestly thought it would be worse. "Even though there's like four other bars within a few blocks of here? I mean, fine. Sure, yeah, if that's the only stipulation, then let's get our money back."

"There's one more," Isa responded, her finger trailing slightly lower on the paper. "They can't financially compensate anyone affiliated with the building, so in order to get the money back, Tyler has to give up her percentage of the business as an investor. They are citing it as a conflict of interest for him to basically pay out his daughter, so she'd need to step away and the money would go to you only, the sole owner."

And there it was.

Isa was already rounding the bar just based on whatever expression was on my face because she grabbed a bottle of tequila that was sitting on the back and popped it open.

Forget the glasses, she just handed me the entire bottle. "Here. Drink."

I drank. No need to tell my therapist about this maladaptive coping skill.

When I came up for air, I let out a loud belch of righteous indignation. "Well, what if we fight fire with fire? I could ask my dad to investigate her dad, dig something up on him and force him to leave us alone."

"Before we get into this fight, maybe you should think about what you actually want." Isa crossed her arms over her chest and leaned sideways against the back bar. "I know you want this bar—but do you want it enough to lose the girl?"

I groaned. "Why does it have to be one or the other?"

"You tell me," Isa replied. "Where is Tyler? She's not here. You look like a sad, kicked puppy. She lives in a penthouse her dad owns and, presumably, loves him. You two have been secretive about everything going on between you, but I've also never seen you this twisted up over anyone. You were ready to tell her you love her yesterday, Yasmeen."

"I've loved women before," I countered, but refused to make direct eye contact with her because she'd see right through me.

Isa lightly scoffed at me. "You and I both know it's never been like this before—at least, not in the time I've known you. Those are *your* words."

Her phone rang on the bar top, and she grabbed it, swiping to answer on a FaceTime call. "Mila, can you take over here?"

My best friend's face appeared on the screen, and seeing her was a breath of fresh air.

Isa handed the phone to me.

"Are you two in a fight?" Mila asked me. "Because I'm not getting in between that again."

"Oh my god, that was one time, Mila," Isa called out from the background, even though she wasn't visible on the screen.

"It was enough to traumatize me for life," Mila replied. "What's going on, Yas?"

I quickly filled her in on everything that had transpired over the last forty-eight hours, and Ari came on screen in the back behind Mila. "Holy shit, Yasmeen. That's so fucked."

"I know, right? Does the Washington Times want to write a story on this?" I asked not so slyly. "I mean, I'll give you the exclusive scoop."

Ari walked closer to the camera, and she was holding their

toddler on her left hip. "I'm about to leave on assignment to cover a trial at a hospital where a baby was decapitated during delivery and the hospital is trying to silence the parents with only ten thousand dollars."

Real story, but this kind of shit is exactly why I didn't chat with them daily. Mila and Ari's life was weird. Period.

I sighed. "Okaaaaay, never mind then."

"I could send someone else to cover it if you want?" Ari offered.

Mila looked at me. "I mean, do you want the story out there? When Ari did the story I gave her, I lost my job and my license to practice law."

"I don't have a job to lose," I pointed out. "Hell, at this point, I don't even have the bar."

Mila shrugged. "Sure, but you have the girl. Or had? I'm confused on if you two are together or not right now. Either way, if you take down her dad in the court of public opinion, she might have some thoughts on that."

Oh, she would definitely have thoughts. "I mean, if *my* dad was doing shady stuff like this, I'd want him to be caught and held responsible for his actions."

Isa barked out a laugh. "That's bullshit. If your dad called and said he murdered someone, you'd be helping hide the body. Anyone in your family would."

"Okay, but that's what family does." I sighed. "Fine. I see your point. I'll talk to her about it first. See what she thinks."

"Gently," Mila added. "Not in an *I-told-you-so* kind of way."

"Fiiiiiine," I repeated. "But just to be clear, I called all of this and you're all witness to that."

Isa rolled her eyes.

"We see you," Ari added. "But in relationships, you either

fight to be right or you fight to preserve the relationship. You can rarely have both."

"If this is about the breakfast cereal for Gracie thing again," Mila began, now turning to look at her wife. "She's way too young for that much sugar."

Ari looked past Mila to me. "See? I could be right and introduce Gracie to the joy that is Cookie Crisp, or I could let Mila have her way on this. Happy wife, happy life."

Good to know the bullshit sayings from the patriarchy have infiltrated queer relationships now. I also hated the fact that it was kind of right...I could prove to Tyler that her dad was the monster I considered him to be, but that was absolutely going to drive a wedge between us that I wasn't sure we'd be able to come back from.

Did I want to come back from it?

The question was swirling around unsolicited in my head. It felt in some ways like I was at a crossroads—my business or my relationship. Guilt swirled in my belly as I realized I didn't know which one I would choose. That was bad, right? Like I *should* be the person who says I'd pick Tyler over anything and everything. That's what a girlfriend was supposed to do. That was the *right* thing to do.

But was it? Something inside of me was screaming self-preservation. I had no control over Tyler, and losing her felt inevitable at this point, but the bar was something that I could have a say in. It might sound dramatic, but it felt a bit like all I had left—even if feelings aren't facts, as my therapist would say.

I pulled my phone out of my pocket and typed up a quick text to Tyler, but I didn't hit send yet. "What if I say this: 'Hey, Tyler. Can we meet up and talk about the opening?' If I can get her in the door at least, then I can bring up the relationship stuff as well."

Isa shrugged. "Seems fine to me. But on that note, we do need to brainstorm."

Both Isa and I said our goodbyes to Mila and Ari. Then she hung up the phone, and I hit send on my text message to Tyler.

"I'm going to have to buy Tyler out of the bar," I said with a long sigh. "As shitty as her dad's deal is, that's the only way I could afford to still make all of this happen."

"I think that's the only choice at this point," Isa agreed. "We're also not going to be able to have the hard launch on the date we'd originally set, but I think we could make a soft launch happen and get everything else in place in the first few weeks of being open. All we need is a liquor license, and we can set up shop."

Thankfully, that wouldn't be the hard part. "We have that already for this location, so we'd just need to find a new location and get the address change approved."

Isa opened up her laptop computer on the bar top in front of me and pointed the screen toward me. "I've got a list of six retail space options that I think we should consider, or at least tour. Three of them are ready to go for a bar setting, but the other three would require renovations up front. None of them have the hair salon component, so that's going to have to come later."

Nothing could ever be simple. "It's literally in the name of the bar—cuts and cocktails. How can we open without that piece?"

"Intentionally," Isa replied. "We state that opening weekend is going to be a fundraiser to start building that side of the business so that as soon as we get it open, we can immediately start offering free cuts and colors and stuff. No one will even know it wasn't always planned that way to begin with, and it'll bring even more press to show opening weekend being a cause-driven event. Hell, we could even extend it out to the first two opening weekends."

Shit, I had smart friends. "That's brilliant. Especially if we're still doing the live podcast, because we could solicit the fundraiser on there and have an option for online giving."

"Now you're talking." Isa grinned. "See? We've got this. This bar is going to be a lot more than just an address."

I smiled and wrapped one arm around Isa's shoulders. "I don't know what I would do without your help on this one."

"Oh, don't worry," Isa said with a laugh. "My bill is already in your inbox."

Whatever it was, she deserved more. "Let me look at those locations."

Chapter Twenty-One

I t had been an entire seven days since I'd texted Tyler, and an entire six days since she had sent me a one-sentence reply that shut it all down.

I'm not ready to continue this conversation with you yet and need time to think about things.

So, that was fantastic.

Tonight was the Ambies Awards, and I was holed up on Nia's couch watching the live streaming of it from Los Angeles on the Amazon Music channel since she had a subscription and I did not.

"Her category is up next," Nia pointed out, though she wasn't completely invested in the show like I was. She had her feet up on the couch next to me, a thick throw blanket over her legs, and a Talia Hibbert romance novel in her lap. "It seems like she'd be a shoo-in to win her category."

My eyes were glued to the screen, and I was frustrated that they didn't pan over to the audience more often. If they did, I was pretty sure I'd be able to pick Tyler out of the crowd, but I hadn't spotted her yet. Although to be fair, I didn't know if they kept nominees backstage part of the time or what the setup was.

Elyse Meyers was currently presenting an award on original scores and the comments scrolling on the right side of the screen were going wild with quoting her quirky and motivational quips.

An X notification popped up on my cell phone screen—or Twitter, I don't know—and I clicked to read what I'd been mentioned in.

@podcastpetty: @thetyleradams spotted at @ambiesawards without a date? If the rumors are true about her being gay AF, someone should check the closet for her girlfriend!

There were two pictures—one of Tyler in a beautiful green gown on a red carpet at the Ambies Awards alone, and the other was a picture of Tyler and me kissing at the DC Pride Parade with my account tagged in the second photograph. My face was mostly obscured so I wasn't even sure how they recognized me or who the hell Podcast Petty was, but apparently, they were big fans of Tyler's show, as well as a few others. The majority of their posts tonight were commentary about the Ambies, and I shouldn't have, but I clicked the photo and began reading the replies.

@ podcastpetty I thought she was dating that Black girl in the parade photo. Who is that?

@podcastpetty why is everybody obsessed with murder f-ing sickos get a real job

@podcastpetty if Tyler is a lesbian, then give her my number.

@podcastpetty she's not even that pretty, who cares

@podcastpetty put me in a threesome with both of them and they'll be loving dick by the next morning

@podcastpetty we stan a celesbian!

@podcastpetty Who is Tyler Adams?

@podcastpetty Are you looking to change your life? Dr. Shaimo gave me an herbal remedy that changed my life, and yours can too. Just click on this link.

Okay, this was getting pointless. The internet was a cesspool of humanity—and I used the word humanity loosely.

"You look like you're about to punch someone," Nia's comment pulled my attention from my phone.

I looked up at her. "People are talking shit online about Tyler showing up alone at the Ambies."

Nia's brow furrowed. "Were you supposed to be her date?"

"No." I shook my head. "I mean, she never asked me. It seems like the kind of thing you'd bring a girlfriend to, but we're also not really talking right now. I'm not sure if she even still is my girlfriend."

"She agreed to still do the live recording on your opening night next weekend," Nia pointed out. "That's got to say something."

"Which I only found out through Isa." I leaned my head back on the couch cushion and returned my gaze to the Ambies Awards on the television screen. "If that's the next time the two of us talk, it's going to be a super awkward podcast."

Nia nodded, looking full well like she did not envy me for a single second. "Did she say anything to Isa about getting off the ownership paperwork for the bar?"

I grimaced. "I haven't asked her yet."

Nia's eyes bugged out of her head, and she put her book down. "Yas, you're opening in one week."

Isa and I had toured all the places she'd found, plus three others. We'd lucked out in the best way possible, and I still couldn't believe it, but we'd found an old diner right by Clarendon Metro that had been closed for over a year. The diner itself had moved locations to another part of Arlington, and the building had just been sitting there the entire time.

We'd ripped out most of the booths and replaced them with high-top bar tables and were currently working on extending the bar to wrap around one side of the diner. The other side we were going to close off for now and later turn it into the hair salon part. There was a huge parking lot out back that we cut down to half size and had tents up for an outdoor area and were working on installing an outside bar.

The license had gone through on the new address, and we were embracing the leftover diner decor on the outside and inside of the building for now. Over the coming months, I'd get a new and better sign up out front and replace the red paneling to be something less obnoxious. But the place had all the bones we needed to open in terms of a working kitchen, table space, and a good-sized bar.

Plus, it came with a jukebox and sound system that we could tap into and revitalize.

"It's a soft opening," I reminded Nia. "It's capped at fifty people and it is only open Saturday night. We'll open both Friday and Saturday nights the week after that, so even more time to finish everything."

My sister wasn't convinced. "Still—you need to talk to her. If you don't get your money back from the last place, then you're going to be so far in the hole before it opens that you'll never dig out."

"As true as that is, I will talk to her. I just wanted to give her the space she asked for." A title bar came across the bottom of the screen, and I saw Tyler's category was up next. "Plus, she probably didn't want to be distracted before the award show. I'll text her again tomorrow to follow up. Or maybe get Isa to."

"Oh, that color works so well on her," Nia commented as the camera panned to the different nominees in Tyler's category.

I could now see that she was seated in the left side of the

audience and was wearing the same green dress from the photo I'd seen online. She did look amazing. Her eyes were glowing in a way I hadn't seen before, and I didn't think it was just the stage lights.

She looked exhilarated and in her element, and *this* was the part of her I heard when I listened to her podcast. Because I had started listening to her podcast—as in, I'd binge listened to eighteen episodes in the last week.

Keep the judgments—I know, okay?

It had brought an interesting new perspective to Tyler to immerse myself in her creative side, however. She was vibrant as she spoke in a way I didn't always see in person—or, I only saw glimpses of here and there. It was like she became unguarded with the microphone because she was playing a role. But...it wasn't really a role. It was still part of her. Specifically curated and chosen parts, but it was very authentically her.

Now seeing her sit in the audience among her peers, I could identify the animation on her face and the hope in her eyes. Someone from Barstool Sports was the presenter for her award and listed off the names of each podcast in excruciatingly slow form. Ironically, they even dropped the envelope halfway through and had to pause to pick it up before they could resume reading the final nominees.

Tyler clapped for the other nominees politely—always the courteous rule follower.

I was sitting on the edge of the couch leaning so far forward my head was practically inside the television screen.

The presenter finally returned to the microphone and cleared his throat. "And the winner for Podcast of the Year is..."

A hush fell over the crowd, and I could hear Nia holding her breath next to me because I was doing the same.

"Tyler Adams of The Deviant Devotee!"

"Oh my god!" I shouted and jumped up from the couch, clapping my hands. I started dancing and swaying my hips from side to side as Nia laughed and offered me a high-five. "She won! She won!"

The excitement was vibrating across my skin like I'd been electrocuted, and I couldn't stop squirming and moving.

Nia was still laughing at me. "Sit down or you'll miss her speech!"

The camera panned back to her, and my girl looked shocked as all get out. Her eyes were wide and her mouth slightly ajar, and it struck me for the first time that she hadn't thought she'd win. This wasn't a posed humility for the cameras. She was completely caught off guard.

Something pulled in my chest, and I sat down heavily on the couch. The Tyler that I knew won everything—that was never a question. In fact, it was one of the first things we fought about because she can be an absolute dick about it. But the woman walking up to the stage didn't look like the confident woman I'd come to love. Something had shaken her, and I couldn't help but feel guilty for the role I might be playing in that.

Tyler took the award from the presenter among loud applause and stepped to the microphone, her face lit up. "Thank you so much. This is...this is truly incredible. I did not expect this at all. I need to thank my production team and agent at Wondery for all their support in getting me here. But most of all, thank you as well to my incredible father, Walter Adams, who has always supported me not only as a daughter, and a podcaster, but a proud and out lesbian. It's with his help and guidance that I'm dedicating a portion of the proceeds from the podcast this year to The Trevor Project to assist and protect young LGBTQ lives."

Excuse the fuck me. I could practically hear a record scratching in my frontal lobe.

"I thought you said her dad was homophobic?" Nia frowned from where she was sitting on the couch next to me.

My gaze panned away from her and back to the screen, and there was no doubt that I was the one with the shocked expression on my face now. "Uh...I...um, he is? He was? She...well, he..."

I literally couldn't even find my words.

Nia sucked her teeth and lifted her book back up to continue reading. "Damn, you lesbians are more drama than this book."

I felt like I was living a book plot. I mean, what the actual fuck?

Tyler was waving goodbye to the audience as she finished the rest of her speech and was walking off. I hadn't even heard anything after the part about her father. In fact, I think I'd partially gone deaf because the irony was ringing in my ears louder than Quasimodo hanging on the damn bell ropes of Rachel's heart.

"I have to call her."

Nia didn't even look up at me over the top of her novel. "She's three hours behind you and on the other side of the country at an awards show. They probably don't even let them bring their phone into places like that."

"Then I'll get on a plane to Los Angeles," I said. "I'll find her hotel and go talk to her."

Now my sister was getting fed up. "Yasmeen, you will not. Go pour yourself another glass of wine, turn on something else to watch, and go to bed like a normal person. When she comes back to town, then the two of you can talk. You're not storming across the country because she said she loved her father. What kind of psycho-girlfriend shit is that?"

Fair point. "I'm not mad that she loves her father! I just—okay, a little annoyed—but to give him credit for supporting her queerness all this time? How? When? None of that tracks. He'd literally lose his evil little career if he pulled shit like that..."

My eyes widened and I gasped so loudly that even I felt out of breath.

"What?" Nia looked at me with concern. "Don't breathe-scream like that, Jesus H. Christ. I nearly fell off the couch."

"She's punishing him!" I clapped my hands together and turned to face my sister—grabbing the book from her hands and placing it down on the table in front of us. I then grabbed her hands and pulled her up to her feet next to me, jumping up and down. "She's punishing him!"

"Ouch! What the hell, Yas?" Nia pushed my hands off of her. "We are not twenty-year-old whoo-hoo girls in a sorority house. Stop jumping around."

"This is a sign, Nia," I replied, finally letting go of her and walking over to the kitchen to pour myself a glass of wine. I returned a couple minutes later with a full one. "Tyler knows what her father did and she's punishing him for it."

I don't know why that was making me so emotional, but it was. I could feel the tears choking up in my throat, and I wanted to cry. It felt like an act of kindness, not like she was picking me over her father. Hell, I had no idea where she and I even stood romantically or platonically or business-wise. I literally knew nothing, except that Tyler had spent her entire life being what other people wanted her to be. She kept everything in—her identity, her desires—and I'd seen the pain it had caused her etched into her flesh.

But she was changing the narrative for herself, and it was the most beautiful thing I'd ever witnessed. I needed to talk to her to find out what that meant for me—for us.

Chapter Twenty-Two

I didn't fly to Los Angeles and track Tyler down at her hotel. After all, I had promised my sister I would tone down my crazy to mild-to-moderate levels. Instead, I was sitting on the floor of the vestibule in front of her penthouse door waiting for her to return from the airport, which was at least four notches less crazy.

Again with the judgment. Stop it.

My phone vibrated in my pocket, and I pulled it out to see my father's name across the screen. I clicked on his message.

The bank confirmed that everything went through. Good luck this weekend. You're going to kill it, kid.

Not that knot back in my throat again. It was.

My dad had helped step in with his lawyers to confirm the return of my finances in the first property from Walter Adams. In fact, our lawyers had been able to fight the entire thing to remove his bullshit stipulations. We got our money clear and free—minus some of the money I'd put into renovations. Still, it was a lot more than I'd expected to walk away with.

Most importantly, Tyler was still part owner of KiKi.

So, me sitting on the parquet floor outside her door was a business meeting. Not crazy at all. Just responsible business.

That being said, we were going on hour three, and not only had Tyler not shown up, but her text messages weren't even showing as being delivered.

I tapped on the bottom of her front door. "Might be time to give up, huh, Larry?"

Even the damn dog was ignoring me. That little shit had never liked me anyway.

Feeling was mutual, taco dog.

The small vestibule I was sitting in had three doors—the door to the penthouse apartment, the door to the tiny manager's office, and then the elevator. And the elevator was dinging with the little box in the top right showing that the car was moving up toward me one floor at a time.

I quickly scrambled to my feet. Someone was coming.

"Shit. Shit. Shit." I pushed at the wrinkles on the flared linen pants I was wearing, trying to get them to straighten out. No dice. I was wearing a dark yellow crop top and adjusted the edges to lay flat against my stomach. There was no mirror around, so I quickly used my phone's front-facing camera to scan my face. It was fine. I looked fine. Everything is absolutely fine.

Ding.

The elevator moved up to the next floor. Three floors left until it got to me.

I shoved my phone back in my pocket, looping my small purse over my shoulder and pushing it behind me. Why was I even wearing a purse? I never used purses. I was a wallet person at best, but most of the time just had a small compartment magnetically attached to my phone for a few cards. But, no, today I had a whole ass purse with me. Tyler was going to ask me why I had a purse with me. She knows I don't use purses.

Oh my God, why am I here? Calm your tits, Yas.

The elevator dinged that she was on my floor.

I should not be here. This is a mistake.

I immediately began looking for places to hide—the property manager's door was locked. I yanked on that door handle like it was a negotiation but the fucker didn't budge.

The door to the elevator opened, and I whirled around, quickly smoothing out my clothes and leaning against the wall like I'd been casually chilling there this whole time.

I leaned like this all the time. This was normal.

I was normal.

"Yasmeen?" Tyler stepped off the elevator with a giant cardboard box in her hands and looked at me like I've never leaned like this in my life.

"I lean." That was all I could come up with in response.

She furrowed her brow and walked toward the penthouse door. Balancing the box on one knee, she put her key in the door to unlock it. "Okaaaay....do you want to lean inside?"

"That would be preferable." Please, God. Strike me with lightning now.

Tyler was unconvinced, her gaze narrowing. "Okay...yeah. Come on in."

I did. I followed after her like a compliant puppy dog and I hated every second of it until I saw what was inside.

Nothing.

Nothing was inside. I mean, aside from some moving boxes and a stray piece of furniture here or there. The entire penthouse was cleared out and devoid of any life. If you'd have told me someone lived here once, I would have said absolutely not. That's how desolate the place looked without Tyler's touch.

"Uh...did you get robbed?" I spun around, trying to take in

every empty corner of the space I'd come to know as her home. "Where the hell is all your furniture?"

"Some of it I moved to my new apartment," Tyler replied as she set the box she was carrying down on the marble kitchen countertop. "The rest my father put in his other properties."

"He...he...wait, what?" Slow the heck down, because someone needed to explain this to me like I was five years old. "This is...this is news."

She didn't respond, but just nodded her head.

I watched her for a few moments before I finally had the guts to ask what I really wanted to know. "Ty, did you mean what you said at the Ambies?"

She looked surprised, taking half a step back and leaning against the countertop. "You watched the Ambies?"

I nodded. "Congratulations. You deserved that win. I don't know why you thought you didn't."

Tyler looked down at her feet, shuffling them slightly as she repositioned herself. "Who says I thought that? I had a winner's speech ready."

I walked over to the counter she was leaning against and matched her body position, but left several feet between us. "I don't know. I saw your face. You looked surprised, and I've never seen you doubt yourself like that before."

"It was a big moment for my career. A lot of hope," Tyler said, her gaze still not quite meeting mine. "But it seemed like a far-reaching hope."

I shook my head. "You deserved the win."

"How do you even know that? You don't listen to my podcast," Tyler countered. It wasn't as accusatory as it sounded, but rather her tone was kind of vulnerable and there was a hint of sadness to it.

I was like a dog with a bone. "Yes, I do. I've listened to the entire last season just in the past week, and already started on the one before that."

Her eyes perked up and the corners of her lips lifted into the tiniest hint of a smile. "You listened to me?"

"I told you I would."

She swallowed hard, looking back at her box.

"I don't understand what's going on here. Where's all your stuff?" I continued, now motioning around me to the empty space we were standing in. "Why do you have that box? What is happening here, Tyler?"

She looked nonplussed. "I moved out."

"To where?" Also, how? Why? *Seriously, why?* This penthouse was amazing. "I didn't know you were moving."

The smallest of smirks hit the corner of Tyler's lips. "Now you look like the worried one."

I cleared my throat and took half a step back. "Worried about what?"

"Me leaving," she clarified. "If what I said in my speech was true. All of it."

I shrugged my shoulders feeling the vulnerability rising up in me. "They are reasonable questions to ask. A lot has happened. We haven't talked."

"I know," Tyler replied. "I'm sorry I wasn't ready when you wanted to. I did need some time to figure out how I feel, and how I want to move forward with my life."

I blew out a low steady breath and looked away from her, focusing on a vent on the ceiling in the corner of the room. "And so...what did you figure out?"

"I meant what I said in my speech," Tyler finally answered. "My dad is my biggest supporter. That's what I have believed my whole life. Now I just decided to hold him to it publicly. That...well, that caused a lot of tension between him and me."

I shuffled my feet, looking down at the toes of my shoe rubbing up against the other. "I'm sorry to hear that."

"I'm not. He lost some of his funding after my speech at the Ambies, and his current organization is trying to figure out how to crisis spin it all." She lifted open the box she'd been carrying and started putting the few miscellaneous items inside that were still sitting around the room—a tchotchke from Hershey's Park, two candles from Pottery Barn, and a row of books that I'm pretty sure she never read. Not that I'm judging.

I mean, a little bit.

"I'd imagine it's a lot to figure out for his staff." I finally met her gaze. "So, that's why you're leaving? They're making you move?"

"No one makes me do anything," she reminded me. "I was going to move out either way. I knew what I set into motion by saying what I did and I knew the potential ramifications of that."

I exhaled loudly. "You said a lot."

She nodded. "Yeah."

I inhaled slowly, just trying to feel the breath in my lungs as I looked at her. "When I was listening to your speech, it felt like a sign. Like you were giving me a sign."

"I didn't say those things *for* you, Yasmeen," she clarified. "I said them because it was the right thing to do. Because it aligned with my beliefs and who I want to be when I look back at my life. I need to make more choices like that. I need to feel like I'm being more authentic to myself."

"Completely. Makes sense." I nodded along like I wasn't breathing solely based on whatever she was about to say. "I'm glad you did, honestly."

She didn't look directly at me. "That's not the same thing as saying I know what I want between us."

A few months ago, I hadn't even known this woman, and

here I was feeling like my heart was being ripped open by her. When had that even happened? The moment I'd given her that level of power over me, over my heart?

"Okay...it's been a whole week, though. That's a lot of time," I countered. Jesus, why was I arguing how time worked with anyone, let alone the woman I couldn't stop thinking about? I'd dated so many women in the past, but never once had I felt like I was the one begging to keep things together. "Can we talk soon?"

I really was begging, and I felt that unfamiliar sinking feeling in my stomach as the pause lengthened between us.

"I don't know if I'm in a position to think about us just yet," Tyler admitted after a few quiet moments. "The award show, coming out, the podcast, the bar opening...life is really in flux right now, Yas."

"Yeah," I agreed because the hell if I wasn't along for the roller coaster, too. "I mean, I definitely feel that, too."

"The only reason I'm still involved in the bar is because I'm not living in my dad's property anymore," Tyler continued. "It was move out or leave the business."

"What do you mean?" I'd assumed she must have figured out her father's ultimatum, but I wasn't sure how much I should say out loud.

"I know what my father did. I know you were right, Yasmeen. You called it from the start." It was unmistakable grief in her eyes as she spoke, and my chest felt tight. "I was just too naive to admit how he was yielding his authority over me— over my entire life, really. I needed to be free of it, and...well, he gave me no choice."

I waited for her to say more, feeling like I couldn't let a single breath out of my lungs.

"I'm starting over on my own," she continued. "I need to.

But I'm also not saying goodbye to my father. I'm not cutting him out—even after what he did."

"Oh." I blinked slowly, trying to process what that meant. "Right. I mean, of course. He's your dad."

"He is." She sighed. "He's the only family I have."

It felt like an elephant was sitting on my chest, and guilt swarmed in my stomach. I had wanted her to see who her father was, but the grief I was seeing now made me realize just how painful that sight was for her. No part of this moment or this version of Tyler felt like what I had wanted. It just felt sad and hollow and full of a history between Tyler and her father that I couldn't ever begin to understand. I'd been the spark to ignite the fire, even though I suspected it had been simmering for decades.

"Tyler, I'm..." I let out a slow exhale. "I'm so sorry. I don't know what else to say."

She shook her head. "You didn't do anything. Don't apologize. I just need some time, okay? I'll see you at the live recording."

I let a few quiet moments pass between us as Tyler returned to packing the last of her things in the boxes. "Isa said she told you about the new location?"

"It's a great idea, honestly," Tyler replied with a nod. "Much better than this location would have been."

I hated to agree in that moment, because it felt like rubbing salt in the wound. But she wasn't wrong. The new diner location was a windfall none of us had expected, and while I would never say it out loud, I was grateful for the shitstorm we'd gone through because of the opportunity it was giving us. We wouldn't open on time, and things weren't going to be as smooth of a start as I'd hoped, but the end result would be infinitely better.

"Okay, well..." I looked around the empty room, trying not

to remember the times we'd spent together here, or the moments we'd been wrapped up in one another. "I'm going to go home. If you need help moving or anything, let me know. My brother is my go-to for moving help. I can call Demetrius any time if you want."

She shook her head. "I hired movers and packers already. These are just the last few items. I'll see you next week, okay?"

"Sure." I headed for the front door of the penthouse and didn't turn around to look back at her.

I couldn't afford her to see the tears brimming in my eyes. I didn't cry over women.

And I wasn't crying over Tyler.

Chapter Twenty-Three

It wasn't even four o'clock in the afternoon and Rachel had straight up ordered a shot of tequila with a lime wedge.

"I admire the hustle, but since when do you pound hard liquor at happy hour?" I asked her as I slid onto the stool at the high-top table she was seated at.

Rachel glanced across the table at me and grinned. "I'm celebrating."

"Oh, Lord. Do I even want to know?"

The waiter walked up and I ordered the house red wine off the happy hour menu and a side of pimento cheese dip and chips.

Rachel held up her shot glass triumphantly. "I just won the case against a sewage company that was using the Anacostia River as a dump site."

"Wait, didn't you say if you won that case, you'd be making partner?" My eyes widened because this case had been all Rachel had been working on for the last several years. All of her friends had heard every single detail, and we'd been rooting hardcore for her to win.

"Meet the youngest partner at Davis, Yung, and now... Blumenthal." Rachel took the shot in a quick gulp then sucked on the lime wedge. She let out a pleased exhale and pumped her fists in the air.

I popped up out of my seat and rounded the table to give her a hug. "That's so incredible, Rach. You've worked so hard for this."

She grinned, and it was rare that I saw her emotion so fully on display like it was right now. "It's been a long few years, Yas. You, Mila—hell, even Isa—really pushed me to keep going when I really didn't think I could stick it through."

I had returned to my seat just as the waiter dropped off my glass of wine and two glasses of water. "Aw. Look at you being all sentimental and stuff."

"I know, right?" Rachel laughed and ordered a beer. "It's not like me at all."

"Big things seem to be happening for all of us lately," I mused. "Did you hear Mila's show was picked up for another season?"

Rachel nodded. "And you're opening KiKi this weekend."

I took a long sip of my wine. "Yeah...that's been a journey."

"You've spent months putting it all together and making it happen." Rachel picked up the beer the waiter had just dropped off for her and took a sip. "I'm excited to go to the live recording of the podcast this weekend. How are you and Tyler feeling about it?"

"Um..." I took another sip of my wine, avoiding an immediate response.

Rachel sat back in her chair and crossed her arms over her chest. "Yas, do not tell me you two already broke up. I thought this one was going to stick."

"It is! I mean, it might." I shrugged my shoulders. "We haven't broken up. I don't think so. I'm not entirely sure, to be honest. We're just taking some time to think right now. Well, she's taking time to think and I'm waiting to hear what she thinks."

Rachel blinked slowly and then leaned her elbows on the edge of the table. "We're not getting younger, Yasmeen. We are in our mid-thirties and it's going to stop being cute real soon if we keep hopping around from person to person like we've been doing."

"So, you're dating someone?" It was much easier to turn the attention on anyone else, and seriously, Rachel telling me to slow down? The irony. "Because I haven't seen you in a serious relationship in years."

There was a devious glint in Rachel's eyes and I narrowed my gaze at her.

"Oh my god, you *are* dating someone. Who is she?"

Rachel shook her head. "They use they/them pronouns. And we can talk about them another time. This is about you and Tyler. I really like her."

I sipped my wine a bit more. "High praise coming from you."

"So, how are you going to fix it with her?" Rachel didn't let up as she dug into the pimento cheese plate the waiter had brought. "Is she still partnering with you on the bar?"

"She is," I replied. "That in and of itself is a whole story. Her father tried to push her out of it, basically didn't want his name attached to anything gay. We had to move locations, but I was able to get the money back I'd paid him and keep Tyler on."

Rachel lifted one brow. "He sounds like an asshole."

"Yeah, he is. But..." I sighed. "I think I put her in a shitty spot. I didn't say it exactly, but I kind of forced her to choose between her father and me. And she chose neither of us."

She swallowed the bite she was chewing. "You did *what?*"

"I know! I didn't mean to, but I kind of walked her into the situation and gave her no other option." I finished off the last of my glass of wine and lifted my hand to the waiter to indicate that I wanted a second. "He's the only family she has, even if he is detestable in like ninety-seven different ways."

Rachel leaned back against the table and lowered her voice just enough to not be overhead by nearby tables. "Listen, I think it's amazing that you come from a family that is so open and accepting of your queerness. Seriously. I look at Nia and Demetrius, and even your dad when he actually does talk, and I'm just amazed that you being gay is not even a blip on their radar. They are so completely fine with just embracing you for who you are."

I felt a lump forming in my throat as I thought of my family. "I know...I'm lucky."

"You really are," Rachel continued. "Because the reality is that you are the exception to the rule. The majority of us don't have familial support like that."

I thought of what I knew of Rachel's family, and how her parents had kicked her out in high school once they'd found out she'd asked a girl to go to prom. She'd felt so deeply ashamed of herself and who she was that it would be another ten years before Rachel would come out publicly to the world. Once she finally did, both Mila and I made damn sure that she felt welcomed, accepted, and embraced every step of the way.

But her family still wanted nothing to do with her.

"Do you miss them?" I asked softly, placing a hand on Rachel's forearm. "Your family?"

"I miss the concept of family. The concept of parents to call or a mother to hug me, or siblings to catch a movie with and laugh with..." Rachel clarified. "But the individual humans who filled those roles for me are not people I miss. Not at all. However, I can understand the desire to not want to let go of them. Walking away from my family entirely was the right choice for me, but it was the hardest thing I've ever done and changed my life in countless ways—good and bad. Doing that might not be the right choice for Tyler."

"It's so easy in the queer community to be like, if they don't support you, cut them out. Boundaries, boundaries, boundaries. That's like a hammer we pound over each other's heads. Not affirming? Adios." I sighed and shook my head. "It's never that simple, though."

Rachel finished another bite of the appetizer and nodded. "It's not. Sometimes it hurts less to be around the person you love even if they don't love all of you than it is to not be around them at all. Everyone chooses their hard. Estrangement is hard. Tolerating hateful or non-affirming family is hard. None of it is easy. You just have to pick your hard, and fuck anyone who judges you for it."

"I really did luck out with my family," I agreed. "But honestly, I lucked out with my chosen family, too."

She grinned at me from across the table and offered me a wink. "Love ya, toots."

"I should apologize to Tyler, shouldn't I?" I finally admitted. "Tell her I can and will accept her for exactly who she is—family and all?"

"Maybe you should talk to her dad?" Rachel suggested. "Invite him to the opening. Mend fences. Who knows? That might go a long way."

The idea of kicking it socially with Walter Adams sounded like a nightmare, but if it showed Tyler that I respected who she was, I'd do it.

Kari arrived just then and scooted onto the bar seat next to me. Today they were dressed fully masc, and giving me full-on lumberjack vibes with all the plaid. "Guys, I broke two million."

"On TikTok?" I asked, waving over the waiter so he could take their order.

Isa was also on her way, but she was usually running a bit late. Not that I would say anything because I owed that woman my entire life at this point and was also never on time to anything. I felt like the older I got, the more I didn't care about punctuality and surrounded myself with people who accepted that about me.

"Yep," Kari confirmed. "And guess who just offered me a sponsored post?"

The waiter brought over menus again and we quickly placed another round of drinks and a few more appetizers.

Kari looked like she'd just won the lottery. "Red Bull!"

"Oh, wow!" Rachel was impressed, but I didn't have the same reaction.

"I truly believe energy drinks are just liquid canned cancer," I replied, but then lifted my glass of wine in toast to Kari. "But that's still really cool. Are they paying big?"

"Five figures for three posts," Kari admitted. "It's the most I've gotten so far."

"Holy shit," I commented, nodding in approval. "Rachel, when we were twenty-five, TikTok didn't even exist and now people are making a living being influencers."

"We could be influencers," Rachel joked, even though neither of us had any actual interest in living our lives online right now. "Is there a Golden Girls fan base on TikTok? Because I think we could have that down."

"Make an account for @GoldenGirlsLoveGirls," Kari replied with a grin. "I don't think that's out there yet, so if you wanted to corner that market, I'd totally help."

"You're twenty-five," I teased Kari. I adored them, but the age gap meant that there was plenty we didn't understand about each other and TikTok was one of them. "What do you know about the Golden Girls?"

"I watched the entire series on Hulu last summer when I was having my top surgery. People really need to stop sleeping on that show," Kari informed us. "There's no way Blanche and Betty White behind the scenes didn't get it on once in a while."

"We stan Betty White." Rachel lifted her glass, and I clinked mine against hers.

"Rest in power," I added. "But speaking of my golden girl, I have to go make some amends."

Kari lifted one brow with a shaved line through it. "You and Tyler are so cute together. It's lesbian goals."

"They're not even talking right now," Rachel informed Kari. "So, readjust your goals."

I shot a look at both of them. "Hey, hey, hey. Conflict is healthy in relationships. It's about how you communicate through them—not avoiding them. My therapist says it's an opportunity for growth."

"See?" Kari pointed at me. "That's the perfect thing to put on a Golden Girls page, because us young folk don't know that therapy talk."

"Your generation invented therapy," I shot back, even though I had a weekly telehealth session with Ms. Maren every Thursday. "I was raised on MTV's Pimp My Ride where every life problem was solved by Xzibit turning the trunk of your car into a giant stereo and adding a flame-painted spoiler. That was my therapy."

"And now you're in a relationship that you don't even know if you're together or not," Rachel pointed out. "So, maybe double up on Ms. Maren visits and stop getting mental health advice from television shows."

I stood up from the stool in a dramatic fashion and dropped a few twenty-dollar bills on the table for my part of the check. "I feel attacked."

Kari laughed, and Rachel got up to give me a hug.

"Go get your girl," Rachel said.

I took a deep breath and exhaled slowly. "I hope she's still my girl."

Chapter Twenty-Four

"I don't know why I'm here," Walter Adams said as he walked in the front door of KiKi six hours before opening.

"Thanks for coming." I offered him my hand for a handshake, but he looked at it like I'd just coughed into it. Swallowing hard, I dropped my hand to my side and pulled on my big girl britches. "Would you like to sit down and talk?"

He gestured like he might as well and followed me over to the old-style booth that we'd left in place from the diner. "Here?"

I nodded and took the bench seat across from him. "Let's just get down to brass tacks: you don't like me."

His face was unchanged, absolutely no emotional reaction to what I'd said. Instead, his beady black eyes just bored through me.

"I'm guessing you also probably think I've been pushing Tyler away from you or into everything we're currently wrapped up in." I gestured around us to the bar. "And, you'd be right."

Walter leaned back against the booth and waited for me to say more.

I was trying not to be nervous, but his squinty eyes were literally cutting holes in me like swiss cheese. Still, I forced the words I'd rehearsed out of myself like I wasn't choking on them.

"I want to apologize, and tell you that I'd like us to start over." I put both hands on the table between us and laced my fingers together. "For Tyler's benefit—and ours—we need to get along."

Walter cleared his throat and looked like he was carefully choosing his words. Finally, he leaned forward and matched my posture, his own fingers interlaced on the table in front of him. "The things Tyler said at the Ambies Awards nearly cost me my career. I've spent the last week doing major damage control that maybe—just maybe—I'll be able to come back from in the far future once all of this dies down."

"I'm sorry to hear that," I replied, even though my inner child was doing a small happy dance. "I hope you know that I wasn't involved in any of that. I heard what she said in live time the same as you did."

He didn't look like he believed me outright, but rather was waiting for my expression to crack or show I was lying.

I held firm and kept my gaze on him, refusing to be intimidated.

"Tyler hasn't spoken to me since the award show," Walter finally said, now leaning back again and letting his shoulders drop just enough to indicate that maybe we had a chance.

I let out a small, strained chuckle. "Me either."

Walter smiled a little at that. "Trouble in paradise?"

I cut my eyes to him. "Don't look so pleased."

A minute of silence passed between us, and we just stared at one another, like we were evaluating each other and neither of us was meeting the other's standards. Which was probably pretty accurate.

He was the one to finally break the silence. "Has Tyler told you about her mother?"

"Bits and pieces," I replied, confused as to where this conversation was going.

Walter looked away from me. "We wanted a second child after Tyler, you know. We loved Tyler, but our family didn't feel complete just yet. We found out she was expecting again around Valentine's Day when Tyler was three years old."

I immediately felt a sinking in my gut, because Tyler had never told me about any siblings.

"When we found out that it was ectopic, she cried and she didn't stop." Walter swallowed hard and inhaled carefully. "We did all the things you're supposed to do—everything the doctor recommended. You might think my political beliefs are awful, but I wasn't about to let my wife die. She was the love of my life."

The skin on my arms was prickling, and I couldn't stop my mind from conjuring up my own mother's face, remembering everything she'd given up to have me.

"I thought postpartum depression only happened after you have a baby," Walter continued. "And we didn't have a baby. We had a procedure, and that was supposed to be it. But when her milk came in and there was no baby to feed, something went off in her head. Some wiring just didn't connect. I came home from work one day and Tyler had just turned four years old..."

The air froze in my lungs, and I couldn't find it in me to exhale.

Walter looked down at his hands now. "My wife was attempting to nurse Tyler, and Tyler was crying and asking not to."

"Fuck." The word slid out of me like a hiss.

"Her little face was so red, so puffy—like she'd been crying for hours and no one was listening. My wife...her face just looked empty. Like she wasn't really there at all." Walter finally raised his gaze to level at me, and his jaw was tight as he spoke. "I had spent my entire life pursuing my wife, loving her, wrapping my entire purpose around her—she was everything to me, Yasmeen."

"I know," I said, because I could feel it. I could feel the love he had for this woman I didn't even know, and I'd heard Tyler talk about their love before. "I know she meant a lot to you."

"But I chose Tyler over her," he finished. "I had my wife hospitalized and when she was finally declared safe enough to be released almost six months later, she made the decision not to come home. She didn't want to be a mother. She didn't want to be my wife. And she could make that choice, but I just couldn't. I couldn't not be Tyler's father. That little girl needed me."

The lump in my throat was cannonball sized at this point. "I...I didn't know all of that."

"Her mother was always talented on the stage, and so she lives in New York City now. She plays random parts on Broadway and lives in a small one-bedroom apartment that I pay for every month."

Shit. "Does Tyler know that?"

He nodded. "Yeah. She sends her a Mother's Day card every year, and sometimes when she visits New York City, I know she stands in front of the building her mom lives in and hopes she'll run into her. I don't think she has yet, though."

For the woman who wins at everything, this felt like the biggest loss I'd ever heard of. My heart ached as I thought of little girl Tyler wanting her mother's love and just...not getting it. My own mother was gone, but she was gone in an act of loving me and giving me everything—giving me life. There was no doubt in my mind that my mother would be here if she could.

The concept of knowing her mother was out there and just didn't want her? I couldn't even imagine that level of grief. Honestly, death sounded easier.

I could understand why Tyler hadn't told me any of this, and why she'd just spoken about her mother like she was dead instead.

"You really stepped up and have been there for her." I let my hands drop to my side, my voice softening. For the first time, I actually believed that sentence. Tyler had repeated it to me dozens of times and I'd brushed her off, but hearing the sincerity in his voice now...I understood her truth a little bit more. "That's incredible, honestly."

"So you understand," he acknowledged. "Tyler is my entire life. I've given everything for her. She is everything to me."

I nodded, because how could I not understand that after a story like that?

"So, for me to do all of that...give up the love of my life, become a single father, set my career back a decade just to become a primary caregiver...and then my only child to tell the entire world that she wants to date women?" Walter shook his head. "It's a slap in the face. I didn't raise her that way. She went to CCD in the Catholic Church for five years. She made a purity pledge when she was fourteen years old, and she was an altar server until she graduated high school. Now she's chosen a life that goes against everything we believe."

"She's chosen love," I countered. "And authenticity."

"We're not going to see the same on this," Walter replied, and the beady eyes were back in full force. Any moment of truth or vulnerability was gone between us. "Despite Tyler's choices, I'm not going anywhere. I love her, and I will be here for her."

"You cut her off," I reminded him. "She can't even live in her home anymore."

He shook his head. "She cut herself off. She still has my credit cards. She still has the keys to the penthouse. She can use them anytime—no strings attached. I may not agree with her lifestyle, but my love isn't conditional. Whatever is mine, it's also hers. Love the sinner, hate the sin. And I love Tyler."

I bit my tongue hard at the fact that unconditional love *actually* meant loving the person for everything they are, not despite who they are. Religious trauma always rears its ugly head, despite the fact that the Bible was some of the most pro-love-everyone shit I'd ever read. But he wasn't ready to hear that, and I wasn't his therapist or his priest. He was not my job.

My job was to love Tyler, and this man also loved Tyler in his own way.

We had at least that one thing in common.

"I have to be honest," I began. "I don't know what to say. I want to be with Tyler...I think I am with Tyler? Either way, she's a lesbian. I love that about her, but I also just love *her*. But part of loving Tyler means loving the people she loves, and she has made it very clear to me that she loves you."

His smile was just smug enough to make me irritated, but I let it go.

"So, I want to foster that relationship," I continued. "I want you in her life if that's what she wants. I want us to be friendly."

He tapped his fingers against the tabletop like he was strumming a guitar. "I'd like that. Honestly, I would."

I nodded and let the air hang between us for a minute before I continued. "So, do you want to come to the live recording of the podcast tonight? I'm sure Tyler would be happy to see you."

He looked like he was considering my offer. Finally, he shook his head. "No, you two have fun. This place is going to do well, and I'm proud of her for knowing when to invest in something that's going to take off. Clearly some of my business sense has had an influence."

He thought we were going to take off? I fought a grin and tried not to feel any pride over that, but for some reason, his verbal approval still made me feel like I was riding on a high I'd never asked for.

"But I would like it if you two would come to dinner at my house, maybe later this month," he continued. "I'd like to get to know you better, and know the two of you together."

"I...I can ask." I didn't feel very confident in where Tyler and I were at all, let alone enough to commit to dinner plans with her father. "If she's open to it, I'm game."

I couldn't believe I was game, but I was. *Ugh.* Why is life so gray? Black and white would be so much fucking easier.

"She'll be open to it. My daughter loves me," Walter said with all the unearned confidence of an old, White man. "And from what I've seen, she loves you, too."

I smiled slightly at that, because it was at least a step in the right direction. A tiny, small tip-tap of a step—but a step, none-theless.

Chapter Twenty-Five

"Why do you look so happy?" Tyler squinted her eyes at me as she arrived at the bar for the live podcast recording a few hours later.

"It's a big day," I replied, shrugging my shoulders like I didn't know what she was talking about. "We're opening!"

Her smile was slow and guarded, but when it finally spread across her face, it looked genuine. "Didn't think we'd get here, huh?"

"I mean, did you?" Honestly, didn't we all doubt it?

After everything I'd faced to make this place open, there had been more than a few times that I'd thought it was all going to come crashing and burning down.

Tyler shook her head. "No, actually. I mean, the space issue was a curveball, absolutely. But there was never a doubt in my mind that you were going to make KiKi's happen."

"Oh." I found myself absentmindedly combing through a stack of menus. Anything to focus my attention on what wasn't the perfect pool of blue in her eyes, or the sincerity in her tone. "Well, thank you. That, uh, that means a lot to me."

That sentence didn't do justice to the feeling, though. Hearing her confidence and assurance in me was like a warm blanket I wanted to wrap myself in.

She walked away from me then, and I watched from the bar as she began setting up the area of the live podcast recording. I'd already set up the basics—a long table with two chairs facing an audience of chairs. She'd brought with her a table banner with the logo of her podcast on the front to display, as well as the audio equipment. Her producer, Riley, was with her as well, helping with the setup and carrying in all the equipment from the van they'd rented.

"You're staring," Isa said to me in a low whisper as she joined me at the bar. "Jesus, you're giving Sting vibes with your stalker anthem."

"'Every Breath You Take' is a Grammy Award winner, thank you very much." This wasn't even the first argument we'd had about music, nor would it be the last.

She just leveled her gaze at me, and I immediately threw in the towel because she wasn't taking my bullshit.

I tossed my hands up in defense. "Fiiiiine. What do you want from me?"

"To talk to her. Tell her you love her. Tell her you talked to her dad. Tell her you want her babies," Isa said, leaning against the bar top like it was just that easy.

"Whoa, whoa, whoa. No one's talking babies," I reminded her, feeling my skin prickle with fear. But also...excitement? No. That would be weird. Definitely fear. Ish. It's got to be fear. "Get that out of your mind right now."

"Are you talking to me or you?" Isa pointed out. "Because those who smelt it, dealt it."

I rolled my eyes with all the exaggeration I could muster. "Are you comparing our love to farts?"

"Depends how much it stinks," Isa quipped back.

I laughed and shook my head. "Oh, my god. Why do I tolerate you?"

"Because I'm a bomb-ass friend, and you know it."

She wasn't lying. I smiled and squeezed her forearm. "Seriously, though. Thanks for everything you've put into tonight. Making this opening happen. Making this bar happen? I couldn't have done it without you?"

Isa looked away, like she wasn't entirely sure how to accept a genuine compliment. "Well, save the thank you for when you see my bill. It's coming, I promise."

"I'm on the lookout," I said, even though no such invoice had once popped up in my email or postal mail.

She was doing this just for me and our friendship, and neither of us would acknowledge it out loud. But I felt it, and I loved her for it. Shit, I really did. The realization hit me hard, because I'd kept her at arm's length for a lot of my friendship with Mila. Not that Mila got in the way of the two of us—she intentionally tried to do the opposite—but when Mila was around more, we both kind of vied for her attention.

But now it was just her and me, and there was no competition.

Adult friendships are a special form of heartbreak. You meet someone who you think is your soulmate in friend form, but then they move away or they get married or life happens and schedules no longer collide and things drift in a way that feels like grief. Even if it's completely normal and completely okay.

It's still a loss.

But then people like Isa pop in, and it's a realization that they'd been there all along, even if my attention had been somewhere else before. And those are the small moments of healing, of reconnecting. Of allowing yourself to close a chapter that meant a lot to you and focus on the one in front of you.

I looked across the room where Tyler was doing a sound check with Riley on all three microphones we'd be using for the podcast—one each for Tyler, me, and Riley to add commentary between takes.

She was the one in front of me right now. And maybe that has always been my problem. I was always thinking of the next project, the next business, the next girlfriend...how often had I actually stopped and enjoyed the now?

"Are you ready for this?" Isa asked, and I knew her question was deeper than just the live recording.

I swallowed hard, nodding my head. "I think I really might be."

Isa beamed at me. "Love makes me happy. I can see it etched all over your face."

I waited a little while longer to walk over to Tyler until Riley had stepped away to get something from the van. The line of attendees was already forming out front, and everything was set up for the most part. We had two bartenders on site, prepping garnishes and bottles to serve everyone during the recording, and everything had been cleaned thoroughly and decorated. We had a backdrop with the KiKi logo on it that people could take pictures in front of on their way in with a red carpet in front of it and everything—the more posts on social media, the better.

"Hey, do you want to grab a photo together before we open the doors?" I asked Tyler as I got to the recording table.

She looked up at me quickly as if I'd startled her. Her gaze went past me to the front window where she could see the line forming. "We should probably do that, yeah. How do I look?"

I stepped around the table to see her full length, but I already knew my answer. The pink blazer and short skirt she was wearing matched her stiletto heels that had little silver buckles on the front. If she'd told me she was on her way to a

Barbie-themed party, I would have completely believed her. Somehow, she made it work and with her hair pulled back into a sleek Ariana Grande-style ponytail, she looked like she was ready to take over a boardroom and lead a pop star concert all at the same time.

"Incredible, of course," I confirmed. I'd opted for black leather leggings under a white, off-the-shoulder top, and my hair loose around my shoulders which was giving more Bad Sandy in the movie *Grease* vibes. "Should I ask Isa to take our picture? Or Riley?"

Tyler glanced toward the back door that Riley had just exited through. "Riley's still finishing the last of set up, so let's ask Isa."

I reached out a hand toward her, and she only paused slightly before taking it. I wrapped my fingers around hers and led her over to the red carpet area.

"Isa, can you take our photo?" I called out to where Isa was pouring herself a glass of wine at the bar.

"Sure!" She made her way over quickly. "Okay, I'm going to need multiple different poses. Tyler, push your left hip out a bit and step back with your right foot. Yas, angle your body and look at me over your shoulder."

We tried our best to follow her instructions as she snapped away on her iPhone. She even made us take some candid-not-so-candid photos of walking across the red carpet and laughing like we'd just heard the funniest joke of all time. Actually, all I could hear was the sound of the freezer behind the bar whirring slightly and the clatter of glasses the bartenders were polishing.

"That's perfect!" Isa finally called out, scanning through the photos she'd taken on her phone as she began to walk away from us and spoke over her shoulder. "I'm going to AirDrop them to both of you now. But talk to me about captions before you post on social media. We need something catchy and cool, even slightly vague."

"I talked to your dad," I finally whispered to Tyler when Isa was far enough away not to hear us.

Tyler turned abruptly on her heel to look at me. "What?"

"It was illuminating, to say the least," I continued, keeping my voice low so our conversation was private. "I'd really like to talk before the recording on where we stand."

She glanced around the room, then nodded her head. "Can we go to your car?"

"Sure," I agreed. We walked over to the bar where Isa handed me my car keys and then headed out the back door so we wouldn't be seen by the line of attendees out front.

My small sedan was parked next to the adjacent building, and I unlocked it as we both approached from different sides—me climbing in the driver's seat and her in the passenger's seat. I turned the air conditioning on and leaned my seat back enough to allow me to angle my body toward Tyler, as she did the same.

"Can I start?" I asked because I wasn't sure what she was going to say but I knew what I needed to.

She nodded, softly nibbling on her bottom lip.

"I told you about my mother a while ago—how she passed and whatnot," I began.

Tyler nodded again. "You did."

"I was talking to my therapist in my session earlier this week about that, and my therapist asked me if I had the choice to have my mother alive again—even if she didn't approve of my sexuality—would I want her in my life?" I swallowed hard, because I'd been sitting with that for a while. "And I'd honestly never thought of it that way before. I'd never thought of your situation like that. And my answer was yes. Without a doubt, yes. I mean, if she was hateful and trying to hurt me, then maybe I'd reconsider. But the surface question itself was easy. I'd want my mother in my life even if she didn't support me as a lesbian."

Tyler looked down at her hands, fidgeting with the edge of her nails. "Is it because you think you'd change her mind? Or she'd come around?"

"Honestly, yeah. I think it is." That might sound childish or fantastical, but it was a part of my personality and who I was at my core. I wanted to see the best in people, and I wanted to love without barriers. "I think I'd have a hard time giving up hope on my mother, giving up hope on the fact that she might one day love me enough to love all of me."

"And if that day never comes?" Tyler looked away through the windshield now. "Because it's been thirty-five years and my dad isn't any closer to changing his mind. I'm not confident he'll ever get there."

"No," I agreed. "He might not. But you haven't given up hope. Or have you?"

When she turned back to look at me, there were tears brimming her bottom lashes. She slowly shook her head. "I have this theory that children will always love their parents more than parents can love their children. Humans can have as many children as they want, theoretically, but you only get two biological parents and that's it. I don't think I was made to give up on them that easily. I think I love them—both of them—more than they'll ever know how to love me."

I swallowed hard as I thought about what Walter had told me about Tyler continuing to reach out to her mother. "Doesn't it hurt though? Doesn't it hurt to keep reaching out and be rejected over and over and over again?"

"Yeah." Her gaze reached me again, and she rested her hand on the console between us. I lifted my hand to hers and drew small circles down her fingers and across her knuckles.

"It hurts so intensely that it knocks the air out of me sometimes."

I squeezed her fingers and interlaced our hands. "Why do it, then? Why not just choose yourself and cut them out?"

"I guess I don't see it that way," Tyler responded. "I am choosing myself by continuing to call them in. I am choosing every day to say that my love matters more than their hate or indifference. I am choosing to not let who they are and what they believe take away a core piece of who I am—my optimism, my hope, my desire to see good in the world. It would hurt so much more to lose those pieces of who I am than the pain I feel every time they say something hurtful or say nothing at all. My choice isn't right for everyone or every situation, but it is right for me."

Shit, I could feel the tears welling up in me now. "That... that makes a lot of sense. I want to support you in that. I want to welcome your father into our life in whatever way he's comfortable, and I told him that. But most of all, I really just want to be in *your* life, Tyler."

She rubbed her thumb against my palm. "You told me when we first met that this isn't the beginning of a love story."

I cringed, remembering that fight in her kitchen. "I guess sometimes I can be wrong."

"Oh, really?" She was giving me a small smirk now. "What a concept."

This time, I leaned closer to her, resting my elbows on the center console. "Tyler, I am head over heels in love with you and this *isn't* the beginning of a love story, but maybe it can be the end of *our* love story."

Her eyes widened. "Oh my god, please tell me you're not proposing."

"What the hell?" My head snapped back, my eyes wide. "Of course not. Are you insane?"

Tyler grinned, and we both started laughing as we returned toward leaning into one another. We just stared at each other quietly for a moment, not waiting for anything but just feeling the closeness between us.

She pressed her lips softly against mine, barely brushing me.

I kissed her back but didn't push further. "I'm sorry I didn't say it sooner, and I'm sorry it took me so long to accept who you are fully when you've been accepting me since day one."

Tyler kissed me again. "Are you ready to come out as a couple live on air in front of the entire world?"

"Beyond ready," I confirmed, kissing her again, harder this time.

We both stepped out of the car and came back together on the other side, walking hand-in-hand into the bar that we were going to turn into a safe space for our fellow queers and neurospicy friends and chosen family.

She was my safe space, and I would be hers as long as she'd let me.

Epilogue

"I'm not walking down the catwalk naked. Are you serious?" Tyler looked at me like I had two heads.

"Why not?" I shrugged. "We get it on in here all the time. What's the difference?"

"It's just *so* on display on stage..." She glanced around. "What if someone comes in? Or looks in the windows?"

"The shades are drawn, and we're the only people in the building because it's four o'clock in the morning," I countered, since we'd only just finished cleaning up after closing the bar. "Who's going to see us?"

Tyler laughed and surreptitiously looked around us. "Check all the shades again. And that all the doors are locked— back and front. Just to make sure."

"Wait, you're going to do it?" I grinned and then saluted her like an army captain. "Yes, ma'am. I'm on it!"

I'd never made my way around the bar faster than I did then, but every shade was confirmed closed and every door locked. We actually had a break-in through the back door last month and the cash taken out of the register, so I'd since upgraded all the locks and was confident that no one was getting in again.

Only one incident after being open a full year was a success in my book, because KiKi: Cuts and Cocktails had absolutely exploded. If there had ever been a doubt in my mind before, this last year had proved me completely wrong. We were always at capacity Thursdays through Sundays and had steady traffic the rest of the week. We hosted events regularly—everything from political rallies to book signings to friend networking events to celebrations. Even Isa's boyfriend performed here twice a month, and I couldn't be prouder of how much she'd stretched herself in this new relationship. She was like an all-new person, and yet, all the best parts of her old self were still untouched. We were still close, and I'd already told Nia she was going to be my maid-of-honor one day because I didn't want to pick between Mila, Isa, and Rachel.

I'm not a masochist.

My proudest moment so far as a business owner was that we'd hosted our first ever wedding reception last month for two regulars who'd met each other on the evening of our live podcast recording and opening—I know, I couldn't believe they were already married either.

Tyler and I weren't at that step yet, but we were living together. It kind of just felt like we were married already, honestly. Eventually we'd make it official, but with how much had been on both of our plates, wedding planning wasn't at the top of my to-do list. Plus, Tyler had already told me she had a guest list of over three hundred people and a binder of ideas she'd been collecting since she was a little girl. So, I already knew I was going to have to psych myself up for something that extravagant.

Not to mention prep my wallet.

"We're officially locked down," I announced to her loudly

as I returned to the end of the catwalk that separated the bar area from the hair salon even though Tyler was no longer standing there. "No one is attending this show except me."

Her face peeked through the curtains at the end of the walk, and she grinned at me. "You ready?"

I pulled up a chair from a nearby table right to the end of the catwalk and sat down, my knees apart with my elbows leaning on them. "Girl, I have never been more ready for anything in my life."

Music turned on as she disappeared and the lights went dim. Colored spotlights hit the catwalk, and I laughed as her song choice hit me—"Nice and Slow" by Usher. I can't believe I hadn't thought of this earlier, because I was literally on the edge of my seat.

The catwalk had been a huge success at KiKi, both for shows and performances, but also for people wanting to show off new cuts, colors, or makeovers from the salon next door. It had taken about three months after opening to get the salon fully functional and ready to go, but now we regularly served people four hours a day for free, and it was entirely funded by the bar and donations. Not only was I getting a crazy good tax write-off, but we were providing a safe, affirming place for anyone struggling with identity, mental health, or anything else to feel good about themselves and enjoy a little bit of pampering.

But taxes were the farthest thing from my mind when Tyler stepped out onto the catwalk when the beat dropped.

She wasn't completely naked. Instead, she was still wearing her button-up shirt—now completely unbuttoned and giving me just enough of a glimpse of the sides of her breasts to get me excited—and her small skirt was lower on her hips.

"Whoo hoo!" I catcalled her, pumping my fist in the air as she kept walking toward me to the beat of the music.

She paused halfway down and did a little shimmy where she let her shirt slide down her shoulders but still held closed in front of her breasts. A few more steps and she let it drop onto the stage entirely, proudly on display now. Some more hip swinging, and her skirt was sliding down next, and she wasn't wearing any undergarments beneath.

I was literally now on the edge of my seat and leaning forward. "Damn, girl!"

Tyler crouched down when she got to the end of the catwalk and beckoned me over with the crook of one finger.

I was up on my feet and at hers in seconds.

She leaned down and let her lips tease mine before she sat on the edge of the stage and wrapped her arms around my neck.

I stepped into her and we kissed like we were starving. My hands slid down her sides, and I pushed her knees apart wider before I began kissing down her neck to her collarbone.

Tyler groaned as she let her head fall back, and she leaned on her elbows as I worked my way down the rest of her body. The song was crescendoing as I gave her breasts some much-needed attention before I kneeled down in front of her. She gasped when my tongue hit her center, and I didn't stop lapping at her until she was shouting out right along with Usher.

By the time I came up for air, we were several songs into her playlist, and I was pulling her onto her feet. Her eyes were slightly glazed over with a lazy smile on her lips as she fell into my arms. I held her in a tight embrace, and we just stayed like that for a moment.

"Let's go home," she finally whispered in my ear, "so we can continue this in bed."

I grinned and placed a kiss on her cheek before she gathered up her clothes and pulled them back on. "Thank you for my strip show."

"Anything for you." She grinned, interlacing her fingers with mine once she was clothed.

I turned off the music and lights, and we headed home together—tonight and every night after.

Interested in reading more in this universe?

The next book DOPPEL BANGER is coming soon!

Check out www.booksbysarahrobinson.com.

Short Story: Waxing Poetic

Demetrius Kiani's Story

This standalone short story was featured in Color Theory 3: Let Love Live, an interracial romance charity anthology, and is being included as a courtesy in the print edition of this book only.

Synopsis

Demetrius Kiani is the stereotypical middle child and tends to find himself going along to get along in most situations—lead the family business, always say yes to his friends' latest schemes, the usual people-pleaser habits—but that tendency puts him in a very hair-pulling (literally) situation when confronted with newly romantic feelings for his non-binary long time best friend and esthetician-in-training, Nicole Flores.

An interracial, queer, short spin-off set in the universe of the Queerly Devoted series by Sarah Robinson.

Chapter One

"It makes absolutely no sense," Nicole said to me as they pointed at the large-screen flat television mounted to the far wall of my living room, their Bolivian accent sharp with their frustration. "They're not even trying to make movies that are believable anymore."

Their legs were sprawled across my lap and a large bowl of mostly eaten popcorn was wedged between us and the back couch cushions.

"It's a rom-com," I replied, referring to the Netflix movie we'd just watched about two dimwitted friends who didn't realize that they were actually soulmates until they accidentally fell head over heels in love—you know, the usual plot line. "They're not supposed to be realistic. Plus, you picked it. The next movie we watch is going to have guns, explosives, and at least one eye patch."

"Oh, because those are *so* realistic. Can you imagine the financial devastation the property damage would cause a city in one of those movies?" Nicole laughed and dropped their head back onto one of the throw pillows that they'd bought for my couch last Christmas in an effort to make my apartment look less "bro-ey bachelor," as they often called it. Nicole wasn't frilly or feminine; in fact, they were non-binary and used they/them/their pronouns, but they still had a lot of opinions on my taste in decor—or lack thereof. "I like action movies, too, but none of your other friends are going to make you expand your horizons, and you can't just watch one genre for the rest of your life."

I patted their shin and then gently pushed their legs off me so I could stand up. "I mean, I could, and probably be pretty happy about it."

Nicole and I had met about five years ago at a happy hour for singles in our area, but we'd somehow skipped dating and landed right in the friend zone. I'm not even sure how it happened or why we never went out on a date, but the friendship piece came so easily that they were suddenly part of my life and my family. Soon Nicole was my plus one at weddings and family functions, and no one even questioned why we weren't actually dating because they were so charismatic that everyone just loved having them around.

It had actually become a saving grace in a lot of unexpected ways. When you have a female-presenting, non-binary best friend that everyone immediately adores, they stop asking you when you're going to meet someone and settle down, or giving you blank *plus ones* to events. It's just assumed that if inviting Demetrius, Nicole's coming too, and everyone feels too awkward to ask anything deeper than that.

And honestly, I'm perfectly fine with that.

Nicole watched me as I stood and stretched. "Can you grab me some water while you're up?"

"Sure." I headed for the arched doorway that connected my living room and kitchen—which was surprisingly large for a bachelor pad. If there's one thing my mom had insisted on when I was growing up, it was that I knew how to cook. To this day, I'm still the only one in my group of friends who can do more than pour a bowl of cereal or slap together a sandwich—well, aside from Nicole, that is. They could cook the hell out of any Latin recipe that I, or anyone else, threw at them.

I grabbed a glass from the cupboard and stuck it under the waterspout on the front of the refrigerator, filling it for them. Before walking back, I scanned the inside of the pantry cabinets for something sweet, but nothing stood out to me.

"What if we order in from that new cookie shop you mentioned?" I suggested as I walked back into the living room and handed them the glass of water.

"Captain Cookie and the Milkman?" they asked.

I tried not to snort out a laugh, but honestly, the names that the young hipsters down in Clarendon came up with were getting more and more ridiculous.

"I've been wanting to try them, but I don't want to pay for delivery when it's so close," they mused then polished off half of the water in a few quick gulps. "Let's walk. I need to get my steps in."

"Fine by me." I switched off the television and slipped on my sneakers by the front door, then I grabbed my keys and wallet out of the bowl on a side table. "Ready?"

I glanced back at Nicole where they were putting on their shoes as I opened the front door.

"Almost," Nicole replied, but when their eyes lifted to mine, they traveled past me, and the flicker of a smirk lifted one corner of their lips. "But, uh, you have company."

I turned back around to see my ex-girlfriend standing in my doorway, her hand raised as if she was about to knock on the front door.

"Rhi?" I was both surprised to see her...and not. "What are you doing here?"

Rhiannon dropped her hand to her side, then pulled tighter at the belt around her waist, cinching her coat closed. It was pretty warm outside to be wearing a coat, but it was also pretty late in the evening to be showing up unannounced so I had a few guesses as to what her motivation might have been.

"Hey, Rhi!" Nicole was suddenly chipper and peppy, and I knew immediately things were about to go south for me. "It's so nice to see you again."

"Uh…" Rhiannon didn't look so sure, glancing between the two of us. "Sorry to interrupt. I thought you'd be alone."

"No interruption at all," Nicole assured her, now stepping past me and linking their arm around Rhiannon's to pull her farther into the apartment hallway. "Come with us! We're headed down the street to get some cookies. Have you tried Captain Cookie and the Milkman yet?"

Rhiannon looked over her shoulder at me, and her expression reminded me of someone being held hostage. I could relate.

"Uh, I haven't tried it yet," she mumbled. "But, you know… I don't need to go."

"Nonsense," Nicole replied, grinning wickedly at me now as we waited for the elevator to come take us down to the lobby. "Demetrius doesn't mind. Right, D?"

I plastered on a smile. "Uh, sure. The more, the merrier."

Rhiannon's eyes had that bewildered deer-in-headlights look as she pulled down on the sides of her coat, trying to cover more of her bare legs. *Is she naked under that?* I tried not to think about it so I wouldn't have any sort of physically obvious reaction to the thought. Instead, I cast an apologetic glance in her direction, but she still simmered with a low-grade anger underneath her flat smile.

"So, you two are still, uh, still hanging out, huh?" Rhiannon asked as the three of us stepped on to the elevator.

Nicole leaned against my arm and patted me affectionately on the chest. "We just don't seem to get sick of each other, do we, D?"

"I wouldn't go that far," I joked, but my skin seemed to heat more and more with every floor we passed on the elevator ride down.

Nicole had long been a source of tension in most of my romantic relationships—including Rhiannon. I understood where they were coming from most of the time, because, hell, I'd feel territorial and jealous too if the shoe were on the other foot. Nicole was drop dead gorgeous, and there were few people—male or female—that didn't find them stunning to look at. But Nicole and I had only always been friends.

Don't get me wrong, I'd considered more than that many times. I mean, how could I not? Nicole was fiery and always kept me on my toes. Of course I'd love to date someone like them, but more than that, I loved being friends with them. My romantic history didn't have the best track record, and I wasn't about to jeopardize losing them from my life entirely if they became just another failed romance. Not to mention, I wasn't sure what that meant for me or my sexuality if we were to date since I identify as straight and have always been attracted to women only. Nicole really tested that boundary for me though, and I was beginning to wonder if gender wasn't more fluid than I had once thought.

Christ, I sounded like that rom-com we'd just watched.

"Doesn't your sister live around here now, D?" Rhiannon asked a few blocks later as we approached the cookie shop. Thank God someone had broken the awkward silence that had been looming over the three of us for the last ten minutes. "I thought I saw her post on Instagram that she'd just moved."

Nicole decided to step in and answer that one for me. "No,

Yasmeen is a bit farther south of here near the Columbia Pike area. She's opening her own bar—did you see that?"

"I've been meaning to go," Rhiannon said, though I could easily detect the insincerity in her voice as I opened the door to the cookie shop for them both. My sister is protective of our family and when I've been in new relationships, she's always put the person through the wringer. Rhiannon had been no exception to that.

"You should definitely check it out some time," I encouraged, feeling that familiar stir of pride for all my younger sister had accomplished. It had been quite a journey for her over the last few years, and Black female owned businesses were far and few between here, but she'd come out on top like I always knew she would. "Yasmeen has done an incredible job."

"She asked me to be a bridesperson in her wedding party, too," Nicole added as we approached the counter.

Rhiannon's face fell for just a split second before she quickly composed herself. She tugged on the bottom of her jacket again. "Oh, I didn't realize she was getting married."

"Next spring, yep," Nicole added, before turning to the cashier and placing their order.

We all separately ordered, and I couldn't help but feel like a dick for not paying for either of them, but it wasn't a date. Picking up the tab for all of us felt weirdly intimate, and I wasn't trying to go there right now with either of them.

Well, not with Rhiannon at least.

Christ, this *was* awkward.

Nicole ushered all of us to a small wrought iron cafe table outside in the courthouse pavilion once we'd grabbed our orders from the counter. Nicole and Rhi sat on opposite sides of a cafe table, and I pulled a third chair over from a nearby table to sit between them.

"So, what have you been up to lately, Nicole?" Rhi was

halfway through her lemon poppyseed flavored cookie before she broke the tense silence at the table. At this point, we'd spent more time as a trio in awkward quietness than actually talking.

Nicole swallowed the piece of ginger molasses cookie they had. "I'm working on my cosmetology hours right now. I need more experiencing in waxing, so I'm doing this part-time apprenticeship at Kim's Bare Limbs in Cherrydale—she's the best waxer in town."

"She's who everyone at my Soul Cycle goes to," Rhi agreed with a nod. "How's it been going?"

"It's okay," Nicole replied as I kept my eyes glued to the rainbow sprinkle Funfetti cookie—don't judge me—I had almost devoured in an attempt to keep my mouth full to avoid conversing. "It's a very homogenous clientele, though. Like, I could strip the hair from a rich white woman's asshole with my eyes closed at this point."

I almost choked on the bite I was swallowing. "What?"

Nicole shrugged like it was nothing. "I really need more experience with other skin types and genders. I've only had one male client so far, and he was already pretty hairless naturally."

"From what I remember, Demetrius is hairy," Rhiannon offered. A small smirk lifted one corner of her lips as she leveled her gaze at me. "Why don't you practice on him? I mean, you guys are *best* friends after all."

The emphasis she put on her words was downright hostile.

Nicole was looking at me now, and the lightbulb in their eyes was terrifying. "Oh my gosh, that is *such* a good idea!"

I've made a mistake in bringing these two together, clearly.

"What?" I pushed back in my seat, the chair scraping the stone a few inches. "That is the worst idea I've heard today. And I am *not* that hairy."

Rhiannon shrugged but her smile only got wider to fit more of her evil idea inside. "I mean, manscaping is all the trend lately, D. Plus, you'd also be giving your friend experience on Black skin, which clearly they are lacking in the sea of Caucasian buttholes."

"That's a very good point," Nicole agreed, nodding along like they'd found their new best friend in my ex. "There are so many Caucasian buttholes, Demetrius. Just so many. I'd have Kim help me, if you're worried. She's an expert!"

"Oh, yeah, because that was my concern—not having enough people ripping the hair off my balls." I pushed up out of my chair. "I'm going to get a six-pack of cookies to go before you two team up on me to paint my nails next."

"We're not done talking about this!" Nicole called out after me. "You need to learn to be more open to things outside of the norm! I'm texting Kim now!"

That's it. I need more male friends in my life.

Chapter Two

I've never allowed someone with a strip of hot wax to be this close to my balls before. But here I am, knees spread wide to either side as someone I am *just friends* with— although that might be called into question after today—stands over me with a flat wooden stick in their hand and the devil in their eyes.

"Wait, hold on," I started, suddenly getting cold feet. Or cold balls—actually more like rescinded balls, because I swear, they were trying to climb right back up inside me to save themselves. "I don't know about this..."

Nicole's eyes moved north from my turtling ball sac to my face. "Demetrius, we haven't even started yet," they reminded me, one corner of their lips lifting into a devious grin. "And you agreed to this. I need the practice, remember?"

They knew exactly what they were doing. There wasn't a lot I'd say no to when it came to Nicole, and after they and Rhiannon had waxed poetic about how friends help each other...it had been basically impossible to say no.

And now I was here in a valley of regret.

I shifted my body, trying to find a more comfortable position. "Right, but that looks really hot," I replied, eyeing the wooden stick in their hand dipped in hard, hot wax. "How many times have you practiced this before on a man?"

Their dark brown eyes darted away from me, avoiding contact. "Uh, well you know, it's hard to get people to agree when you're new in general, and then men are even harder with machismo bullshit and all that. That's why I'm so grateful to you. You're really doing me a *huge* favor here."

Their emphasis on the word *huge* was not lost on me, and I was grateful for their generosity in this moment of fear-induced shrinkage.

The instructor, Kim, was standing next to Nicole and nodding her head. She was probably only ten to fifteen years older than Nicole, but the exhaustion etched into her face made her look much older. "It really is a *big* favor. I've never seen a boyfriend agree to do this for a partner before."

"He's not my boyfriend," Nicole informed Kim way too quickly for my liking. "We're friends."

Kim's eyes widened and she glanced at me with what can only be described as a guilty expression. "Oh. Okay. Hey, um... Demetrius, you signed the waiver up front, right?"

I nodded, deeply regretting that decision now because despite how many times in the past I'd had this fantasy of them both standing over me naked, I had never been more flaccid now.

"You ready?" Nicole asked, their accent trailing across their words in a rumble that could have convinced me to do anything and clearly had. Good freaking Lord. Hard to convince myself after this that I only saw Nicole as a friend because I sure as shit would not be doing this for any of my other friends.

I nodded slowly, focusing my eyes on the ceiling tiles as hard as I could. "All right. Just one strip."

"We'll see," they teased, and got to work.

What the hell did I just get myself into...and why?

The first strip went on smoothly and the heat of the wax wasn't too terrible—neither was their hand rubbing across the wax strip to push it on harder.

"Are you ready?" Nicole asked from somewhere near my ball sac.

I kept my eyes glued to the ceiling, and my voice was suddenly catching in my throat. "Go for it," I croaked.

The room was silent for what felt like an eternity as I waited for the sting, but it didn't come. I turned my gaze away from the ceiling and looked down at them. "Are you going to—"

Nicole's hand yanked the strip away from my body with a ferocity that could not have been human. This was feral. Straight feral.

I opened my mouth to scream, but no sound came out. My vocal cords must have been attached to those specific pubes because I was mute now.

They quickly rubbed their hand against the bare skin, which actually did make it feel the tiniest iota better. "That wasn't so bad, right?"

Kim chuckled. "I'm not sure he'd agree with you."

My voice croaked out of me like I had betrayed it. "Thank you, Kim. Always so helpful, Kim. KEEP ENCOURAGING THEM, KIM."

My tone only hardened and escalated with every repetition of her name.

"Oh, he's getting mad. You should hurry up before he changes his mind," Kim advised as Nicole slathered on the next patch of wax and placed a sheet on top.

"Do you need a countdown each time or should I just go for it?" Nicole asked.

"Just do it." I gritted my teeth and the next two went by just as painfully.

And if that's all it had been, then maybe I could have handled it. Maybe I could have been like, okay this wasn't great, but it's done and here we are. But then they asked the next question.

"Are you okay with me stretching your balls?"

My head popped up so quickly, I almost had whiplash. "What?"

"They need to stretch your balls," Kim clarified, but that wasn't any more helpful. "There's a lot of little hairs on the ball sac that you can't see without pulling the skin taut. Otherwise, it's just too wrinkly."

Did she just call my balls wrinkly? I blinked twice and then put my head back down on the table. "I...I guess I've already gone this far."

"Great!" Nicole's hands were now on my actual balls—stretching them down.

It didn't hurt, and honestly...it didn't even feel bad. I almost kind of liked it until what could only be a pair of tweezers grabbed a single hair and ripped it from my loins.

"Ah!" I shouted and bucked up off the table. "What the hell!"

"Some of the smaller hairs won't come up with the wax," Kim said as she put a hand on my leg and tried to rub comfortingly. It wasn't comforting. "So, we tweeze them."

"Was I told that?" I nearly panted out my question in between heat waves of pain as Nicole kept their face buried somewhere close to my now-burning balls. "Tweezers?"

Nicole popped up and looked at me with a confused look.

"Okay, well let's switch to the strip for right now if you want to start there."

They slathered on wax and applied the strip before I could protest. When I'd thought the wax strips on my inner thighs or that fat pocket above my dick that never went away despite how often I worked out was painful, no...no, it was not even remotely painful compared to this.

A hot wax strip yanked from my ball sac is probably the same level of pain as used in torture scenarios during war crime investigations.

"Ahhh!" My screams echoed off the walls and hit me like a tidal wave.

Nicole's hand was pressed down on the skin immediately but that only offered brief relief. "Sorry. I know it's uncomfortable."

"Uncomfortable?" I panted out the word as sweat broke across my forehead. "I think I'm dying."

Kim laughed, and she must have thought I was joking but rest assured, I was not. "It's never very fun, but you'll love what it looks like after. Smooth as a baby's bottom."

Please don't compare my balls to a baby's ass. I just let out a puff of air, trying to psych myself up for the next strip.

"You'd be surprised how many men get erections during this," Kim continued as Nicole was continuing.

"How?" I asked, more in a strangled cat type of way than in actual curiosity. "How could anyone get hard during this? This fucking hurts."

Nicole was the one laughing now. "You never got a little thrill out of a little discomfort or pain? Or power differential? I'm like a dominatrix right now."

"A dominatrix gets paid. You're doing this for free," I reminded them, my voice cutting off with a groan at the end as the next piece of my balls was yanked hair-free. "Shit! Am I bleeding? I swear to God I feel like I'm bleeding."

"You're not bleeding," Kim assured me, and her maternal tone actually did border on comforting for a moment there. "Actually, Nicole is doing a really fabulous job. It's looking wonderful down there."

Should I take that as a compliment?

Kim went on to give Nicole some more instructions about specifically tailoring their work to Black male hair follicles and now both of their hands were on my balls, but this time lifting them to get underneath. Seriously, I can't believe I agreed to this.

A few more hair-wrenching strips and deranged Tweezer pulls later, Nicole was powdering the area and giving me a run-down of what to expect over the next day or so and how to be careful of irritating the skin more. Then both Nicole and Kim left the room, and I could hear them comparing notes in the hallway, including one where Kim was remarking on my ball size. *Good lord almighty.* I deserved several drinks after this entire situation.

I hobbled off the table slowly and put the bottom half of my clothes back on carefully, trying to not touch the afflicted area much. Surprisingly, though, it wasn't too bad. A little sore, but not excruciating. I finished putting on the rest of my clothes before stretching and joining them out in the lobby of Kim's salon.

"How are you feeling?" Kim asked as I entered the well-lit room that faced the strip mall parking lot where we were located. "It's good, right?"

I wiggled my hips a little, trying to adjust myself in my boxer briefs. "I feel cold."

Nicole's brows lifted. "Cold?"

"Yeah, it's like...bare." I glanced down at my pants and then back at them. "Everything feels heightened and colder."

It really was a very odd feeling. I'm not saying I hated it though.

Nicole grinned and shook their head. "I owe you a drink. Let's go."

"You owe me *many* drinks," I corrected them, because I was about to run up their bar tab like a professional.

Chapter Three

When we arrived at BARtanical—a plant-themed pop-up bar that Nicole insisted we had to try—there was already a huge crowd of people blocking the bar.

"Maybe we should try somewhere else," I commented. "This place is packed, and I guarantee you their cocktails are like fifteen dollars just for having grass in it or something."

Nicole shot me a look then rolled their eyes. "Artisan cocktail making is a craft, D. You have to appreciate the artistry. Plus, I'm paying for it."

I couldn't argue with that last part.

I hung back for a minute, looking around the space and trying to scope out a place for us to sit as Nicole went up to the bar to order our drinks. It had to have been less than three minutes, but by the time I'd found an open seating area and turned back to look for Nicole, there was already a man up in their personal space trying to hit on them. Brown sandals, a Vineyard Vines shirt, and Madras shorts told me all I needed to know about the future Hill staffer burnout who'd probably be back on a flight to his hometown in the Midwest before the next election cycle.

"Demetrius!" Nicole waved me over and the panicked look they were giving me made my body tense as I immediately understood the assignment. "Over here!"

"Hey." I intentionally dropped my voice an octave as I walked up to them and slid my arm across their shoulders, pulling them tighter into my side as I kissed the top of their head. "Sorry I'm late, baby."

The pale prep boy next to them was immediately sizing me up. "*This* is your boyfriend?"

I lifted one brow and cleared my throat. "Thanks for keeping my favorite person company, but you're welcome to leave now."

Nicole just gave him an apologetic grin that I didn't buy for a second. "Sorry. I told you I was with someone."

He finally got the hint and slinked away with his tail between his legs. As soon as he did, Nicole stepped away from me, letting my arm fall to my side. I immediately wished they hadn't.

Where the hell did that thought come from? I tried to shake it off.

"I swear to God, some men are so aggressive, D. Like why isn't *I'm not interested* enough? No, instead I have to prove I'm already spoken for." Nicole shook their head. "As if that's the only reason I'm allowed to not want him, just because I have boobs and a vagina."

"Goddamn patriarchy," I replied, because this certainly hadn't been the first time they'd had me step in to ward off someone skeevy at a bar. "Did you order our drinks yet?"

They nodded and pointed toward a bartender, who was

currently sticking sprigs of herbs into tall cocktail glasses before handing them to us. "You're going to love it."

I took one, but I was not convinced. Lifting the edge of the glass to my nose, I smelled the heavy scent of herbal fragrance and when I took a sip, I nearly choked on the intense amount of alcohol permeating the drink. "This is strong."

Nicole took a long sip through their straw. "It's good though, right?"

"It's not horrible," I conceded, but that was the most they were going to get out of me. I led her over to the free seats I'd seen earlier, and we got settled in. Someone dropped off a menu and I perused the food items but didn't see anything I immediately wanted.

"Nicole?"

A man's voice caused both Nicole and me to lift our heads and look in his direction. It wasn't the same man from the bar. Instead, the guy in front of us was wearing a suit, but the jacket was draped over his arm and his cuffs were rolled up like he'd just gotten off a long day.

"Jeremy?" Nicole's eyes lit up as they sat up taller in their seat. "Oh my gosh, how are you?"

A smile split his face and, goddamn it, even I had to admit the man was a looker. Something about the way he smiled was mesmerizing, and I couldn't look away even as Nicole hopped up out of their seat and threw their arms around his neck. I tried to ignore the bristling sensation on my skin as I watched his arm slide around their back.

"It's been forever," Jeremy said, finally pulling away just long enough to look Nicole in the eyes, his arms still around their waist. "You look incredible as always."

Nicole's cheeks darkened, and holy hell, were they blushing? Nicole was always calm, cool, and collected and I'd never seen them go mushy over a guy before. Something about it happening now was really pissing me off, but I couldn't pinpoint exactly why.

"Uh, hum." I cleared my throat loudly to get the attention of them both.

Nicole glanced back at me as if they just realized I was there—and seemed inconvenienced by it. "Uh, Demetrius, this is Jeremy. Jeremy, meet my friend Demetrius."

Friend. Okay, I wasn't liking any of this. *What the hell is going on with me right now?*

Jeremy barely looked at me before returning his gaze to Nicole. "Nice to meet you, Demetrius."

"Do you want to come sit with us? We have to catch up." Nicole was already pushing my shoulder so that I'd move down the bench to give him a spot. "There's plenty of room."

"Yeah, pull up a chair, Jer. Let's catch up." I motioned for him, the disdain in my voice certainly not escaping him. I tried to ignore the discomfort in my boxer briefs as I slid my recently bared ass down a seat.

Jeremy eyed me a moment longer than he had before, sizing me up and down. He then pointed to each of our cocktails. "Are those good? I can get the next round."

Of course he could.

"Delicious," Nicole confirmed, taking another sip. "Do you want to try some of mine?"

They pushed their glass toward him and batted their lashes just a little too intently at him for my taste.

"Sure." Jeremy reached for Nicole's glass, and I didn't miss the way his arm brushed against their arm as he did.

"Actually, you don't want to drink that." I reached forward and grabbed Nicole's glass before he could. "Nicole's got a nasty cold sore. Amazing what makeup can hide, right?" I motioned to the server walking by and quickly ordered another cocktail just for him, asking him to close out Nicole's tab at the bar and open one with my card. "I've got you covered, Jeremy."

Something sharp hit my shin and I jolted, quickly finding Nicole giving me a death stare.

"Funny story, Jer. Can I call you Jer?" I continued, because honestly nothing could stop me right now and I had no idea why I was acting manic.

"I prefer Jeremy," he replied.

I nodded as if that was obvious. "Of course you do, Jer."

The waiter was back almost a little too quickly with the cocktail for Jeremy and a black checkbook from the bar. "Uh, ma'am. Here's your tab from the bar. We tried to run the card you had on file, but it was declined."

I bristled immediately at the use of the word *ma'am* which I knew was going to bug Nicole later once they processed everything else the waiter was saying.

Nicole's face went beet red as they took the checkbook. "Oh. Uh, thanks for letting me know. Sorry about that. Let me get a different card."

"I can get that," Jeremy quickly offered, leaning in to take the checkbook.

I beat him to the punch and swiped it, sliding my card inside and handing it back to the waiter. "Here you go."

Nicole looked mortified and for a second I wondered if I'd gone too far. "I don't know why it got declined. I just got paid so I know there is money in there."

I immediately wanted to provide comfort. "Check your banking app on your phone. I'm sure it's just a glitch."

Nicole was holding their phone in their hand already, a frown pulling down on either corner of their lips. "It's frozen."

"Your phone is?" Jeremy asked.

They shook their head, and the bottom lash line of their eyes looked like it was beginning to brim with tears. "No, my bank account. It says I emptied out everything at an ATM in Columbia Heights earlier today."

"Let me see that." I took the phone from them and began scouring through the transactions.

This was exactly my area of skill being part of a security organization. In fact, my father had founded Kiani Security before I was born and had grown it into one of the biggest and most profitable security firms in the metro area. We now covered everything from physical security to cyber security, and were ranked as one of the top Black-owned businesses on the East Coast. I'd spent my summers working for him when I was in high school and college, but after I graduated and proved myself doing a few years of grunt work, he had brought me on as a Vice President of Operations. I'd been handling the day-to-day happenings since, which allowed my father to focus more on the research and development side of the business.

"I think you've had your identity stolen." I pulled out my cell phone and began typing out some quick messages to teammates. "I'm going to get someone on this right away."

"Between the cold sore and identity theft, it sounds like you guys have a lot going on right now." Jeremy ran a hand across the back of his neck then stood up. "I'm just going to pop into the bathroom for a second."

I've never seen a man shuffle walk out of a place so fast in my life.

"I think your boy is going the wrong way. The bathrooms are to the left." I pointed toward Jeremy's retreating back. *How odd.* "Should I tell him?"

Nicole's expression was frazzled at best. "He's definitely not coming back. He's already ghosted me once when I told him I wanted a commitment last year."

"He really doesn't like to stick around for the hard stuff, does he?" Jer was a real disappointment for the male species, but I was also grateful that he was gone along with the love-struck look that had been plastered on Nicole's face a few moments before. "You're better off without him, Nic."

Why did I feel like a dick right then? I mean, Jer *was* shitty. Clearly. But also...I wasn't blameless in this interaction either. I hated how easily the threatened alpha male part of me could be triggered, and I knew from previous lectures from Nicole that they wanted nothing to do with toxic masculinity.

"You always do that when I'm talking to guys." Nicole shook their head but had already returned to looking at their phone screen.

"Do what?" I shrugged innocently, like I had no idea what they were talking about. I didn't honestly have an answer for her question anyway, but probably best not to open that can of worms right here and now.

They placed their phone down on the table with a loud sigh. "First, I'm going to be single forever, and now, I'm completely broke."

"To be fair, you were pretty broke before someone stole your identity, too," I teased, trying to pull a smile out of them.

I was met with an angry glare instead. "That does not make me feel better."

A protective instinct burned hotter in my gut as I took in the anguish in their expression. The last thing I ever wanted to see was them upset, and despite the fact that they were supposed to be the one who owed me right now for letting them wax my balls, all I wanted was to do more.

I placed my hand on their knee and gave a comforting squeeze. "We're going to fix this, okay? I've already got my team looking into it."

They nodded slowly, and I could tell they were refusing to allow tears to fall despite how close they were to doing so. "Can

I stay at your place tonight? This whole thing feels so...violating. Like what if they have my address?"

"Of course," I agreed immediately. "That's probably a good idea until we figure this out."

I wasn't ready to let them be alone either.

Chapter Four

"It doesn't look like all bad news," I began as I plopped down on my couch next to Nicole.

They were already burritoed into two of the throw blankets that they'd bought for the back of my couch as decor—I had no idea blankets even could be decor, but here we were.

"What do you mean?" Their gaze perked up and swung over to me. "Did they find out who it was?"

I shook my head. "That will probably take some time, but everything has been frozen for now and the credit bureaus have been alerted. No further damage can be done at this point."

"No *further* damage," they repeated my words with a tone of frustration. "That still means I'm out everything in my checking account."

"And, uh..." My words trailed off for a moment as I considered how to break the rest of the news to them. "Your savings account was also emptied."

They sat up straight suddenly, the blankets falling to their waist. "Please tell me you're joking. D, say right now that you're joking."

"I wish I was." God, I hated seeing them like this. I was doing everything I could on my end to unravel this nightmare they were experiencing, but even I couldn't make her money come back from the black hole it had vanished into. "You can stay here as long as you want, though, and if you need help making bills meet over the next few weeks or months or whatever, I'm your man."

Nicole frowned slightly, and I immediately felt like I'd said something wrong. "I'm not taking your charity, Demetrius."

"Why? Or why not? It's not like this situation is on you, or something you did," I reminded them. "You're a victim right now. You need help."

Nicole's eyes flared like I'd just slapped them. "I am *not* a victim. Yeah, obviously I didn't cause this or want this, but nobody makes me a victim."

The intensity in their tone took me by surprise. "It's not a bad thing, Nic. Life happens. Shit happens. It's okay to ask for help."

"This isn't the same thing as asking to wax your balls," Nic shot back. "We're talking about my entire ability to provide for myself and be independent. I don't need some man sweeping in and saving me from...from what? We don't even know what's happening right now. It would be stupid to jump to conclusions. Maybe it's just a mistake with the bank and on Monday morning, it'll all be back in my account. Completely solved."

I scooted a few inches closer to them on the couch. "Nicole, it's not a banking mistake. I've had my agents speak with the bank, with your account representative. There's video footage of someone at an ATM withdrawing your money with a duplicated version of your debit card."

Their face paled slightly, but then they set their mouth in a thin line. "How is that even possible? My debit card is on me at all times. It's in my wallet right now—I already checked."

"That doesn't matter." I leaned a bit closer and slung my arm across the back of the couch behind their shoulders. "There are shitty people out there who know how to clone that shit or steal your card numbers and replicate it. It's not impossible. It takes skill, and it's not something that the average pickpocket thief could do, but it's still possible. I'll get you an RFID blocking wallet going forward to be safe."

Their lip quivered, and I saw their eyes darken as they turned away from me. "So, you're saying that someone targeted me."

I waited a beat before I responded. "It's looking that way."

Nicole curled into my side, pushing away the blankets that were taking up space between us. "This is so fucked up, D. It's not like I'm out there rolling in it. Who targets an average Joe? That's just...that's just cold."

A sigh escaped my lips as I let my arm drop down around their shoulders. "Unfortunately, that's the most common type of scam out there. It's a lot harder to steal from the rich and famous, so thieves are often targeting low-hanging fruit."

A sharp elbow dug into my ribs. "Did you just call me low-hanging fruit?"

"But, like, really nice-looking fruit," I offered, laughing now and edging away from the sharpness of their elbow. "Christ, your elbows are sharp. I think you cracked my rib."

"I did not," they insisted, leaning away to look at me. A pause fell between us for a moment as Nicole's eyes dipped down to my mouth, then returned. Their tongue slid across their bottom lip and then they cleared their throat. "I'm sorry, Demetrius. All of this is totally unfair to you. It's not your job to take care of me."

"I'm not taking care of you, Nicole." Something about the way they'd said that didn't sit right with me. "You've done everything for yourself your entire life, and it's...it sucks, honestly."

Their eyes lifted to mine again. "It's not the end of the world."

Bullshit. I was calling absolute bullshit. My family history had its issues—for example, my mother passed away during childbirth with my younger sister. Being raised by only a father and having two sisters certainly shaped me to be a specific version of myself—one that I was proud of. But Nicole? I knew their back story. Nicole's parents had stopped speaking to them after learning that Nicole identified as non-binary right before their fifteenth birthday when Nicole had refused to wear a dress at their Quinceañera. The moment Nicole turned eighteen, their parents had sent them on their way and never checked in again. The term non-binary itself can mean a lot of different things as I'd learned since getting to know Nicole, but for Nicole it simply meant the absence of any gender identity at all. They didn't feel akin to male or female or any other type of gender identity. They just felt like...Nicole Flores.

And I really liked Nicole Flores just as Nicole Flores.

My younger self might not have been as open, but between Nicole and my sister Yasmeen being a prominent lesbian in Northern Virginia who owns a lesbian queer bar, I'd been more than a little exposed to a diversity I hadn't allowed myself to experience before. That also included asking myself some hard questions about who I am, and who I want to be perceived as. I wouldn't say I have those answers entirely yet, but I'm working on it.

Watching the way Nicole had battled familial hardship and gender discrimination was something that stuck with me and pushed me to explore for myself.

"I didn't say it was the end of the world, but it was the beginning of the rest of yours." I turned my body just enough to be partially facing them. "I'm not trying to sweep in and rescue you. You don't need that, and you've spent your entire life proving exactly that."

A shadow of hurt passed across Nicole's expression at my words, like the memories of their own past were coming back to haunt them in that moment. "When you say it like that, I sound like some sort of freakish loner."

"Not even remotely," I continued. "I'm just saying that no one sees you as some sort of easy target, Nic. I know that this might feel that way—and we're going to find whoever the asshole is that did this—but you're still one of the strongest and most impenetrable people that I know."

"Impenetrable?" Their brows furrowed as they looked at me. "What do you mean?"

I paused for a moment to think about what I meant, but whatever I was saying, I wanted it to be positive. Hell, I saw it as positive. Nicole was a fierce entity to tangle with and despite how close we were, there was no doubt that they lived their life in a silo. "I just mean, you're your own person. You don't need anyone else, you know? You just...you're Nicole. You're like an island in this insane fucking ocean of people and drama in D.C. You're a league of your own."

The expression on their face could only be described as crestfallen. Nicole shook their head emphatically and then stood up from the couch, immediately turned around and saddled my lap—one knee on either side of my thighs on the couch.

I leaned back and placed my hands on Nicole's waist, unsure what else to do or how to react. Hell, I was unsure how we'd gotten in this position to begin with—not that I was complaining.

"I don't want to be an island, Demetrius." Their voice was throaty and desperate and sexy and sad, and when Nicole's mouth pressed against mine, I didn't know how to do anything else except bask in their embrace.

Soft kisses exchanged between us as I welcomed them into my space and my hands slid up their back, pulling them closer to me. A groan left Nicole's lips and I felt my core ignite at the rumbling of their vibrato against my skin.

"Is this too much?" Nicole's words whispered against my mouth, but they didn't pull away and they didn't stop, and I didn't want them to.

I could barely find my voice in that moment, but when I did it was barely above a whisper. "Absolutely not." I sat up straighter and pulled their chest against mine, trying to remove any gap or hesitation between us. "It's not close enough, actually."

I don't know where that admission came from, but it was out there and Nicole's response was everything I could have hoped for—and everything I hadn't even known I was hoping for. My validation seemed to charge the air between us, and electricity sizzled like we were plugged into one another...and in every way, it felt like we were.

Their fingers gently slid down one side of my face, and we took a moment to just stare into the other's eyes—as if daring one of us to blink and stop all of this before it starts.

But this had already started.

"Should we go to your room?" Nicole asked, a breathless-ness to their request.

Holy f-bomb, yes. Yes, we should absolutely do that.

I nodded furtively because words had dried up in my throat and speaking was the very last thing I could handle in that moment.

Nicole's lips returned to mine, and I tightened my grip on their waist as I lifted us both off the couch. I could feel their thighs clenching against me so as to not fall, but there was no worry about that. I wasn't going to let go even if the entire world imploded in that moment.

When we reached the bedroom, I waited until I felt my knees hit the side of the mattress before slowly lowering Nicole to the top of the bedspread. Again, a fucking bedspread that they had bought me because apparently seeping with just a bottom sheet and that light blanket I'd stolen from a Holiday Inn once was unacceptable.

There was literally nowhere I could go in my life—or in my own house—that wasn't touched by Nicole. This felt like a moment we'd been waiting for forever...or maybe it was just what I'd been waiting for.

I stayed vertical for a moment, grabbing at the collar of my shirt behind my neck and lifting it over my head before tossing it to the floor next to us.

There was no confusing the fire in Nicole's eyes when my shirt was off—and I was damn proud of how hard I'd worked at the abs and pecs they were currently looking at. I could be honest for a moment and point to the pressure my father always put on me to have the perfect physique as someone in security, but none of that mattered right now. When Nicole was looking at me, none of my normal body insecurities came up—the ones that a man, let alone a Black man, could never talk about. Instead, I felt like Nicole's eyes turned me superhuman.

I was electric in their presence, with an energy surging through me that felt underserved, but everything about the way Nicole looked at me told me that wasn't the case.

I lowered my body across theirs as they shimmied out of their shirt as well—no bra, because Nicole didn't believe in those, and I fucking loved that about them. Their breasts were perky and perfect, and begging for attention as I lowered my mouth around their nipple.

"Ah!" Nicole gasped the moment I made contact with their skin, arching their back to bring themselves closer to me.

I obliged, because how could I not? My lips closed around their supple skin, and I pulled it into my mouth with light suction, allowing my tongue to flick back and forth across the tip.

They were groaning again, and this was the most intimate thing we'd ever experienced together. It had been years of platonic friendship, and somehow, somewhere, that seal had been broken in an instant.

I didn't have the time or attention to consider how that had happened. All I knew was that I was here, we had crossed the line, and I didn't want to ever walk back to where we were.

Chapter Five

I've never regretted buying a king-sized bed as much as I did in that moment.

After last night with Nicole, things had been in another category all of its own. And I'm not just talking about the sex. That had been nothing short of incredible...and just in case we weren't certain, we'd made sure to repeat the entire act several more times.

Final result: worth it.

Worth it a fucking lot.

But it's now just past eight o'clock in the morning, and Nicole is bunched up in the covers in the spot farthest away from me on the bed. Like, I'm on the left and they are on the right and there is a valley of emptiness between us.

How the hell did that happen?

It didn't seem like Nicole had awoken yet, so I moved to get closer to them but the moment I did, they roused.

"Hey." They pulled the covers around their naked body tightly, as if trying to hide themselves.

I immediately felt weird. I'd seen every inch of Nicole last night, but that move alone had felt like...remorse?

"I, uh..." Nicole cleared their throat. "I have to get to work soon. It's, um, it's busy on weekends, you know? Plus, with literally nothing in my bank account, I have to work every moment possible."

"Of course." I nodded my head like I understood, letting my arm fall on the pillow as if I'd never been planning to wrap it around them and pull them in closer. "I'm sure weekends are when most people want appointments since they aren't at work."

"Yeah. Not everyone works a nine to five," they added, now sliding out of the bed and taking one of the throw blankets with them to cover their body. "It's hard for those of us without a trust fund."

I blinked, taking a beat. *What the fuck?*

We had never spoken to each other that way. There'd never been a moment when Nicole had made a point to emphasize the difference between my background and theirs. Yes, I knew it was there and Nicole certainly knew as well. I wasn't stupid and neither of us were blind. My mother had put things in place before she died to make sure her children would always be okay, and then with the success of my father's business and bringing me on board...yeah, money wasn't something I'd have to worry about anytime soon.

But they'd never thrown it in my face like that before.

"Uhm, well...yeah, I know." My words stumbled out of me as undiplomatically as possible. "I was just thinking it would be nice if we could grab some breakfast together. After last night, I've definitely worked up an appetite."

Nicole was already sliding their clothes back on as discreetly as possible, as if I hadn't already seen them naked.

"I'll grab something on the way to work. I'm sure you can find something to eat here, right?"

"Sure." I mean, yeah, I had a fridge like every other person over college-aged in the Goddamn country. *Seriously, what the fuck is happening right now?*

"I'm going to head out, but uh...let me know if you find out anything about my account." Nicole was pulling their hair up into a messy bun and glancing toward my bedroom door like the exit was going to save them.

I didn't try to keep them from leaving. "I'll catch you later, then."

They didn't even look at me as they nodded, sliding their phone into their pocket and making their way out. "I'll text you later."

And with that, Nicole was gone. I heard my apartment door close quietly a few moments later, and there was a sinking feeling in my chest I hadn't felt before.

My phone pinged from the nightstand, and I rolled over to check it. I needed the distraction in that moment, and if that meant working on a Sunday, then I was absolutely on board.

We found her.

The text message made me sit up quickly. I swiped across the screen and brought it to the front, quickly typing back a response to the colleague who I'd been communicating with about Nicole's identity theft issue.

Her?

Three dots in a text bubble appeared before his response pinged through. *Have they mentioned anything about trouble with a coworker previously?*

Not that I've heard. Nicole is an independent contractor.

At least, that's what I'd thought. Was I wrong? She'd been doing her own work as an esthetician-in-training for a while, and I was pretty sure that there wasn't a specific boss or coworker she interacted with. I mean, aside from Kim. But that couldn't be who he was talking about because I'd let that woman rip the hair off my taint.

Looks to be a woman named Kim, works in the same business that she does. It would make sense that their paths have crossed somehow.

My stomach sank as I sent a quick response back to clarify. *Kim from Kim's Bare Limbs? The esthetician? Nicole is training under her.*

Ding, ding, ding, he responded back within seconds. *Sounds like we found our guy.*

I thought of the way Nicole had just run out of here, like they couldn't get away from me fast enough. There weren't a lot of people that Nicole trusted, and I knew that I had solidly taken one of those spots, but I also knew that Kim had as well.

Telling Nicole about this was not going to be easy.

You're sure? I texted back, but he responded quickly with screenshots and proof that was pretty impossible to deny. Kim was Nicole's mentor, and she'd stolen her identity as well as her entire bank account.

And, damn it, I'd let that conniving woman touch my balls.

I opened a blank text message and typed Nicole's number at the top, beginning a text to try and explain what had just come to light.

But I couldn't hit *send.*

I tossed the phone down on my bedspread instead and got up, in search of something to eat. Maybe it would feel easier to rock their world on a full stomach.

Spoiler alert—two bagels later and a tall glass of orange juice, none of it felt easier.

Hey.

I sent the message out to Nicole, letting it linger in the universe with an unspoken hope that maybe they wouldn't see it. Maybe they wouldn't respond, and I wouldn't have to crush a relationship in their life that means a lot. They were so selective on those, it felt terrible to take one away.

But what other choice did I have?

Got to work fine. Thanks for checking in!

Nicole's response was quick and abrupt, and I hadn't even asked about whether or not they'd gotten to work. I didn't regret a thing about last night, but the way Nicole was talking to me now almost made me consider it. Had I ruined our friendship? Had one night of impulse torn down what half a decade of friendship had built?

I need to talk to you.

I knew my response was cryptic, but how else was I supposed to handle this? There was no playbook for how to break the news and somehow keep a friendship—or maybe more—intact.

I'm pretty busy with work today.

I shook my head and typed a response. *Are you staying here again tonight?*

The three dots appeared again, but no response came to fruition for several minutes. Fuck it, I wasn't about to let this die out.

Nicole, you need to come back here after work. We need to talk. I've got information about the entire incident.

I knew that was low, throwing in the promise of information about the identity theft situation. Of course, Nicole would want that information, and of course I could have just texted it to them. But also, could I? It felt like something I needed to say in person. It felt like something I needed to watch them process and hold their hand while they did.

Several unanswered minutes went by before a quick response pinged through.

Ok.

Nicole was coming back, and I was ready to stop playing games. I was going to tell them what Kim had done, and I was going to tell them the truth about last night and right now. That this hadn't been just a one-off. This hadn't just been a moment of vulnerability where two friends had tangled in the sheets as a way to avoid everything that they were actually feeling.

If there was one thing that had been solidified for me last night, it was the fact that I didn't just want to be Nicole's best friend. I wanted to be their lover, and I didn't care what that fucking meant. I didn't care how my family might react to me being in a gender fluid relationship or that my sexuality might not be as heterosexual as I'd once assumed. I didn't even care that my friends and coworkers who all currently saw me as some sort of muscle-bound alpha male would undoubtedly be surprised to hear that I wasn't the womanizing player that it was easy to paint me as.

And maybe I'd painted myself that way, too. Maybe I'd been as unfair as I expected others to be.

Maybe I was ready to change that.

Chapter Six

Nicole knocked on my front door that evening, and it honestly felt offensive. We didn't *knock* on each other's doors. We had keys. We had permission and authority and precedence, and there hadn't been a time I could think of in years where they had rapped their knuckles against my door.

I opened it anyway, trying to keep my irritation at bay.

"Hey." I welcomed them into my space, and Nicole walked in slower than I'd ever seen them do before. It was like I was pulling them in, as if they didn't really want to come in.

Yeah, I was fucking hurt by all of that.

"Hey," Nicole responded without meeting my eyes. "You said you had some news?"

That's not exactly what I said, but I understood their desire to skip right to that.

Actually, no. No, I didn't understand.

"Are we really going to do this?" I asked as I closed the door behind them.

They placed their bag down on the side table by the front

door but refused to move farther into the apartment. "Do what?"

I wanted to roll my eyes, but I was a full-grown adult. "Nicole, I'm not an idiot. You basically ran out of here this morning like you were on fire. It was...it was fucking weird, honestly. So, I have to ask...do you regret last night? Do you regret what happened between us?"

Even as I asked the question, I was willing them to say no. No, they didn't regret any aspect of it. They'd wanted it as much as I had, and it had been as life-changing for them—or maybe relationship-changing is a better word—as it had been for me.

But Nicole's eyes avoided mine. "I mean, it's complicated."

Fuck. The sting of tears tried to broach my eyes, but I wasn't about to give them the satisfaction. "It's not *that* complicated."

"D, I love you. You know that." Nicole sounded sincere in those words, and the way they reached out a hand to grab my forearm. "We've been friends for a long time. That's not something to just risk after one night without some serious thought."

"I am giving it serious thought," I replied, the tension in my voice pulling even tighter. "This wasn't just a one-night stand. I don't regret what happened between us, Nicole."

"I know..." Nicole averted their eyes. "There's just a lot going on...I need to focus on getting my money back."

That was an excuse and we both knew it.

"It's Kim." I blurted the news out like a barbarian. "Kim stole your identity and took all of your money."

Nicole took a step back from me, an audible gasp leaving their lips. Their expression was vacillating between hurt and confusion, and I wasn't sure if it was aimed toward me or the actual perpetrator, so I didn't pause to find out and kept talking.

"I spoke with my colleagues, and we've done the fact checking. It's true. Kim must have either stolen your debit card or cloned it or I don't know what...but she's who emptied your bank account." I was putting it all out there now, and I couldn't stop. "Her brother is the one we caught on camera at the ATM, and he's already admitted that she's the one who gave him the information. The way they went about this whole thing, it doesn't sound like this is their first rodeo. I'm guessing they've done this before."

"Kim?" Nicole's voice was barely above a whisper. "*My* Kim?"

We were still standing in my entryway, and there was nothing comfortable about this moment. I wanted to reach out and pull them to me. I wanted to let them know that they weren't alone, and that I was going to support them through every moment of this heartache even though I wasn't sure where the hell we stood right now. I could only imagine how it felt to trust someone with your career and then have them steal your entire history—financially and more.

I pulled out my phone and brought the screenshots and ATM photographs up, handing the entire thing to them to see for themselves.

Nicole took the phone and swallowed hard as they swiped through every ounce of proof I'd accumulated. Finally, they seemed to nod as if they'd fully accepted the situation I'd just presented them.

"So, what now?" There was a glimmer of tears on the lower brim of their lashes. "I press charges? I get my money back? I end my apprenticeship and never get my hours because my mentor has completely fucked me over?"

The last sentence was said with a harshness that bordered on yelling, but the moment of anger was immediately replaced by a frown pulling down on their lips.

I slipped my fingers around their wrist and pulled them

farther into the apartment, bringing them to a seat on the couch that was only a few steps from the front door.

I could feel every protective instinct inside of me flaring to full capacity. "Nicole, we can take this wherever you want it to go. If you want to press charges, I'll help you do that. If you want to put her in jail, I'll help you do that, too. We can take this as far as you want."

Nicole shook their head. "I don't want to do any of that."

A moment of silence settled between us as I waited for them to explain further.

"Kim's been really helpful in teaching me about this industry," Nicole finally continued. "I honestly couldn't have learned what I've learned without her."

"Okay." I tried to find the words but felt like I was stuttering over them. Who gave a fuck that the woman was a good teacher? Good teachers didn't steal your life savings. "That might be true, but, Nicole, she stole from you. She literally conned you."

"How much did you look into Kim's life?" Nicole moved to the edge of the couch and turned their body to face mine.

I wasn't sure how to answer that question. "What do you mean?"

"Kim has an adult daughter," Nicole began. "She has Rett Syndrome and everything Kim does is based on taking care of her—like, doing everything for her. Her daughter requires around-the-clock care. She doesn't talk about it much, but I've seen what she's given up. I've seen her have to leave early to let the caretaker go and come in late because her daughter had a rough morning and couldn't be consoled."

"That sounds incredibly difficult," I admitted. Realistically, I wasn't sure how else to respond to that, but I still felt defensiveness in my gut at someone hurting Nicole.

"Having children was her dream," Nicole continued, and I

wished they wouldn't. I didn't want to normalize or humanize this person who'd hurt her so badly. "She spent six years going through IVF before she had her daughter. That alone cost her a fortune."

That sinking feeling gripped me again. "And then her daughter ended up being disabled."

"Another cost she never saw coming, and one that doesn't have an end date." Nicole nodded, seemingly more affirmed in her decision. "I don't want to press charges."

I had eighteen responses to that, but I closed my mouth and said nothing.

"Can we just change my account information and whatever else is needed so nothing else can come out?" Nicole's eyes were definitely lined with tears now and all I wanted to do was wipe them away, but I knew better than that. "And maybe I should find a new supervisor."

My lips slid into a grimace. "Yeah, maybe a different supervisor would be a good idea.'

Nicole leaned back deeper into the couch and let out a slow, long exhale. "I...I might need a little help. Nothing huge, but...covering next month's rent as I rebuild. If that's okay."

"It's always okay," I responded faster than I could even think. I knew what a big step that was for Nicole to ask me that, even if it was because they were protecting someone else. It was a step in the right direction still. "I can help with whatever."

They nodded and their tongue slid across their bottom lip. "Can you ask your colleague to delete the information? Just delete everything in the case? Let this not even be an issue anymore?"

I swallowed hard, trying to find the words in my throat. "Nicole, I can't just...I can't just ignore it. She broke the law. She stole from you. She hurt you."

"I don't want to pursue anything, though," Nicole clarified. "Just let this be it and we'll all move on."

I understood charity, but for fuck's sake, this was too much. "Okay, but moving on means us changing all your account numbers, all your cards, everything. It's not some small task."

"Okay, well that's enough work for now then. Change the account numbers. I can't afford this to happen again, obviously." Nicole was nodding now, and I finally felt for a brief second like maybe they weren't completely insane. "But everything that's already happened? Let it go. Do not involve the authorities."

"Nicole, she could be doing this to other people," I added a moment later, trying to keep my voice as low and friendly as possible. *I mean, were we seriously going to just ignore this?* "I'd say it's actually quite likely she has before and will do it again."

"Demetrius, I'm asking you." Nicole turned their gaze to me again, but this time with a seriousness I didn't see often. "Let this go. Let Kim go. I'll talk to her, and I'll ask her not to do this again. But we are going to let this go."

I swallowed hard, trying to figure out how I wanted to proceed. I literally was a VP at a security agency—letting criminals go was not in our modus operandi. If they did something illegal, we pursued with every harshness that the law afforded us.

"What are you going to do, then?" I asked. "Because without legal recourse, that money isn't coming back to you. You can't claim it as an insurance loss, or anywhere else. You can't recoup it from her. You're just out everything that you had."

"I know." Nicole didn't meet my eyes this time. "Can you respect that this is my decision?"

Everything in my gut screamed against it, but I also

Sarah Robinson

couldn't say no. "Nicole, you're taking a huge loss for this person."

They didn't give me a chance to finish that thought. "Can you respect my decision or not?"

I took a deep breath, letting the moment wash across me as I considered what Nicole was asking me. "If that's what you think is best...if that's what you need...then, okay. Okay, I'll let it go."

"That's what I need," Nicole repeated. "Please."

I nodded my head, less out of acceptance but more out of submission. "Okay. I'll drop it."

Nicole seemed to release a deep exhale that they had been holding on to. "Thank you, D."

I turned my back to the couch and pushed backwards, allowing myself to lean against the cushions. I didn't have anything to say in that moment, and I was just trying to find a way to breathe through it all. It was a strange feeling to be both somehow letting them down at the same time that I was also respecting their choices.

"D?" Nicole's voice broke through the silence a few moments later.

I turned my head to catch their gaze, but didn't respond.

"Can I stay here tonight?" they asked, this time their voice sounding like a timid mouse afraid of the answer they were going to get.

I pushed forward and turned my body toward Nicole. "I don't want you to stay anywhere else."

They didn't respond immediately, but I could see the vulnerability spilling across their face.

"Nicole, I don't want you to stay anywhere else ever again. I want you here, with me," I continued, just letting the words tumble out of my mouth in a manner I hadn't planned or expected. "I don't think I can keep going as we have been. I

274

can't just be your friend, and I know that's a risk. I know it's the biggest risk we can take—but, if anything, you've proven you don't shy away from those. I think we could really be something."

Nicole swallowed hard, but then the smallest glimpse of a smile pulled at the corner of their lips. "I think I'm okay with that."

My brows lifted in surprise. "Really?"

They nodded. "D, I think we've known this was inevitable for a long time."

"Did we?" My voice caught in my throat, and I pulled them into my arms. "I really wasn't sure."

"Oh, you were always sure," Nicole continued, letting me bring them close. They wrapped their arms round the back of my neck and slid onto my lap with the confidence of someone who was always meant to be there. "I'm the one who took a bit longer to catch up."

"Always gotta be the hold out, huh?" I grinned, a small chuckle parting my lips at their resistance to vulnerability. "You could just say...*yeah, me too.*"

"Demetrius..." Nicole said my name like they were licking the sound across their lips, and I wanted to slide with every syllable they pronounced. "I want this, too. So, yeah, let's do this."

My mouth pressed to theirs and I made a vow to myself in that moment that this was forever. Nicole was forever. Everything we felt...I wasn't going to let this go.

They were my person, and I was theirs.

Mini-Epilogue

"You can't be serious," I said as Nicole shrugged their shoulders in front of the white board where all of our wedding plans were located.

My sister Yasmeen looked as bewildered as I did. "Have you seen Demetrius dance before, Nic? I don't think you want that."

A fair assessment since she'd seen me dancing a few times after having one too many drinks at the new lesbian bar she'd opened in Arlington, VA. Obviously, not my normal scene, but I always wanted to support my sister's business ventures. Plus, Nicole and Yasmeen's wife were already super close friends after everything that had happened at Yasmeen's bar last year.

"Let alone in unison with my friends—none of whom are going to be jumping at this idea," I added. "We're not dancers without multiple tequila shots first."

It had been two years since we'd turned our friendship into a romantic relationship, and wedding plans were already in full swing. Nicole had been the one to propose to me—shocking, I know—and there was no way I could say no. Once we'd bridged the gap from friends to lovers, there was no going back and no way in hell that I wanted to.

"Flash mobs at weddings are all the rage, you guys," Nicole insisted. They pointed a finger at the song list they were proposing on the white board. "And this medley will be perfect. You and your groomsmen only have to do the first two, and then my party will finish the number out. The guests will love it!"

"As someone in your party, I'd like to put my vote in for absolutely not," Yasmeen told Nicole, but the smile on her face seemed to say otherwise. Yasmeen shot me a devilish grin, and I knew she'd rather suck it up and do it just so that she could watch me do it. Sisters are evil, and I cannot be convinced otherwise. "But like...if we have to do this, then there better be an open bar from the beginning of the ceremony on to give D a little liquid courage."

Nicole laughed and nudged their elbow into Yasmeen's arm. "There will be no shortage of booze, I promise."

"If Mike is already going to be doing a performance, isn't that enough dancing?" I asked, trying to find any loophole to get out of this flash mob dance. "You know he's going to go all out."

"The drag show is completely separate," Nicole clarified, referencing a good friend of mine who is a straight male fire-fighter and also happens to be a drag performer on the weekends. That was a whole story for another time, but Mike was already slated to be my best man. "The flash mob dance will be our entrance into the reception and the drag show will be after the cake cutting."

"Remember that time so, so long ago when you didn't want to spend all my money?" I teased with a sarcastic grain of truth.

Nicole shot me a glare. "Remember that time so, so long ago when you were single?"

I immediately zipped my lip.

"Okaaaaaay," Yasmeen butted in as she dragged out her words. "Before the wedding is called off entirely, have we at least agreed on the cake flavor yet? The baker said they need the final call by tomorrow morning to get their orders in."

"Cookies and cream," I said.

"Lemon," Nicole said at the exact same time.

Yasmeen grimaced, lifting her eyebrows. "You know what? It's too soon to decide on cake. Plus, I think we should consider a different bakery because my best friend Mila used this one for her baby shower cake and it was a lot. What about the general colors for the wedding?"

"Coral and navy blue," Nicole replied.

"We need colors?" I asked at the same time.

Nicole shot me another look and then began ushering both of us out of their home office. "Okay, that's enough wedding planning for today. Out, out, out. Let's get some food."

Yasmeen left first, and I lingered for a moment in the doorway.

"Hey, you know I'm kidding, right?" I asked Nicole, shoving my hands into the front pockets of my jeans. "Lemon cake, flash mob dance...I'm in for whatever as long as I get to say I *do*."

Nicole grinned and pushed up on the balls of their feet to reach my lips with theirs. They gave me a soft peck. "Wait 'til you hear what I have planned for your tuxedo."

"Shit." I grinned and kissed them back before following them out of the office in search of something to eat. "You know I must really love you to be willing to go through all that."

"You secretly love all of it." Nicole squeezed my hand.

And they were not-so-secretly right. Embracing the side of me that wasn't as strait-laced as I once pretended to be had opened up an entirely new world to me—one where people accepted each other for every queer and quirky part of themselves.

I was proud to call these people my family, and even more proud to soon be calling Nicole my spouse.

Want to read more about Mike, the firefighting drag queen, or Mila, the best friend who fell in love with her sperm donor's sister? Check out the Queerly Devoted series by Sarah Robinson!

About the Author

Contemporary Romances Across the Rainbow

Sarah Robinson first started her writing career as a published poet in high school, and then continued in college, winning several poetry awards and being published in multiple local literary journals.

Never expecting to make a career of it, a freelance writing Craigslist job accidentally introduced her to the world of book publishing. Lengthening her writing from poetry to novels, Robinson published her first book through a small press publisher, before moving into self-publishing, and then finally accepting a contract from Penguin Random House two years later. She continues to publish both traditionally and indie with over 25+ novels to her name with publishers like Penguin, Waterhouse Press, Hachette, and more. She has achieved awards and accolades including 2021 Vivian Award Finalist, Top 10 iBooks Bestseller, Top 25 Amazon Kindle Bestseller, Top 5 Barnes & Noble Bestseller, and sold successfully in digital, print, and mass market paperback. She has been published in three languages.

In her personal life, Sarah Robinson is happily in a mixed-orientation marriage with a gentle giant and they have two beautiful daughters. Their home is full of love and snuggly pets in Arlington, Virginia.

Find Sarah on Facebook and Instagram at @booksbysarahrobinson or TikTok @mentallymama.

Also by Sarah Robinson

Mall You Need is Love

Mall Out of Luck

Mall American Girl

Mall-O-Ween Mischief

Mall Year Long: The Box Set

The Photographer Trilogy

(*Romantic Suspense*)

Tainted Bodies

Tainted Pictures

Untainted

Forbidden Rockers Series

(*Rockstar Romances*)

Logan's Story: A Prequel Novella

Her Forbidden Rockstar

Rocker Christmas: A Logan & Caroline Holiday Novella

Kavanagh Legends Series

(*MMA Fighter Standalone Romances*)

Breaking a Legend

Saving a Legend

Becoming a Legend

Chasing a Legend

Kavanagh Christmas

Standalone Novels

Not a Hero: A Bad Boy Marine Romance

Misadventures in the Cage

One Night Stand Serial

Second Shot of Whiskey